FIREBORNE

(RAVEN CURSED BOOK 1)

MCKENZIE HUNTER

McKenzie Hunter

Fireborne

© 2019, McKenzie Hunter

McKenzieHunter@McKenzieHunter.com

ISBN: 978-1-946457-04-2

ACKNOWLEDGMENTS

I am forever thankful for my friends and family who continue to support me unconditionally and make sure I leave my writer's cave. I can't thank Elizabeth Bracker, Sherrie Simpson Clark, Stacey Mann, and Robyn Mather, for taking time out of their busy schedules to beta read for me. You all are the best.

Thanks to Meredith Tennant and Therin Knite, my editors who worked so diligently to help me tell the best possible story, and Oriana for the beautiful cover.

Last, but never least, I want to thank my readers for following Erin's adventure and allowing me to entertain you with my writing. You allow me to do what I love and I appreciate that.

CHAPTER 1

"Come out, come out wherever you are. There's a crimson martini waiting just for you." I peered through my night vision binoculars. Crouching behind the thick manicured shrubbery and planted flowers that enclosed the rooftop café allowed me to keep a careful eye on the front and side entrances of Kelsey's, the city's premier restaurant for the supernatural elite—or those who'd like to appear to be.

They say pride cometh before the fall, but I beg to differ —the indulgence of an overpriced drink available only at Kelsey's would be Grayson's fall. Ridiculous.

Two things I knew about my bounty: He was arrogant, which would surely lead to his capture, and undoubtedly he was enjoying the chase more than I was the hunt.

What the hell was he thinking stealing the Crelic? He was thinking the way he always does. He wants, he takes. Toddler rules. Except this particular man-toddler grab required careful planning and high-end equipment to get in and out of the heavily secured location, to get to his desired toy.

Trouble was, it wasn't some toy he took but a magical object banned by the Supernatural Task Force. In the wrong hands it could be deadly. That's the last thing I wanted my sister to have to deal with. If the Crelic was used to commit a crime, that old debate about supernaturals needing to be policed by human police, not the Supernatural Task Force, would reignite. It always did when things like this hit the media. The rationale baffled me—supernaturals with access to magic from all denizens and technology couldn't prevent the theft or misuse of magical objects, but humans with only technology at their disposal could?

The theft wasn't public knowledge and it needed to stay that way. The STF were good about keeping supernatural secrets and mishaps quiet, but leaks happen.

Shifting to a more comfortable position, I continued to watch the procession of people filing into Kelsey's, the alabaster stone building that stood out among the surrounding rows of brown and tan buildings. Floor-to-ceiling windows in the front gave passersby a peek of what they were missing. A mere glimpse was all you were afforded, because carefully placed artworks prevented a full view of the establishment and gave the patrons privacy. If the swanky exterior hadn't tipped me off, the doorman should have.

If I tagged the bounty, the money paid to the manager for my rooftop location was well spent.

I did another quick equipment check and made sure my rifle with scope was close.

Doubt reared its head after ten minutes had passed. Bounty hunting had taught me to never underestimate a person's arrogance and that their desire to satisfy their id made them careless. I was counting on both to be true about my mark . . . but what if I was wrong?

I gave a quick shake of my head. I was rarely wrong about this sort of thing. Grayson thrived on his id and satisfying his self-entitled desires. He was just the type of person who'd steal a priceless magical object on Tuesday, catch a movie on

Wednesday, have drinks with the fellas on Thursday, and be truly shocked that someone dared to apprehend him. Grayson was a man-toddler with an Amex black card.

The appearance of a tall, self-assured figure had me grabbing my rifle in a reflexive response to the anger that rose immediately at the sight of the man. He was talking into his phone a few feet from the side door of the restaurant I was watching, complying with Kelsey's no-cellphone rule. It was one of the few rules he followed. He wasn't my mark, but someone I wanted far worse.

Asher. I hissed his name like a curse. If only the rifle had rubber bullets instead of a tranq. The shots wouldn't be fatal, but they'd hurt like hell. I wanted him to hurt.

Asher slowly scanned the area, as if he'd heard my furious whisper into the darkness. He ended the call, tilted his chin up, and noticeably inhaled the air. His silver eyes narrowed, glinting like an animal's. He pushed a hand through a tuft of wavy russet hair, his lips easing into his signature smile, charismatic and disarming. He used his smile like a weapon. It allowed him to be blatant with his improprieties and crimes without fear of being questioned or apprehended. I wondered how many illegal and rare magical objects he had in his possession, ones that were never found during warrant searches but that everyone knew he had. Getting these items was a game to Asher, even though he, like all shifters, didn't possess the ability to use their magic for anything other than changing to his animal. So acquiring the objects was just a flagrant disregard for rules and laws and to see what he could get away with. As far as I was concerned, he got away with way too much.

His smile moved into a smirk. And his look said it all: "Yeah, I did it. And?"

Jaw clenched, I relived that day. It was *my* job. *My* find. I did all the work, and he poached it from me. The worst part was that I still hadn't figured out how he did it. I leveled the tranq gun at him. I wanted to shoot him for no other reason than to see his face twist into a grimace of pain and astonishment.

Mr. Arrogance's tongue moved lazily over his lips, but his gaze wasn't homed in directly on me, just in my general direction. Could he see me or was it just his predator's instinct, sensing someone was near? His need to be the hunter and not the hunted.

Clearly amused, he slipped his phone into his pocket, relaxed his arms at his sides, and widened his stance.

Is this jackass posing?

It made me want to shoot him not once but twice, and possibly junk punch him. My voice of reason told me I was above such behavior, but when it came to Asher, I wasn't. I glared at him through the scope of the gun.

He mouthed, "Hello, Erin."

The urge to race across the street to knee him in his man berries was almost irresistible.

As if he sensed my intentions, his brow hitched up and he gave me a lazy two-finger salute before backing his way into the restaurant. As he turned around, he pulled out his phone and started tapping at the keys. Moments later, I got a text notification. I glanced at him and saw the grin he was giving me over his shoulder. If he knew how perilously close he was to being shot in the back with a tranq, that smile would have vanished. I didn't have a lot of rules—it's hard to in this line of business—but shooting someone in the back was a no-no. But for Asher, I could make an exception.

Could he see me, or did he sense me? Was it my scent? Shifters were good at tracking people by their scent. That was one of the innumerable things about them I found annoying. My hair couldn't have been seen, too dark, but to be cautious I'd twisted it into a messy bun and covered it with a black slouch hat.

The leather pants I was wearing were an occupational

requirement, but I still scowled at the cliché of being dressed in all black and leather, complete with a tote crammed with weaponry and my violent little toys. Black washed out my olive-colored skin, so I didn't like to wear it, but what should I have worn to catch Grayson? I couldn't just bring hand-cuffs, a winning personality, and a smile to a fang fight. I would have loved to be wearing a comfortable pair of jeans and a t-shirt or tank top that allowed easier movement, but black blended with the night, and it only took being dragged across concrete once to know I needed leather pants. I scowled again. Dealing with Grayson, being dragged down the street was the least of my worries.

Knowing that I now had a message from Asher made it difficult to ease out of my Asher rage. A wave of embarrassment swept over me. Each time I allowed him to get to me like this, he won all over again. I couldn't let that happen. I deliberately released his taunting look from my mind, refocused on the job, and peered through the binoculars again.

He'll show up. Whatever it was about Kelsey's, it called to people's pleasure centers. Grayson would answer the call and risk capture just to have a sip of the crimson martinis he loved so much.

"My indulgences do get in my way." The smooth, rich voice came from behind me.

"Grayson." I whipped around, grabbed my projector pistol—better for shorter distances—aimed, and shot. The dart whirled through the air and was plucked out of the air by his deft hands before it could touch him. Crushing the dart in his hand, he then tossed it aside.

"I broke your toy," he mocked, moving slowly to the right out of my line of sight.

"No worries, I have more." In a flash, I snatched up the other projector pistol, that I had stored on my right side, and shot. I knew it was going to miss. It was a distraction. While he was busy picking it from the air, I lashed my whip out at

5

him. It wrapped around one leg, and with a tug, I sent him crashing to the ground. Vampire speed was fascinating to watch but infuriating when on the receiving end of their mesmerizing graceful swiftness. Grabbing hold of the whip, he tugged me several feet closer to him. I released my hold on it so when he yanked on it again, the loose end snapped back in his direction and narrowly missed hitting his face. His contemptuous glare bore into me.

He was on his feet, my whip ripped in half, and the left side of his mouth quirked into a smile as he waved me forward, inviting the ass kicking I was so ready to deliver. Yes, now I could vent my Asher aggression on him. He grunted when a round kick caught him on the left side of his jaw, hard enough to make his head jerk back. He flipped backward out of reach before I could deliver another.

The magic he'd stolen was obviously still new to him because that would have been a perfect time to use it.

"Strawberries and Riesling," he purred into the silence, reminding me of how he'd described my scent on more than one occasion. Why were vamps and shifters always smelling things? Didn't they realize how disgusting that was? He casually looked me over, the leer on his face reminding me that we'd seen each other naked, far too many times. It was a tactic to throw me off, and another time it might have worked. But I was too focused on the stolen magic that wafted off him. I shuddered.

He slowly rounded me. I shuffled back a few steps, keeping my attention on him and trying to anticipate his next move, which was nearly impossible. With the exception of his fascination with whatever was in Kelsey's, Grayson was unpredictable. His impulsiveness was thrilling and made for some memorable nights. Vampire bites were exhilarating, intoxicating, and a great distraction from thinking about my curse. I refocused. Tonight he wasn't a fun distraction—he was a bounty.

"I hate when we're on opposite sides," he said, his voice velvety smooth. "We play so well together."

That we did.

I wasn't sure if the smile that bared his fangs was an invitation or a threat. I remembered the feel of them against my skin, the prick of them against my body, the adrenaline that rushed through my veins at being so close to death. The endorphins from the bites. The combination was hard to resist. I'm not proud of my response.

A harsh breath pushed out of me, along with the desperate need. *Do the job, Erin,* I scolded myself. This was the story of my life. Bring me close to death, set me in the middle of a disaster with little to no chance of survival, send me on a job where I'm not likely to return, and I feel alive. Adrenaline was a poor substitute for what I really craved, but adrenaline was all I could go for because the other was forbidden. Magic. I couldn't have magic, so I was left to find inadequate substitutes.

I yanked out the gun from behind me and shot. He moved back, dodging the first bullet, then jerked to the left to avoid the second. I was a menace to anyone who didn't have vampire speed; to Grayson, I was merely an annoyance. When the final round had been shot, he turned, tugging at his shirt to straighten it. Bullets didn't kill vampires, but they did make them bleed. There was too much paperwork when a bounty's blood was spilled. It was a real pain in the ass.

"How much?" Grayson asked.

"You can't buy your bounty." Really, the man was exasperating. "What were you thinking?"

He shrugged. "That I wanted the Crelic to see what all the fuss was about."

"What the fuss was about!" Screw it. I snapped the grenade from the belt and lobbed it at him.

His shock at the sight of the explosive gave me enough time to run at him and snap one cuff end on him and the other on me. I jerked him to me. He was hissing at the pain from the rune-spelled cuffs. They weakened him enough to make apprehending him manageable. Silver weakened shifters, iron wreaked havoc on fae, iridium rendered witches and mages magicless, and zirconium worked against vampires, but they made horrible cuffs and came with a hefty price.

"I guess that thing was a decoy," he murmured, looking at the green pineapple-shaped object on the ground. *Why do people keep falling for that trick?* I thought it would have gotten around by now. "Hey, she uses a fake grenade to distract you —don't fall for it." Yet they all fell for it.

"Grenade? It would have killed me too and destroyed the building. That would have been reckless."

Taking advantage of our proximity, he leaned in. "But you are reckless. That's the most alluring thing about you. Every moment with you an adventure, isn't it?"

I ignored him. "Of all the things you have taken, the Crelic is the one you should have left where it was." Grayson was a young vamp—or younger, just under a century—and hadn't quite settled into the insipid life of immortality. Really old vamps just existed, afraid of true death but bored by the banality of vamp or pseudo-human existence.

"What fun would that have been?" Grayson's smile was roguish. This was him in all his glory. If he wanted something, he took it with expectations of impunity. And before my sister took on her position at the Supernatural Task Force, he might have been able to donate the right amount of money or schmooze the necessary person to get away with whatever it was he wanted.

He studied the manacles, looking for a weakness in them, I was sure. I was in the presence of a fellow adrenaline junkie, so his theft was about more than just obtaining the Crelic. It was about the thrill of it, the joy of getting away with it, and for the past two days—the chase. Of course, I wasn't going to rule out good old-fashioned self-indulgence and arrogance, too. Never underestimate how much of those qualities vampires possess.

"Whatever the bounty is, I can double it," he told me.

I considered it. Double the amount? Did he know how much it was? That's probably what added to the excitement of the chase. The chase could have gone on for several more days, but he sacrificed it for one night at Kelsey's. What the hell was it about that place?

Sensing my resolve faltering, he grinned. "I can triple it."

That got my attention. No one would have to know I came this close. I could tip the STF off that he'd return to the very place that led to him nearly getting caught the first time. But would he? *Erin, you took the job, so do the damn job.*

"No." My rejection wiped the cunning smirk off his face, replacing it with a moment of surprise. He was about to be taken in. Actually punished for one of his reckless acts. It was probably a first.

Because he wasn't used to magic, I saw on his face the moment he realized he might be able to use it to help him escape. His intention showed in his eyes and I felt the energy of the magic suffuse the air. He opened his mouth to speak the spell, and in haste I invoked my words of power, inching in closer to him with each word.

Mistaking my words of power for more than what they were, his lips lifted, welcoming me. I should have kept it strictly personal, but I didn't. I gave him a kiss, *the* kiss. He hadn't realized that now he was susceptible to the same weakness as magic wielders, even if his magic was manufactured. It was linked to him, part of his life and not-death—or rather, pseudo death.

The arrogance drained from his face and was replaced by shock and then somnolence. I eased him to the ground as he slipped into the state of in-between, tethered in the liminal state between life and death.

With Grayson lying peacefully, I easily found the Crelic, which he had fashioned into a bracelet. The engravings of the spell in a long-abandoned language harnessed the witch magic in the flat, round, opal-colored stone.

I started to remove it but then stopped. It was linked to him; I wasn't sure what would happen if I severed the tie. Would he go through true death? Not wanting to risk it, I uncuffed myself from him and bound his hands together with the cuffs. With him still on the ground, and taking advantage of the magic I had taken from him, I extended my hand to my supplies, willing them toward me. Nothing. I did it again. Nothing. The magic was there; I felt it in me when I pulled it from Grayson with the kiss. Why wasn't it working?

After making another futile effort to use magic that I would only have for a limited time, I started the timer. The small stack of supplies looked like I was planning a mini siege: whip, double-edged karambit, bola, runed cuffs, belt holding three sheathed throwing knives. Hauling the bag of weapons and my rifle downstairs, I quickly loaded them into my car and returned to Grayson.

All the while, I was thinking. Why was the magic not available to me?

If I had been a hundred percent positive he would be caught, I would have brought help because both Grayson and I were going to have bruises from getting him to my car. His would heal quickly, probably by the time he awoke in a cell, whereas mine would linger for days.

Once he was loaded in my backseat, I leaned forward and whispered in his ear, hoping he'd remember the statement. In this state some people have been known to hear voices. Sometimes they remember, but usually not.

"Magic has consequences. Even for you."

Magic had consequences; I knew that only too well.

CHAPTER 2

"*T*his is for you." Catching me as I left a scowling Grayson with the booking agent, Claire handed me the envelope.

She was smiling overenthusiastically, as she always did. I opened the envelope and glanced inside. The bounty was more than I had expected; object retrievals came with a flat rate, and I figured the bonus was probably for expediency and preventing a scandal for the department.

"Thanks." I stuffed the envelope into my pocket and headed for the exit, pretending that I hadn't heard her call my name. I could feel sweet freedom, when she caught hold of my arm.

"You can't leave without saying hi to your sister."

That's exactly what I had planned to do. I was going to get out of there before she had a chance to interrogate me about the catch. I didn't want to see Madison yet. I hadn't had a chance to come up with a plausible story that conveniently left out giving Grayson the kiss—total misnomer, by the way. Kissing wasn't necessary, but the process was easier and more controlled if I did.

"If she's still here this late, I'm sure she's busy. I'll call her later."

"Nonsense." Claire held on to my arm to prevent a getaway. "She's expecting me for a meeting, anyway. You can just pop in. I'm sure she's interested to hear the details of catching Grayson."

Of course she would be, which was why Claire was there bright eyed and bushy tailed handing me the check instead of me picking it up from the Collections Office. No way was her presence a coincidence.

Madison might have wanted to see me, but she was definitely busy, which was why Claire was taking the circuitous route to her office. One of the best agents in the agency was on sister-babysitting detail.

The scenic route through the building allowed me to experience firsthand Claire, the Supernatural Task Force's most profiled witch. She greeted everyone with an energetic "Hiya," her arms flailing like one of those advertisement balloons. Her wide contagious smile was difficult not to return. If she weren't such a stickler for the rules, I would have bet she was using her witchy magic to evoke such a response.

"Madison's obviously busy, I'll catch her later. It's not a big deal," I said, once our route took us to the break room for coffee.

"Want some?" she asked, ignoring my comment and filling her bright-pink coffee cup. I wanted something stronger, but coffee would have to do. She busied herself grabbing coffee and a few cookies from the open package on the counter, oblivious to the looks of confused amusement of the few agents in the break room. Their reaction reminded me that Claire's appearance was a series of contradictions. Dark-brown asymmetrically styled hair was shorn scalp close on the sides. Her heavily lined azure eyes were enhanced by the coating of mascara. Multiple piercings decorated both ears. Her dark-brown jacket almost hid the happy face on her t-shirt. Well, at least she was halfway dressed professionally—she had on a nice suit jacket and slacks.

The scenic route, coffee, and snacks might have been enough time for Claire to fill the silence with STF updates but was not long enough for me to come up with an edited version of Grayson's apprehension.

When I heard a male voice coming from Madison's office, I took it as a sign that the universe was working in my favor, but after Claire knocked on the door to announce her arrival and peeked in, Madison invited us in.

The owner of the voice had on an ill-fitting suit that didn't flatter his tall, lanky frame. His squared jaw was clenched tight, and a bloom of color brushed the tip of his aquiline nose. He pulled his intense, amber-colored eyes from my sister long enough to give Claire a disdainful look. Definitely a police detective.

The bridge that linked the two buildings and allowed the departments better access to each other didn't improve their working relationship. They were in a perpetual state of contention. My sister and the man in the suit looked as if they'd rather fight a tiger than have a conversation with each other. It was tight smiles, dulcet pleasantries, and use of their titles like they were evoking a curse. The strained relationship between the police and the STF didn't show any prospect of being resolved anytime soon. I couldn't help smiling, although it really shouldn't have brought me joy to see her so perturbed by him—better him than me.

"Hello, Adam." Claire's voice returned the hostility he'd just sent her way. *Take that, Adam.* He definitely wasn't ever going to be treated to one of her high fives or fist bumps with accompanying explosion. Actually, no one should be treated to them, but anyone around her long enough would get one.

Madison had been promoted to Chief of the Supernatural Task Force's Runes and Recovery Department two years ago. They policed the darker side of the supernatural world that involved illegal magic, magical object recovery, and deaths as a result of illegal magic use. The latter seemed to make up the majority of their work. Whenever there was illegal magic, a death always seemed to follow.

Adam gave a gruff greeting, then instead of returning his attention to Madison, his eyes traveled over her office. Madison's massive office, like her home, didn't have one thing out of place. The large space was enlivened by the muted peach walls decorated with inspirational quotes framed in the same walnut wood as her desk that, with a click of a button, elevated to a standing desk. It was practical because, being always cautious and in a perpetual state of attentiveness, Madison couldn't sit down for long. Adam's gaze traveled to Madison's chair and eyed it in the same manner I had the first time I saw it. A fully customized chair, with arms and adjustments that allowed it to be positioned in ways I wasn't sure the body moved—or should move. It was an impressive chair, which undoubtedly cost a great deal of money.

Adam's frown deepened. I wondered if it was her office that bothered him, or the STF budget that allowed her to have such an office.

"Unfortunately, we need to continue this discussion later," Madison informed Adam in a breezy, professional tone, subtly letting him know it was a ceasefire and nothing more. Not a surrender or acquiescence. It was a good demonstration of why she was the youngest person to have ever held the position of Chief of Supernatural Task Force.

"We need to work together. If we think you aren't being forthcoming with information, how can our agencies trust each other?" Adam said. The creases in his face deepened with his scowl.

"I agree. You asked if the Crelic was missing. I answered.

The Crelic is in our possession, and I confirmed the rumor wasn't true." He opened his mouth to speak, but Madison held her hand up, halting further discussion. "This conversation will be continued at a later date." Her tone left no room for debate.

Adam's huffy departure caused the tension in her face to relax. Out of habit, she lifted her hand to her hair but quickly remembered that her mane of deep-sienna curls was gone. She'd complained that the mass of hair, a result of her Irish father's shockingly red hair and her Haitian mother's thick dark coils, made her look too young, and worrying about it coming loose from a holder or bun was a distraction. Her hair was darkened to brown, just a shade or two lighter than mine, complementing her copper skin. It was cut short enough to draw the eye to the button nose that softened her features—too much, she said—and made her look cute. It was a contradiction to her cool disposition that some found off-putting.

"He's always so concerned about our agency. It's like he has a crush," Claire teased.

"Crush, my ass. I suspect he's behind any and every leak and rumor about us. I don't trust him." Madison glared at the door with the same ire and frustration I'd seen only once before, when she found me next to a dead body. I had called her first, even before my mother, who had been cleaning up my messes far too long. At twenty-five, I'd needed to start handling situations better. But calling Madison hadn't been any better than relying on my mother. Instead of my mother making my problem go away, it was my mother's best friend's daughter.

Shaking off her frustration, she moved closer and gave me a quick squeeze. "Erin, it's good to see you."

Sure, I'll play your game. No one called you the moment I let them know I had Grayson. You being here is just a coincidence.

"Always," I said, returning the hug. "It's late, don't you

want to get home? We can talk later." I glanced at the clock again. I needed time to construct a story. One that she couldn't poke holes in; one that wouldn't make me falter during her interrogation.

"I'm fine. Let's go have a drink. You caught Grayson in *two days*. I want to hear about that." Censure and sibling pride struggled to get the upper hand and resulted in the weirdly rigid smile on her face.

I'd have a drink or two and she would have water. She wasn't going to drink on a work night. Not this late.

"It's late," I repeated. "Go home and rest. We can chat later."

"No, I'm fine. Let's get a drink and you can tell me about your tag. I knew the moment I heard you were on the job that we'd have the Crelic."

"I don't want a drink," I told her, which was a lie. I wanted a drink or three and a night to relax and come up with the story I'd tell her. Her light-brown eyes studied me. I fidgeted under the weight of it. Our history and friendship gave her an unfair advantage and an uncanny ability to see when I was hiding something.

"Fine. Let's have waffles. You're always in the mood for waffles."

Our unusual relationship was forged by our mothers' friendship. They were inseparable and raised us as sisters. We pointed out on numerous occasions that if they were sisters, we'd be cousins—not sisters. That always earned us scathing looks of reproach and chastisement about being "mouthy," and when they were feeling settled in their martyrdom, they'd looked abashed while saying "is that any way to speak to your mother." Our answer was always yes, especially when there were flaws in the genealogy. Despite the irregularities in our lineage and no recognizable traits that would identify us as sisters, people readily accepted it.

The six-year difference in our ages meant Madison took

on the role of older sister—protecting me at all costs. I owed her for so much, especially my freedom. If it weren't for her intervention, I would be serving time in prison instead of having been sent to the Stygian, where they house misbehaving supernaturals who manage to avoid jail time.

She was my sister in every sense of the word, but we were polar opposites in nearly every way.

I looked over my shoulder at Claire. "I thought you all had a meeting?"

"It can be discussed later," Claire said hurriedly and ducked out of the room with a quick wave.

"Waffles it is." Madison looked at a packet on her desk and frowned. "I need to take care of this, but I'll meet you at Tallulah's Grille." The smile that emerged moved in phases until it was wide and lively. I witnessed the inception of an idea, something I had a feeling I wasn't going to like.

"I have to approve this job." Madison was giddy. As giddy as she was capable of being. It was the animatronic move of her shoulders—a shimmy but stiffer—that gave me pause. Seeing a spirited, carefree Madison was fun because it wasn't something I saw often. This was her little happy dance. This off-beat, stiff shoulder shake with rhythmless jazz hands didn't fill me with the same joy it did her but was a reminder that I was willing to go many lifetimes without seeing it again. On a child, it's cute—on an adult woman, it was a reason to call the EMTs.

"You'll be perfect for it. You're a great bounty hunter and I appreciate you helping me out, but this is a steady job."

"In an office?"

She nodded, eyeing me apprehensively. I suspected the job would entail me being in an office, surrounded by humans, to remove any temptations of being around magic. My plaintive smile surely looked as forced and fake as it felt.

"We'll discuss it at Tallulah's," she suggested, and I knew that while she was dealing with the details of the job, we would both be preparing our deliberation and ready to engage in a lively—possibly hostile—debate.

She raised her desk to the standing position, moved the mouse to wake up the computer, and shifted her gaze to the corner to look at the clock. "We'll meet in forty-five minutes."

It never failed. Whenever I left the Supernatural Task Force building, my attention always went to the adjoining police station. Technically, it was all the police department, and the Supernatural Task Force was a division. The overt symbolism of the building wasn't lost on anyone, nor the contradiction. The skyway joining the three-story sister building presented a unified front, a symbiotic relationship born from mutual respect and social dedication.

The STF center was gray brick with undertones of browns and beige. The police department: brown brick, undertones of gray and beige. It seemed like they'd have a harmonious relationship working in conjunction to keep the city safe. The PR spin and the big production they made of the momentous event when the buildings were complete dominated local news and social media. We were inundated with verbose speeches, people in suits presenting their most endearing smiles while making promises that only the most naïve would believe would be kept. We all returned the fake smiles, graciously accepted the platitudes and the grandiose speeches, although supernaturals and humans alike knew there would be no amicable relationship.

The police officers still sneered at the building as if it had feelings and could tell how much it was detested. They seethed about the multitude of issues that they had with the laws they thought protected the supernaturals. Not all of them held animosity for the supernaturals, but the ones that did weren't adept at hiding it.

The man approaching me, River, was at the top of that list. The detective with rumors of political aspirations pulled a smile onto his face when he saw me. His tone started neutral but quickly acquired a cold edge, and if a person was observant enough, his dislike of me soon became clear. I was very observant, especially of him. He'd need to control that. It made him sound insincere, although when it came to dealing with me, he probably was.

"Look who it is. Always a pleasure." It wasn't. He hated me. Arriving second on the scene after the *incident*, he saw the spin Madison had put on it and the beginning of her goal to get me off for murder. He hated my guts, and maybe he should. In his mind, I was a blatant example of how the supernaturals "got away with murder." In his mind, and technically, I had.

"Hi," I pushed through clenched teeth, keeping my tone light and overly saccharine.

"Staying out of trouble?" he asked, taking a sip from his coffee cup. Working in his favor was his dazzling smile that hit all the right notes to make him seem warm, caring, and endearing. Perfectly aligned teeth. The smile of a potential politician. His beach-sand skin had a healthy glow, but the lines were possibly sun damage, not age. Definitely the outdoorsy type. In his early forties, I guessed, with dark hair salted so nicely that it wasn't ridiculous to think a stylist was involved. Tall, broad build and the assured grace of a person who could handle himself and had the requisite training and real-life experience to hone his skills. But he wasn't in the field in that capacity. In a year, he'd moved up to detective.

I searched for a way to end the conversation. There wasn't one, because whether intentionally or not, he was blocking my path. His oaky cologne wafted from him and small lines around his mouth and lips formed from the strained smile that he worked to make look genuine.

"Congratulations on getting into law school," I said, wanting badly to end the encounter. *Move one: I show you I'm keeping as close tabs on you as you are on me. Your move.*

"Thank you. It's been my goal to do more in the system. To right some terrible wrongs." *Move two: I plan to eventually bring you down one way or another.*

And there it was. That would be the platform he'd run on, and I was willing to bet my story would be the one he spoke of. Sucking in a ragged breath, I kept the snide remarks that were threatening to emerge to myself.

"I'm sure you'll be an asset wherever you decide to work." I was still acting sunshine and syrupy sweet.

"I already know where I plan to work." His intense cognac-colored eyes slowly drifted over me until they met mine and narrowed with an unspoken promise. District attorney's office.

"Good for you. Later." Our shoulders brushed as I slid through the sliver of space he'd given me.

"You too. I'll see you around." His voice held the threat of a vendetta. He didn't know the person from the *incident* personally, but the few degrees of separation made it personal enough for him to be holding a grudge. As far as he was concerned, the man had been murdered by one of those "rogue supernaturals." In his opinion, not all supernaturals were reprobate, immoral wielders of bad magic with no instinct control—just me. The nebulous nature of my magic bothered most supernaturals, and freaked out humans. My magic caused donors to slip into an obscure state between life and death, and that bothered people plenty.

CHAPTER 3

*M*adison studied the menu as if there would actually be something new on it. For the past five years, Tallulah's Diner and Grille had been our breakfast spot. The menu, like the cozy retro appearance, remained unchanged. Black-and-white tiled floor, turquoise bottle cap-shaped stools on a wide silver base at the long counter with complementing benches throughout the restaurant. Decorating the aqua walls were cutesy pictures and stencils of the word *diner*. I suspected it was their late hours and breakfast food that kept them in business.

I placed the menu on the table without looking at it and finally checked the message Asher left me. *Black is your color.*

Sheer, raw will and the presence of an STF agent in front of me was all that kept me from hauling my butt out of the chair and going after him. *Another time,* I thought. Another time, and I couldn't wait for that time to come. Asher rage had to be a condition caused by just knowing him. I couldn't be the only person suffering from it.

"I think I'll get the farmhouse special," Madison finally said after moments of deliberation.

"Really? Like every other time," I pointed out, grinning.

A blush reddened her cheeks and the bridge of her nose. "Then you should have ordered for me."

"I considered it, but you would've claimed you wanted something else just to prove you're not predictable."

Once we placed our orders, we sat in weighted silence as Madison stared at the cup while stirring her tea. I sipped on my decaf coffee.

"So . . ." She dragged out the words. "Grayson?"

"Grayson," I responded, ignoring her look of censure.

When I didn't elaborate, she scrutinized me.

"Details," she urged after several more moments of silence. Madison's face was devoid of emotion as I told her every detail of the capture, breezing over being distracted by Asher, because that was embarrassing.

Madison shook her head after I finished.

"Indulgence goes before the fall." I grinned.

"That's not how the saying goes, Erin," Madison said with a smirk.

"I know, I'm making it my own. It's an Erin-ism."

I couldn't make out the Haitian French she muttered under her breath, but I was positive it wasn't kind.

My French was rudimentary, learned from Madison's mother, who spoke and interchanged French and English words mid-sentence. During game night, French was spoken more often to counter her husband's Irish brogue that thickened when he was joined by his sister and brother. They spoke English and knew some Irish Gaelic. Then game night devolved into seeing who could embrace their language the most. It made for an interesting evening. They all had more than their share of stubbornness, and they'd passed it on to Madison.

"It was his indulgence," I said. "Whatever Kelsey's putting in those crimson martinis needs to be investigated. I don't know a vampire who isn't enamored by them. I camped out there because I knew he'd be there. It's nothing short of an addiction."

The word *addiction* brought a wry smile to her lips. I was constantly dealing with mine, and it was the source of many of our conflicts and the reason I was forever indebted to her. I swallowed.

"He was bound to show up there...but he found me first."

"Found you first?" Her brows inched together.

I nodded and prepared for an interrogation.

"You must have been distracted. People don't sneak up on you. What distracted you?" she said rapid-fire, scrutinizing me.

"Asher," I breathed, warmth from my embarrassment creeping up my cheeks.

"He really gets your hackles up, doesn't he?" She laughed at my expression.

"Yours too. You just live vicariously through my frustration. You want him taken down a peg or two as well."

A smile flickered across her face at the thought, although she'd never admit it. Just the thought of that arrogant shifter dismissing me made me want to grab my tranq gun and go find him. I might have snarled a little.

"Why isn't he in jail?"

"He hasn't broken the law and you disliking him isn't an arrestable offense. We have no proof of his wrongdoing or that he is in possession of any of the items you claim he has. The last time he was linked to one and we proceeded on your lead, we ended up having to settle a lawsuit," she reminded me.

I wasn't in the position to pass judgment on anyone for not having a clean record, but Asher's was as spotty as a leopard. It wasn't his questionable dealing that bothered me; it was the smugness with which he committed his indiscretions.

Twirling a fork, Madison asked, "You said you placed runed cuffs on Grayson. Then what?"

Of course she hadn't missed how I glossed over the cuffing, apprehending, and getting him into my car.

"I took his magic," I mumbled. The server placed a plate of waffles in front of me, and I busied myself drenching them in syrup as a distraction from her disapproving gaze. She waited until the server left before continuing.

"You didn't just take his magic, you put him in a state of in-between," she said. She pushed her food away. I'm sure the word conjured up the same images for her as it did for me. The fear sparked by the onlookers as I was taken away in handcuffs, my face plastered on the television, the DA's speech about a plea deal. And me being the wrong face of my kind: death mages. It wasn't even actually what we were. We were considered cursed by the raven. Linguistically the same, but Raven Cursed sounded innocuous, almost poetic. Not really how one would describe a person whose only magical skill was to bring death.

That wasn't quite true. I didn't bring death—well, I did. In a way. Sometimes. I could only use the energy produced while the donor was in a state between life and death and I borrowed their magic. If the donor died, I had use of their magic but only for a limited time. Technically, I didn't possess my own active magic; my magic was a result of taking it from others, which was probably why the craving for it was so intense. Wasn't it our nature to want the things we couldn't have? Being able to hold the power, feel the surge of it, and control it, even for a short time, created a terrible void when it was gone. It was more than an empty space: It was a consuming desire that I hadn't been able to squelch. Some might go as far as to call it an addiction. Sometimes I felt like it was. Most of the time, I felt that my magic was a curse. My curse was my magic.

Madison's lips pressed together into a tight line, and she eyed me with a mixture of sympathy and disappointment.

"I called you in on this job because I knew you could apprehend him quickly. I didn't think you'd use your magic. You've caught bounties before—many times before—without doing it. Why can't you work without using it?"

My gaze drifted away from her. "You have the Crelic," I reminded her softly.

"If it had gotten out that it had been stolen from us, there would have been backlash, a scandal, and calls for a reassignment of duties. I'd weather that crap storm if it meant you'd stay away from using your magic."

Silence was my response. Nothing I could say would change her mind. This had been debated too many times.

"You missed your appointment with Dr. Sumner," she said, tapping her fingers on the table. "I rescheduled it for the day after tomorrow. Don't miss it."

The command threaded its way through her words. She wasn't being overbearing without merit; it was just getting tiring because they wanted me to be something I wasn't, and no matter how I tried, I just couldn't walk away from magic. My body craved it like water—like oxygen. I lived in a constant state of appetite but unable to satisfy my hunger without someone dying. I wasn't reckless—it was just the nature of my magic, and it couldn't be fixed by chatting it up with a therapist. I wished I could get them to understand that.

"What time?"

"Same time. Nine thirty."

I made a face. "I don't need him anymore. He's not working."

Dr. Sumner's weekly appointments were becoming a huge inconvenience. My arrest led to me going to the Stygian, then released on the contingency that I had weekly therapy sessions until I was deemed "cured." The memories of the *incident* rushed to the forefront of my mind, but I pushed them back. I was out and about, gainfully employed —well, employed, anyway—and I sort of, kind of, most of the time stayed on the right side of the law.

The therapist at the Stygian argued against my release, citing that I had been tested and found to have an "antisocial personality disorder." In layman's terms, a sociopath. A death mage who might be a sociopath wasn't exactly an award-winning discovery. Finding one who wasn't sociopathic would probably be harder. When magic could only be gained by death, toeing the line between acceptable and unacceptable behavior was hard. I knew killing was wrong; I wasn't a monster, but I had a hard time fighting my desire. Life didn't seem as important when I had the potential to gain magic. It should be; I knew that. I wasn't a monster. Just weak. And flawed.

"Do you think it's not working because you're still borrowing magic?" Madison's eyes narrowed, studying me.

"I meditate, exercise, and do everything possible to get it under control."

"Except *not* borrowing magic and staying well away from it."

My mouth snapped shut and I looked quickly around the room to see if anyone heard her. Madison would never willingly make a scene, and her elevated tone showed how little control she had over her mounting frustration.

"I borrow it from one person, Cory, and you know I would never do anything to hurt him. I have things under control."

With a weak smile, she stood, her eyes soft. "Until you don't. You're not just borrowing from Cory. You borrowed magic from Grayson, too."

"To subdue him." Yeah, right. I had him locked in runed cuffs. I didn't need to borrow his magic—I wanted to, just to feel it pulse through me, if only for the few minutes it took to get to the STF department.

Madison sighed. "I know it's not fair that your magic is so dangerous. Erin. Sometimes life just isn't fair and that sucks…" She paused, considering her words. "But sometimes we have to just live with what life hands us."

Did we? Madison didn't understand. She was an earth fae and she drew her magic from the earth. Limitless and boundless. When weakened, she could pull energy from the rich soil, the verdant trees and vibrant flowers, leaving them lifeless. Not very different from my magic, but the consequences weren't grave. No one wept for the fallow soil, withered flower, depleted tree, or lifeless plant. If by some chance her magic was restricted by iron, she knew it was just for a moment. It wasn't a permanent loss.

I wondered if she had ever considered what it was like to be divested of magic. To feel the loss and miss it in the way a person would miss any essential part of them—a limb. She had to understand, but she didn't. The therapist had downgraded my desire for magic to nothing more than a magic lust, but it wasn't that simple.

"I can use magic without killing people. You know that." I hated that I sounded like a petulant child. I made my voice drop lower, deeper. I wouldn't be reduced to the screw-up sister begging for a chance to prove herself, nor did I want Madison in a state of readiness for cleaning up yet another mess of mine.

"Sometimes I need magic for work. Not only can I adopt the donor's magic, I can mimic other types of magic, too. Once I shapeshifted."

I didn't tell her I had no freaking idea how I'd done it and probably couldn't do it again.

She still didn't seem convinced that I needed magic to do my job and was clearly unimpressed by my shapeshifting. Her lips moved into a wry smile.

27

"Erin, you don't just use magic, you borrow it, putting that person in a near-death state." That part she wouldn't let me brush over. "It's dangerous, and every time you borrow, you put someone's life on the line."

"Not *someone*. Cory. You know I wouldn't do anything to hurt him."

"I know," she responded quietly as she came around to my side of the table and pressed her lips to my forehead in a light kiss. "I know you wouldn't do anything *intentionally* to hurt him. But"—silence lingered for a long time—"things can happen. You need to stop borrowing, period. Erin, I know you can."

She didn't sound confident, and regardless of whether she said it or thought it, for just a few seconds her face displayed her concern over having to clean things up again. This time it might not be with a neat little bow. Part of me wanted to continue the debate, but I couldn't because my defense was weak. Madison made an effort to shift her worried frown into something that resembled a smile.

"Make sure you go to your appointment. It will help." Her brown eyes flickered with amusement before dropping the check on the table. "I know what the bounty was for finding the Crelic. You can afford it."

The heaviness in her smile lingered with me long after she left.

CHAPTER 4

*T*he contract job that I'd accepted from a frequent client definitely wasn't what I'd expected. As I leaned against the desk in my small office, which felt even smaller due to the overpowering presence of my new clients, I wondered if it was too early for an Irish coffee. Their narrowed eyes watched me with the same level of intensity with which I watched them. This seemed like a really bad joke: A shapeshifter, a mage, and a vampire walk into an office. But it wasn't a bad joke; it was a bad situation.

Finding lost magical objects and catching bounties were my preferences. I hated cleaning up messes. It was what people paid me to do, but sometimes I felt like telling people to clean up their own crap. This was one of those times. But it was a job, and I needed the money if I was going to move out of my apartment and work on earning my freedom from weekly counseling. I needed every job I could get.

"Gentlemen, who won?" I was having a difficult time tempering my sarcasm.

I looked at the shifter. The light glow in his hazel eyes warned me that he was not amused. He ran his hand over his nut-brown beard, several shades lighter than his hair. He was

29

ruggedly handsome and aware of it. I wasn't going to let that distract me from how lethal he could be—those good looks were just as dangerous as the animal that shared his body. Slim, angled features mirrored his tall, well-defined physique: a wolf, stealthy and deadly.

Standing next to him was a person who rivaled the shifter's lethality. While the shifter was solid muscle, visible through his shirt, this man was wispier. I assumed, because he was a vampire, that he was just as strong. He grinned, baring razor-sharp fangs, and his onyx eyes sharpened. Another warning.

"Won what?" he asked as he shoved his hands into his pockets, stepping closer to me with the grace and stealth typical of his kind. My reaction was to slide my hand close to the knife at my side.

"The pissing contest," I said. "You guys whipped it out big time."

I looked at the mage. His hunter-green eyes didn't seem dangerous, but he possessed the same level of menace as his companions. I could feel his magic, and it took everything in me to stay in my spot and not get a taste. I closed my eyes for just a moment, inhaled it, let it wash over me. *Ignore it,* I told myself. Just thinking about it was a slippery slope. When I opened my eyes again, his inquiring gaze held mine. I'd piqued his curiosity as much as he'd awoken my urges. It was a bad combination. I couldn't tamp down my curiosity, my desire to experience his magic, and his interest was making it even more difficult to resist. I wanted it. He wanted it. But "it" could get pretty bad for both of us.

The mage gave me a charming smile. Broad features were offset by sharp cheekbones that reminded me of the many sculptures in the park. This was Kieran, an elemental mage, gifted with the use of fire. My fingers tingled at the thought of feeling the sparks, of controlling something as noncompliant and dangerous as fire.

I needed to break my train of thought.

"I expected better from you, Kieran," I chided.

His grin widened.

"These two"—I waved a hand toward the vampire and the shifter— "can't help themselves. They just can't help whipping things out for people to get a look-see, but you usually exercise restraint."

"They came here for help, Erin, not a lecture," said the deep, cultured voice of the man who emerged from the corner like an elusive wave. Ignoring his presence was easier when he was out of sight; now he overtook the room. This was my job and he had been relegated to the corner to be a quiet observer. Obviously, he had no idea what that meant.

He inclined his head in my direction, his eyes focusing on me hard, as they always did, with a mélange of curiosity and aversion. Yes, they were definitely important clients, because he usually didn't leave his side of the city, where the homes cost more than the building that housed my rented office, and his home reminded me of a downscaled castle.

He greeted each person as he languidly walked closer. Dark eyes glinted, and his lips beveled into a wicked smile. He guided me away from the clients, excusing us. I kept my voice low, aware of the vampire's and shapeshifter's enhanced hearing.

"Satan."

I greeted him in the same manner I did every time we met as he closed the distance I had strategically placed between us. I put on a bravado that I didn't actually possess when dealing with him. The unknown was always scarier than the known; I knew what every other person in the room was, but I had no idea about this man. I could feel his magic, but I didn't desire it as strongly as I did Kieran's. The same curiosity that piqued whenever I was around magic was present, but most times I was near him, my apprehension was enough to subdue it. I was skilled at controlling many forms of magic, but I wasn't sure I could wrangle his enough for it to be of any use to me. Warning signs flashed through me at the very thought. I didn't need Dr. Sumner when I had this.

There was something dark and foreboding about his magic. The ominous air that surrounded him made it seem even scarier, but I worked hard never to show fear. He struck me as the type who thrived on people feeling uneasy around him, and I wasn't going to give him that satisfaction.

A grin spread across his face, baring the edges of his perfectly aligned white teeth.

"I still prefer my name, Mephisto, but for you, I will accept 'Satan' as a term of endearment."

He looked at me in the appraising way he always did, and seemed pleased. I hadn't made an effort to look pleasing. Prepared for anything, I kept my hair pulled back into a ponytail. Makeup I only wore on special occasions, and I didn't count seeing Mephisto as one of them. I'd settled on a simple fitted teal button-down shirt, with the sleeves rolled mid-arm, jeans, and silver slip-on shoes. His gaze lingered on my lips, which must have been a little pink from me trying to bite back sardonic words, and then slowly over my curves, the few that I had. My tall, lean frame didn't allow for the pleasing curves that many men adored. Long runs, constantly slipping into tight areas, and having to fight— often, for my life—had shaved off any voluptuousness that I could have possessed.

When he finished his assessment, he seemed more wolf than man. For years, I thought he was a shapeshifter and was rather surprised to find that he was a mage—well, that's what he'd told me he was. I suspected it was just to stop my questions. His magic wasn't remotely similar to that of any mage I'd encountered. Mephisto was an award-winning ass and wore the title as if it held the same prestige as nobility. However, I couldn't deny he was handsome. Midnight-and-indigo hair and a strong jawline so sharply defined it could cut metal. Winged cheekbones and clear, emotive eyes that sparked with knowing when he smiled, which he did a lot.

I had tried to distance myself and restrict my interactions with him, but my business couldn't thrive without him. It wasn't like I had a line of people willing to give me work. Most people steered clear of me. If I wanted to work, I had to deal with him. I wasn't his employee, but he often had more work than he could handle, so I got his overflow.

But this job wasn't overflow. I was surprised he was allowing me to work with these three. Then again, I had never failed, which was why Mephisto often tried to recruit me as an employee instead of a contractor.

"I applaud your parents' commitment to being unique," I said. "Why in the world would they name you after the devil?"

His lips lifted into a smirk. "My parents didn't name me Mephisto," he said in a low teasing tone, regarding my curiosity with a peculiar pleasure. "We've had this discussion many times."

"Then what *is* your name? It's been three years. Don't you think I should know it?" Even payments were made from *Mephisto*. It was frustrating. I wanted to know the man behind the name.

Amusement played at his lips, and in seconds he had taken up all the space between us that I had managed to create. His tall, imposing body folded slightly as he whispered into my ear.

"That's something I only share with lovers and friends, and you are neither." He took a step back and winked. "But I am willing to change that."

"No thank you, I have enough friends. I'm not looking for more. And regarding the other thing, the amount of liquor I'd need would cause alcohol poisoning. You don't want to be responsible for my death, now, do you?"

He continued to smile as he moistened his lips. He probably thought there was an implied "not yet" behind my denial. He looked back at the group of men.

"I wanted this job, but they actually requested that I set things up with you."

I wished they had come to me directly, then Mephisto wouldn't get his fee, and it might also pave the way for more direct clients.

He was still too close, and when he directed me to our clients again, his elbow nudged me in a reminder to play nice. I wasn't going to play too nice, because it was like petting an unfamiliar animal. I had to stay on my guard and not be dominated by people who were clearly used to dominating.

"Landon, you lost a Dracon dagger. Why on earth didn't you destroy it the moment you had it in your possession?" I asked the vampire. But I knew why. Staking a vampire didn't lead to death if feeding was possible, and good luck trying to sever a vampire's head without them taking a chunk out of your neck. But being nailed by a Dracon dagger ensured death.

Ignoring the look Landon gave me, which clearly indicated he was unaccustomed to being called out on his behavior, I looked at Alex, the shifter.

"And you lost . . .?"

"A moon ring," he admitted in a tight voice.

I gave myself a headache rolling my eyes so hard. Those rings were invaluable. They helped shifters prevent changing, which could be quite helpful around the full moon if they didn't want to shift. Because there were so few of the ancient rings, one could hold a price tag close to seven figures.

And then my focus went to Kieran. His lips twisted and he took a long time to answer, which meant it was going to be a doozy.

"Summoning stone."

My gaze moved between the three of them. "You all do realize most people play poker with money, right?"

"Erin," Mephisto said calmly, "they understand the severity. That's why they asked for a meeting with you. You are one of the best retrieval specialists I know."

He made being a professional thief sound so eloquent. But I did have to admit it had a nice ring to it. I'd bet he called an assassin a director to the afterlife.

I should have known that the items were going to be priceless when Mephisto offered me the job. He had his own company of investigators and professional thieves—or, rather, retrieval specialists. I wasn't totally confident he didn't employ afterlife directors.

I crossed my arms and rested against the desk, my gaze sweeping over each one of them before landing on Landon. His tongue ran over his fangs and his hard eyes flattened. I narrowed my eyes at the way he kept eyeing the veins in my neck and wrist. *Don't even think about it.*

"What happened?" I asked Landon, since he'd hosted the game. Apparently, when you're a century-old vampire, that's what you did. You hosted poker games and bet with priceless magical objects like they were just junk you found around the house.

He shrugged and approached me slowly as if he'd forgotten he was in my crappy office and instead was strolling down a catwalk. And he was still eyeing my neck. I wished I'd asked someone who was a little less dramatic. His slow and overtly seductive moves were too much for a morning meeting. I definitely should have had an Irish coffee.

"It was a typical game," he said in a tone as silky and refined as the Italian suit he wore. "The stakes had gotten rather high—"

"Wait." I glared at each one of them. "You all just keep priceless objects with you for the hell of it?"

Alex nodded. "I keep mine on me, yes."

That made sense, but it didn't make sense that he'd been irresponsible enough to bet it in a game. Maybe he'd been sure he had a winning hand. Among the benefits of being a shifter were acute senses that could be used to assess others' responses. I figured he'd initiated the high-stakes bidding. I hated dealing with manipulative assholes, and I was dealing with three.… Wait, I forgot Mephisto. Four.

"Then what happened?"

"Lights went out, not even for a minute. A bright flare made things blurry, and when it cleared, everything was gone, the objects and the money." Landon made a face. "They even took several bottles of 1850 Pierre Chabanneau."

Because expensive cognac is what this is all about. Getting his cognac back wasn't going to be a priority, although it seemed to be one to him. The egocentricity of vampires never ceased to amaze me. I wanted to point out that no one steals cheap cognac, so maybe he should waste his money on that. Instead, I asked Alex, "You didn't smell anything?" Not too many things got past a shifter. I didn't want to question him too much—I was sure this was embarrassing for him. A hunter being preyed upon couldn't be a good feeling.

"Magic?" I asked Kieran.

He nodded but didn't elaborate.

I thought for a moment, then looked at Landon, from whom I'd garnered a great deal of attention. "I'll be by your home later to check it out." Then I addressed the others. "Give me a couple of days. I'll get your items," I said with a confidence I didn't feel. This wasn't just someone sending me out to steal stuff, or a run-of-the-mill acquisition where they told me what they wanted and I tried to find it. Those jobs were easy. I just asked around and usually found whatever it was without much effort. Rich people with more money than time paid me to find something they wanted. Most of the time they didn't mind if I found it in someone else's home. Usually I could negotiate a purchase . . . and if I couldn't, well, sometimes things got "lost."

The thieves had managed to circumvent a shifter, vampire, and mage—they were good. And I wasn't too arrogant to admit they were probably better than me.

"What do you think?" Mephisto asked once we were alone. The olive tone of his skin deepened his dark eyes. Like Landon, he enjoyed his suits. He usually wore black, all black. He'd changed a little for this meeting. His suit was dark green, with a black shirt with one button open in an attempt to make him seem casual. I stifled a laugh. There wasn't anything casual about him.

"It would have been a great inside job. All the person had to do was up the ante. After all, he knew the type of people he was dealing with, men easily persuaded into showing how big their tools are and only too willing to have a size contest. 'Look, my priceless object is better than yours.'"

"Do you always have to do the eye roll?" He looked amused.

"Do you always have to stand so close?" I stepped back.

Mephisto considered personal space optional, and regularly invaded mine. He stepped closer again. His odd brand of magic prickled at my skin as if inviting me to test it.

"You're curious, aren't you?" he whispered.

I moved back. Again. "You don't want me to be," I warned him.

He smiled. "It might be fun."

"I can assure you, dying is not fun," boomed a deep baritone from the door. My best friend's voice was just as commanding as his size. Six-five with thick, striated muscles that stretched the seams of his t-shirt. His dark-brown hair was cut scalp low. Tawny skin brightened when he smiled. His impressive presence was a clear reminder that he was an ex-Marine, but his gentle smile made it easy to forget. Our friendship had been forged out of convenience while I was learning to use my magic. He'd been the only person who managed to miss ending up on the floor, unconscious, with a team of people trying to bring him back from the clutches of death. Returning magic to its donor has nuances I hadn't quite mastered back then. The moment a person starts to ease from the death state to true death, their body revolts, sending them into shock. Even when the magic was returned, most of the time medical attention was needed. I couldn't blame the school for encouraging me to pursue my education elsewhere and abandon using my magic. The incidents should have scared me into compliance, but instead I perfected the technique. Now the donor didn't revolt against the somnolence but welcomed it.

"Hey, you said it wasn't that bad," I teased, grinning.

"It's cleansing," Cory said. "Like being punched in the chest. It's a reminder of how nice it is to breathe without it hurting. Every once in a while, people need a reminder of how good they have it." He was still smiling as he took a position next to me, crossing his arms over his chest, mirroring my stance.

"Satan's here, where's the check?" he asked as he looked at the desk. Cory helped me a lot between working at his full-time job. When I knew I needed magic for a job, he was there to help and, worst case, offer me his own magic.

He looked up from perusing the desk. "What happened?"

"Landon, Kieran, and Alex had a moon ring, summoning stone, and Dracon dagger stolen during a poker game."

"Most people play with money. Do they not realize that?"

"That's what I said." I laughed.

Mephisto didn't find us amusing. He frowned. "As you were saying," he urged.

"It just seems like it would be ideal for someone to plan

this game only to have things stolen and then claim innocence. What if Landon planned it?"

Mephisto didn't take a beat to consider it. "Something like that is beneath him. Despite the long-standing mythology, vampires and werewolves get along just fine, and Landon and Alex are friends. I don't doubt that if he'd won the moon ring, he would have sold it back to Alex . . . at a hefty upcharge." He smiled at the idea and I figured he'd probably do the same thing, too.

I dismissed the inside-job theory.

Cory was the constant skeptic. "It's really odd that they came to you, Mephisto, and not the police."

I shook my head. "Think about the nature of the three objects. We'd be discreet. It's doubtful the police would be, and then you'd have pandemonium. How many people would be hunting for them? You're looking at objects that combined could easily command three million dollars. Let's say the police found them. How long would it take for them to get the objects back to their owners? And you know the summoning stone is going to be confiscated. Technically, they're illegal."

"There's nothing technical about it. People just frown upon objects that can summon magic from other realms. You know the whole apocalypse-by-magic thing tends to make people a little jumpy," Cory offered.

"I know, and if the stone were owned by anyone other than Kieran, I wouldn't be comfortable returning it."

Eyes narrowed, Mephisto watched the exchange. He smiled. "Do I detect desire? Kieran or his magic?"

"Neither. He just seems like someone who could be trusted with it," I said a bit too quickly.

Mephisto snorted. "Yes, trust the man who used such an important and dangerous object as currency in a game," he pointed out, derisively.

He was right. Was my interest in Kieran's magic—or even

the man himself—clouding my judgment? I shook off the thought. I needed to be open minded and ready for anything, because there was definitely something to this story.

"Is it possible they wanted all the objects, or just one, and the rest were easy targets since they were all there?" Cory asked.

That, my friend, was a very good question.

CHAPTER 5

"*Y*ou didn't move anything," I stated as I entered Landon's house.

"No, I did as you asked and left things as they were."

Any lingering suspicions I had about him being involved in the theft were put to rest.

He couldn't use the summoning stone—he wasn't able to perform magic. Unlike Asher, he wasn't known for collecting things he couldn't use. The moon ring was no good to him, either, and I was sure he was very unhappy that someone else now had the Dracon dagger. There were very few people who could kill him, but it had just become a lot easier.

He showed me around the spacious room where he'd hosted his guests. It was as nicely decorated as the rest of his home. A large wooden table sat in the center, and modern chairs were placed in the corners. A long sofa was a few feet from the table, and to the far right a bar was stocked with top-shelf alcohol and wine that I would probably never be able to afford. I scanned the room and decided it hadn't been a job of convenient circumstance. There were other things that could have been stolen. Landon had magical objects casually placed throughout the space—as if they were after-thoughts. Some could be dangerous in the wrong hands. They might not be of any use to vampires, but if he entertained anyone who performed magic, they could be.

I perused his collection. Affixed to the walls were katanas. They weren't magical, but the blades were made of iridium, a metal that prevented magical beings from using their magic. Want to stop a magic wielder? Shove one of those in them. I supposed just being impaled by a sword would stop them, too.

A calling stone, something necromancers used during spells and rumored to have the ability to compel vampires into compliance, decorated a side table. It didn't seem like something you'd display willy-nilly, but Landon was egotistical. He practically begged someone to steal from him. If the rumors about him were correct, the thief would regret it dearly. Landon wasn't the Vampire Master but was sired by him and one of the oldest vampires in the city. The Vampire Master was aged to the point he found humans and their more entertaining counterparts—other supernaturals—so dull he rarely interacted with anyone. And when he did, his boredom was blindingly apparent.

Landon often represented the Master. Possessing the same aloofness and views of human existence, Landon preferred the company of other supes for his social needs, and humans to satisfy the others.

He was handling things well—too well. I decided then and there that once I found the objects, I wasn't going to give him the name of the person who'd taken them. I wouldn't have their blood on my hands.

As I continued to look around, the lights suddenly blew out. A gust of putrid wind filled the room, and then fog so thick I couldn't see my hands in front of me. Panic flooded me at the sensory loss. I listened hard for the sound of steps near me. Nothing. My hand went to the knife sheathed at my waist. Before I could do a blind search, the room was again brightly lit, the air clear, and every one of Landon's valuables was gone, including all the alcohol off his middle shelf.

Landon glared at the empty shelves, the spots where swords had hung on the wall, and the bare tables. If he could have turned red, he probably would have. His eyes blazed. "Who the hell is doing this? I'm going to rip their arms off."

"No need to do that," I feebly reassured him. But based on how quickly the person had gotten in and out of a vampire's home with a ton of valuables, I wasn't sure he was going to be able to rip anything off them. I inhaled the air. I could feel the magic—dark, fiery. My skin tingled with it. I took another whiff. Magic felt different, depending on its source, the scent and feel as unique as a fingerprint or snowflake. Witches' scent was earthy with hints of cinnamon. Fae's florid with undertones of dark chocolate—the good kind. Less than fifty percent cocoa. Anything with more cocoa than that made me feel like I was snacking on dirt. Mages' magic was breezy and cloying, like fruit with a tang of mint.

There were distinctions within each group. One witch's magic could remind me of a meadow, another the forest, or clay sand. A mage's magic could range from the light crisp smell of a pear or apple to something potent and invigorating like citrus. A fae's magic could envelop me in hints of lavender, juniper, or lilies. The various scents I could still enjoy; it was the variation of the magic and how it felt when I had use of it that I could no longer experience. With the exception of my attempt to borrow magic from Grayson, Cory's magic was all that I knew and felt now.

"We need to get Alex here," I said.

"Why do I need him? I have you."

"I'm not a shifter. My sense of smell isn't nearly as keen as his. It would be a good idea to call Kieran as well."

Vampires' sense of smell was extraordinary, but unexceptional when compared to that of a shifter.

Alex's expression was stern as he walked around the room, visibly inhaling, and then he frowned.

"Just like the last time, nothing. I just smell smoke. Everyone has a scent, but the smell of smoke is masking theirs." His inability to get their scent was disappointing, but the intel I gathered was priceless: Shifters couldn't track scent over smoke.

He scanned the area and his eyes went to a small mark on the floor: a partial footprint.

"What do you all do with your phones when you play?" I asked.

"They aren't allowed," Landon said. "No devices are allowed during the games."

I looked for my phone; it had been taken. I turned to Landon. "Do you have your phone with you?"

He shook his head. At his age, he was probably used to a simpler time, so it might have been easy for him not to be attached to it. That wasn't the case with me. The moment I realized mine was gone, I felt naked. I really needed to find the bastard responsible, now.

"The person wasn't that stealthy. They put a spell on you all, and what you thought was them moving at lightning speed was actually you not moving—stuck in that single moment in time. They changed the clocks, watches. My phone is thumbprint protected; they took it so I wouldn't have any idea how much time had passed," I explained.

Brilliant. Now I had to find out who had the skill and magic to do it. And they would need to transport, too.

"You're dealing with more than one person. One probably transported the other one here. The person who froze time wouldn't be able to do that and also cast the transporting spell and leave without needing to rest in between. Magic like that extracts too much energy."

"How did you come up with that?" Alex asked with a half smile. It was the first time I'd seen his predatory alertness; it reminded me of Asher. His eyes were focused keenly on me, and I didn't like it. I looked down at the partial footprint, which had been modified. I used something similar on the bottom of my shoes during jobs. Alex's eyes followed. I didn't offer any more information.

"When I—" No. It wasn't a good idea to disclose how I *retrieved* things.

He smirked, moved closer, the haunting glow of interest sparking in his eyes, and a brow rose. "When you what?" he asked, a hint of playfulness in his voice.

"When I deliver toys to small children on the twenty-fourth of December," I said, then directed my attention to Landon, who only seemed interested in getting his things back.

"I have to go. I'll call—" *Dammit, I need a phone.* "Once I have another phone, I'll call you," I told Landon.

Alex walked out with me.

"Do you need any help?" he asked as he headed toward a sleek, black, expensive-looking sports car. I hadn't seen one like it before, which probably meant he wasn't hurting for money. Owning a moon ring was additional evidence of his financial solvency, and if he'd been invited to play with Landon, he obviously had enough money to lose it frivolously. I figured Mephisto had probably charged a lot more than he'd offered me for this job and took out more than his typical referral fee.

I didn't have time to dwell on my pay rate; I had thieves to find, ones with better resources than Mephisto. What I really hoped was that when I found the crooks, I could resist trying their magic for myself.

Cory and I walked slowly through the alleyway, looking at his phone as we attempted to track mine. The little dot flickered, alerting me to the location of my phone and possibly that of the thief who took it.

"It has to be a witch," Cory said after several moments of deliberation. As a witch himself, he had to be reluctant to accuse one. He felt witches were always the first ones people considered when strong magic was performed.

"It could be a mage," I suggested, but it lacked conviction.

Cory's face twisted and his eyes scrutinized me.

"Name one mage that can do a spell that powerful."

"I can't think of one," I panted as we started running full tilt toward the location of the phone. I could see the back of a hoodie peeking out from around the corner. Hints of pine lingered in the air, mingling with the putrid smell of refuse. Our pace quickened to close the distance between us and the hooded figure.

Once in striking distance, I lunged at the figure, my arm outstretched. If I couldn't grab the thief, at least I would be able to see their face, hair, or some distinguishing feature. But I didn't get anything more than a flash of skin from the hand that flicked back in my direction. Just a little magical shove to get some distance, then the phone thief vanished. Cory was a couple feet behind me—solid and slow. Getting hit by him would surely knock you out, but if you could run fast, you were likely to avoid that fate.

"Pine," I announced to the empty space. Apparently, other supernaturals didn't have hyperosmia when it came to magic —just me.

"Still think it might be a mage?" he questioned in his mocking I-told-you-so voice. The rivalry between mages and witches was bewildering. Their magic was closely linked and mirrored each other's, yet both races pretended their magic was so different that they didn't understand how it could be confused. There were elemental mages, but there were witches who could control the elements, too. Depending on who was telling the story, one race originated from the weaker sister.

Ameritis, the goddess of magic, had two daughters: Verne, the forebearer of witches, and Prae, the forebearer of mages. Whoever was giving the history lesson, mage or witch, determined which sister was the weaker of the two.

The debate didn't make sense to me. They were sisters who both conceived children with human men, the results were the same: Ameritis was their grandmother. Pointing out their similarities was useless because doing so led to an unrequested and rambling history lesson. Because obviously me and the rest of the world were too simple-minded and inept in our magical knowledge to see the nuances in their magic.

We didn't have time for a debate, so I let it go.

"We're looking for a witch or witches." But something gnawed at me about everyone smelling smoke. Why smoke? Smoke covered most other smells. An elemental mage could control it without setting the whole place aflame, so it could be an elemental mage, but I didn't know that they were able to transport themselves. I thought only witches could do that. On the other hand, a vampire had borrowed magic from the Crelic, and the magic it imbued him with would allow him to Wynd and magically transport.

"Text Madison and find out if the Crelic is still in their possession," I asked Cory. While he contacted Madison, I processed all existing information: The smell of smoke lingered long after the assailant was gone; a partial footprint was left. Whoever had my phone was a witch—the hint of pine—and had likely been part of the heist. They also had the ability to transport, which meant either the witch was one of the strongest witches I'd ever encountered, or they were in possession of an object similar to the Crelic to boost their magical ability.

CHAPTER 7

*M*y need for a quick departure from his office had me nearly jogging to my car. Mephisto was leaning against his car, waiting for me.

"Have you had breakfast?"

"No."

"Why don't you join me?" It wasn't the first time he'd made an invitation like that, but it was the first time I accepted. I was surprisingly hungry, or perhaps in need of a distraction.

We walked just a couple of blocks to a small café that made me forget that we were in the suburbs of Pine, Indiana, rather than downtown in a major city. The chic café touted an industrial look. White brick made up the back walls. Dark-wood tables complemented the rustic wood seating. Eclectic metal art from local artists covered the walls. Despite the industrial look, the atmosphere was warm and inviting. A place you'd feel comfortable chatting with friends over a cappuccino or a mimosa.

After we were seated, he rested back in his chair. "We have a thief terrorizing the good folks of our city," he said with a wry frown.

"I think calling them 'good folks' is using those words rather liberally. They robbed Landon and Alex and some of your friends, after all."

He shrugged. "We have a thief among us, and he's very active."

"Did you smell smoke at your client's place? Smoke and a leathery odor?"

He considered for a moment before nodding in confirmation.

When the server came to our table, Mephisto ordered a Bloody Mary. He raised his brow, asking me if I wanted something to drink. I declined. When I ordered a crepe and coffee, he suggested I make it Irish. I declined. I needed a distraction, not my inhibitions altered.

His drink was placed in front of him, and he pushed it in my direction. Had my face betrayed me again? Did I look like I needed a drink? I really wanted one . . . possibly two. I couldn't stop thinking about Dr. Sumner's upcoming meeting with Dr. Wilmer. Plus, drinks with Mephisto implied a casualness that I didn't want. Things needed to be strictly professional between us.

"I don't drink," I lied, pushing the drink to the center of the table. Why the lie? I could have just said I didn't want the drink. It was him; he studied me too hard, seemed way too interested in my life, in me.

"Aren't you the principled one? I can honestly say that you are the first of your kind I've met who doesn't. Is there a reason? It seems like such a difficult magic to have, surely sometimes you need something to take the edge off." His lips lifted in a mirthless smile, his honed gaze showing that he knew I'd lied.

Magic wafted off him and laced around me, strong and unique. Hints of it were always present whenever he was near—with effort, I could ignore it. This couldn't be ignored. It drew me to him, the magic swirling between us like a bouquet. An alluring, intoxicating scent of the many variations of magic that melded to create his unique brand. The intensity of it was more potent. Enrapturing. My senses nudged me at the trap laid before me. No magic. The many times I said it to Dr. Sumner, I didn't mean it. This time I did.

"Fine, I drink." *Too much at times.* "I just don't want to drink with you."

That amused him far more than offended him. "Ah," he mused, taking another sip from his glass. "You need to be at your sharpest when you are with me. Should I be flattered or offended?"

A person like him would be flattered, and he was. I could see it in the curve of his smile and the amused assurance in his eyes. He thought I'd relax around him and he could easily coax any information he wanted from me. He was so wrong. I got the server's attention and ordered a sangria.

I took a long draw from the glass as soon as it arrived, keeping my gaze fixed on him the whole time. I realized the hypocrisy of having our own version of a pissing contest after chastising Landon, Kieran, and Alex for doing the same thing.

Eyes locked, we drank in silence for several minutes.

"Death mage." Disdain laced the words. "I despise the bastardization of language and the devolution of words, ignoring the intent and symbolism of the original context. Cursed by the raven has a more elegiac ring."

"But death mage is more accurate. Raven Cursed makes it seem like my magic is more harmless than it really is and causes the danger to be overlooked or dismissed by the beautiful wording. I'm not unaware of how dangerous I can be."

He took another sip from the glass, then pushed it aside. His hands rested on the table as he leaned in. A smile tugged at the corners of his lips. "It's unfortunate that your kind has two modes: docile or sociopath. Most just slip into a pedestrian life as though they are simply human. It has been instilled in them to fear their magic, so they don't explore it. Such a destructive way to live, withdrawing from the supernatural world and ignoring that essential part of themselves. There really isn't a middle ground with your kind, is there?" He gave me a sullen smile. "Those of you who explore it seem to love it too much and end up in institutions, prisons, or worse. But..." he drew it out, "I shouldn't speak in such absolutes, after all you've managed."

He carefully watched me. Mephisto knew damn well I hadn't found that majestic middle. Oftentimes I found myself hanging by a tendril, trying not to find myself in the "worse" situation. If a death mage went on a bender, lost control, or indulged too much, then more than likely he or she "accidentally" died while being apprehended. I've known of three. One never explored her magic, settling for a pseudo-normal life, pretending to be just human. Two went to magical school with me. I lasted a semester longer than they did. Being surrounded by magic wielders and knowing that one whisper of power and their magic was ours was too much for them, and they returned to human schools. Considering that we could easily walk through the streets, moving upon people like a wraith and leaving corpses in our wake, the level of restraint we exercised every day should have been but never was acknowledged: "Hey, good job, you didn't kill anyone today. Here's a cookie."

Mephisto ran a finger along the rim of his glass. He looked up, studying me with renewed interest. "I suppose you're the unicorn. The one who loves their magic and how magnificent it is." He leaned toward me. "And learns to manage it. People like to say your kind are some evolution of evil, but that's because there are so few of you and no one can truly appreciate the many layers and nuances of your magic."

What was the purpose of the last part? Was I supposed to

revel in my specialness? Do the snowflake dance down the street, embracing my unicorn-ness?

After a long pause, he finally said, "Has it always been easy to manage, or have you had the same problems as others?"

Fine, I'll play your game. He knew damn well I had problems. There wasn't any doubt that he knew everything about me, even the records Madison had been able to get sealed.

"No." I lied with the confidence of someone swearing on a Bible. I winced inwardly at how easy it was. I saw the word flash before me: sociopath. But a lie just to end an uncomfortable conversation didn't hurt anyone. I didn't want Mephisto's attention; his apparent fascination with me made me feel uncomfortable.

He smiled. "Good for you." A knowing smirk played over his mouth and made it all the way to his eyes, which seemed to glint with mischief. "Personally, I don't see your magic as evil. In fact, I'm in awe of it."

Of course you are, Satan's little helper. But it wasn't just a morbid curiosity; there was more. Why was he so intrigued and was that interest reserved for me, or all people like me?

His voice dropped to a low drawl. "It's such a strange and enchanting gift to be able to use death in a constructive way." He looked past me, drawn into his thoughts so much that he held his breath. Then he returned his attention to me, and there it stayed.

I spent most of the meal trying to ignore both his gaze and the refreshed sangria a couple of inches from me. I didn't want to admit it, but Dr. Sumner was right: Alcohol did lower inhibitions. I only had one donor, someone I would never kill, and yet I didn't want to risk losing control. Perhaps there was something sociopathic and sadistic in me that wanted the tenuous vine that kept me fettered between control and unrestrained recklessness to break. No boundaries, no rules.

"How many like me have you known?"

It didn't take long for him to answer. "Four."

I'm sure the question showed on my face, which led to him answering without me asking. "All the ones I knew are dead," he said.

As soon as I placed my empty glass on the table, both of our glasses were replaced with fresh drinks. The devil was enjoying our day drinking.

Between sips, I ate. Did I want to know more about their deaths? Yes, but I was afraid of what might be revealed. I hoped by the time I'd finished my meal, I'd be prepared to hear what happened to them. I felt like it would be a biopic of my life: bender, arrested, died during apprehension. A reminder of what could happen and how many people didn't like what I was. I switched the subject to the robberies.

"I need you to have a poker game, something as obnoxiously extravagant as Landon's," I told him.

"The one that Landon had wasn't that extravagant, and the attendees weren't what I'd consider the top echelon of society."

"Is your tie in a twist because you weren't invited?" I watched his smug, elitist moue twist into a scowl. "Well, you can make your little game the most extravagant in the land and invite all the heavy hitters. Bet a bald eagle, Alexandrite and black opals, and objects that most believe are just rumors. Go for gold. May your party beat up Landon's party. Be discreet enough to get the thieves' attention, but not so discreet that they don't find out about it."

"As you wish," he said softly, in false compliance. If I had my wish, he wouldn't be getting ten percent of a job he wouldn't be helping with. As I drained the last of the liquid from my glass, I saw Mephisto signal the server to bring another.

Mephisto started doing something with his magic again. Potent and captivating. There wasn't any denying that he possessed a great deal of magic, and it was as intoxicating as the drinks. All the things I could do with it. The thoughts of how I'd use it became more forceful and my awareness of it more acute. When he leaned closer, I wondered how much he knew of the mechanics of my magic. He was close enough; all I had to do was whisper the words and snatch the magic from him, leaving him in a state that could be mistaken for a health emergency, the people around none the wiser as to what I'd done.

If he was worried about the consequences of being so close to me, he wasn't showing it. His face was a slate of cool indifference.

"*But* you would never do that," he said, "because you have better control than to leave me in a state of lifelessness."

Eyes narrowed, I wondered if my expressions were that easy to decipher or whether Mephisto had other abilities.

"Can you read my thoughts?"

"No. I'm quite perceptive, and even if I weren't gifted in that, I know you."

"Do you?" I challenged.

He nodded. "More than you'd ever give me credit for." His attention went to the window as a black car pulled up. "You've had three drinks. I have a car ready to give you a ride if you'd like." I glanced at the black sedan outside and nodded.

His fingers traced the rim of his glass again. "Ask your question, Erin."

No need to be coy. "You didn't have anything to do with the deaths of the other Raven Cursed, did you?"

Pulling his eyes from the glass to meet mine, he didn't respond as quickly as I wished, but eventually he said, "No."

What good was his response if I didn't know how to read him? Was that the truth or was he a good liar? His answer just created more questions.

CHAPTER 6

*F*ive more minutes and I was going to be late for my appointment with Dr. Sumner. I reached for the door handle and stopped, needing a few more minutes. I was stressed. Madison had sent me a text. She was looking out for me and it was hard to be irritated with that, but I was all the same. It was a less than subtle reminder that she didn't have confidence in me and that it was only a matter of time before she would need to fix another situation of my making. I took out my phone and stared at the link to the job in archives she'd sent me and her comment. *It's yours if you want it.* I shoved the phone back into my purse and frowned. Archives? They had state-of-the-art technology, everything was digital, why the hell did they need someone in archives? I pulled out my phone again and looked at the duties. Ah. It was to make everything digital.

I got a headache just thinking about how mind numbing and boring that job had to be. Could I function shut away in an office, uploading things into files, logging information, and never getting my adrenaline rush? Maybe my life would be infinitely easier with a dull nine-to-five job, and being confined in a room away from magic, with just paper and a computer to keep me company. Briefly, I considered the possibility, but I knew the answer.

"Erin."

The familiar deep voice pulled me from my thoughts. On my right, Mephisto was getting out of his car. He'd traded his customary black suit for one in midnight blue, a woven dark patterned tie, and a shirt just a shade or two lighter than his suit. He looked at the building and then back at me. His brows arched, but he didn't ask and I didn't tell.

"You have business in this area?" I asked.

He nodded. "It seems that someone has been very busy claiming items that aren't theirs." His tone was rough, agitated. Perhaps he thought he would be next. The thief did seem to have a type: supernaturals who prided themselves on their collection of valuable magical objects.

"What was taken?"

"I'm not sure. I'll have more information when I meet with them."

I glanced at my watch, hesitating. Given a choice, I would rather continue to talk to Mephisto than to Dr. Sumner. But I didn't have that choice.

Our session went as it always did, me looking at him for the first ten minutes as he waited for the metaphorical dam to break and for me to reveal all my feelings to him. It had been over two years and he was still waiting. Initially, I'd been going to the Stygian, but Sumner had condescended to take me on as a client. I'd always thought it was peculiar that a human would distinguish himself as the preferred therapist for supernaturals. It wasn't as if there weren't any—supes were in all professions—but ten years ago, when the city was plagued with young shifters who had difficulty controlling themselves and the city experienced a rash of vampire attacks, he'd been instrumental in helping manage the mayhem and his role became defined. I remained unconvinced his intervention was the reason for the cessation of attacks, which coincided with a change in the Alpha of the Northwest Pack, and the return of Landon and the Master of the Vampires to the city. I suspected a visit from the local Alpha and the Master did more to manage the shifters and vampires than anything Dr. Sumner did. But Dr. Sumner lavished in the accolades that came from his great work. His brilliance as a therapist and physician wasn't in question—I'd give him that. I was, however, skeptical of his ability to deal with supes with the expertise for which he'd been celebrated.

He pushed his glasses up his nose, crossed his right leg over his left thigh, and looked up after he finished reviewing his notes. We started with all the same questions.

"When was the last time you borrowed magic?"

"A while?" Grayson didn't count. I didn't use the magic, and as far as I was concerned, it only counted when I did.

"Meditation?"

I shrugged. "Meditation." It worked sometimes, but my mind drifted too much to my desire for magic, that initial feel of it coursing through my body. The euphoria of possessing it, having it at my fingertips. Meditation didn't work as expected—not for me. But at the Stygian, I put on an award-winning performance about the therapeutic wonders of meditation.

"Are you drinking?"

"More than I'm meditating because it works better."

He went on his spiel about alcohol decreasing inhibitions, masking problems, blah, blah, blah. I'd heard variations of the same line over the years. Eventually he noticed I'd zoned out and was staring at the closed drapes, which were never open during my sessions because, apparently, I'm too easily distracted. Now I was distracted by the patterns in the curtains.

"Wine comes from grapes, whiskey and bourbon from barley and corn. If I can farm it, is it that bad?" I asked.

A disapproving moue formed and disappeared.

"Drugs?" he breathed out in a stiff voice, poorly veiling his irritation.

"If it can be grown in my apartment, is it really a drug?"

My attention going to the door earned me a stern look. His glasses inched to the bottom of his nose so he could look at me over the top of them. My money was on the glasses being fake, worn solely to add to the stock therapist look he had going on, straight from central casting. I snorted.

Reasserting his neutral demeanor, he pushed his glasses farther up his nose in such a practiced sweep, I knew it was something he did often as an alternative to showing his emotions. His face didn't show them, but his glacial stare did.

"You don't have to tell Madison when I miss an appointment. She's not medical power of attorney. I am."

"These sessions were court ordered. The confidentiality requirements are different," he said coolly. "It's been over two years, and we aren't making progress. I'd like you to go without using your magic as a choice. Like you're human. Humans don't have the option to use magic."

Human. The word seemed so obtuse in describing me and my magic. Saying what people considered me was too simplistic. I only had magic when I borrowed magic from others, so many supernaturals didn't consider me one of them. But I had the ability to borrow magic, something humans couldn't do, so I would never be considered human either.

"I can get you a prescript—"

"I don't need a goddamn med, sorry." The sorry was punctuation, not an actual show of remorse. "I don't even think about possessing magic for myself anymore. I know that it will always be fleeting. That I will never have it indefinitely and at my disposal. And when I do use magic, I only borrow it from one source, Cory, my best friend, and I would never take his magic as my own."

I didn't elaborate because Dr. Sumner knew what it

entailed to take someone's magic. He didn't need reminding of it, of what I was, or my past transgressions.

"Let's explore your relationship with Cory. Are you two lovers?" He tilted his head before scribbling something on his pad. The unreadable look on his face bothered me. His low and even tone bothered me. It was the way they spoke at the clinic. But this wasn't the clinic. His office had light walls and a nice-sized window that looked onto the street. Dark wooden bookcases filled with books lined one wall. His desk, just a few feet away, was neat. Everything had a place. Structure.

I didn't want to "explore" my relationship with Cory. I let my eyes meet his light-blue ones again. They always held a hint of disgust.

"You don't like me?" I asked. Sumner didn't say it—I doubted that he could as a professional—but I wondered if he thought I was nothing more than a woman who'd gotten away with murder. A death mage.

His eyes widened and he moistened his lips. "Would you like another therapist? Perhaps a therapist from the Stygian?"

Refusing to succumb to the anxiety that accompanied any thoughts of returning to that place, I took several slow, measured breaths. He knew I didn't want to go back there. He was losing patience with me. I was just one psychological test, angry word, or inappropriate joke from being put back in there. Continuing with Dr. Sumner was my best option.

"You didn't answer my question."

He looked me over slowly. I had made sure my hair was neat, a few soft curls framing my face. I had on a fitted white shirt. I liked white. It was calming, pure. But only for clothes. I hated white walls. His gaze roved over my jeans and lace-up boots and then back up to my face. I had on lip gloss, and his eyes rested there while measuring the smile that it high-lighted as I waited for him to answer.

"Why does it matter?"

"You always look like you're disgusted with me."

"I'm not disgusted with you. I don't think you realize how fortunate you are. You could be locked up right now. And because of your condition—"

"It's not a condition. It's what I am."

He gave me a slight nod. "Because of what you *are*, you probably would have been in isolation. I would like to see you take this more seriously."

"I am."

"No, you're not. Will you take it seriously when someone else dies?"

When it came to giving advice about denying the use of my magic, people became a Nike slogan. *Give magic up—just do it.*

"Everyone thinks I can just stop and not want it anymore, but it's not that simple," I admitted. "Have you ever been dehydrated?" I didn't wait for his answer. "That's what it feels like. A thirst that can't be quenched, and when I'm around magic, when I finally get to have it in me for that moment, that thirst is satisfied."

His wide-eyed shock at my admission flared for a mere second before fading. I dropped my gaze to my hands clasped in my lap. That was a far cry from the evasive tactics I'd unsuccessfully used before. That was raw, real, and uncomfortable.

I glanced up to find Dr. Sumner studying me with what looked like sympathy. It was the first time I'd seen anything other than disdain, aloofness, and at times even poorly suppressed contempt.

He relaxed back in his chair, took off his glasses, and placed them on the side table next to him. I was right: At the angle he positioned them, I could tell they weren't prescription. He looked younger now, with a studious appeal. And perhaps what I was doing at the moment, inappropriately ogling him, was the reason he was Clark Kent-ing and wearing them.

"Dehydration is physical. The body is deprived of something vital it requires to survive and has deadly consequences if not remedied. That's not the case with you. You've gone months without magic, and you didn't die. Your body doesn't need it to sustain itself. I suspect you are confusing it with appetite. You can live through not having magic if you choose to. One step is to stay away from it. The more you deny yourself and not give in to temptation, the easier it will become. The best way is to take yourself away from temptation. A different job, more human friends, a hobby." His voice was low and earnest. A shadow briefly passed over his face and he slipped his glasses back on.

Was I looking at him like I wanted him to be my new human friend or next hobby? I wasn't good at preventing my feelings from showing on my face, something I'm often chastised for, but I hadn't been thinking anything salacious. A simple observation. My therapist was a good-looking man.

"How do your parents deal with it?"

He'd asked the question before and I skated around answering it. It made me examine that I was even more than an anomaly among my own. My mother was half mage and my dad was human. She could borrow magic, but her abilities were limited. Incredibly limited—minor offensive magic that she described as weak. Her account was all I had to go on. Magic meant so little to her that I'd never seen her actually use it. She just lived her life as if she were human—no urges, no desires. It should have been motivational.

"Tell me about that night." His voice had dropped; it was low and somnolent, as if the gentle timbre would ease me into the discussion without hesitation.

"You're a psychiatrist, too?"

He nodded.

"Why not work in a hospital just dispensing drugs? Why do this?"

"We've talked about this before. Medicine is an option, but I prefer getting to the root of a problem and fixing it without medication if possible. You"—he halted, searching for the right words, maybe kinder words—"already made it clear that medication is not something you're willing to consider. Let's talk about the *incident*."

The *incident*. The night I lost control and someone died. The night I called Madison with my confession. The night she was swept into the whirlwind that had become my life and had to clean up the mess. The night my face was plastered on the TV, news, and social media, making me the poster person of the problems with magic.

I glanced at the clock on the wall. "Maybe next time, my time is up." Once again, I'd successfully run out the clock.

The disapproving smile had reappeared. "I don't have another client. We have time."

"I don't. I have a meeting," I lied, standing and heading for the door.

I was just through it when he said, "I meet with Dr. Wilmer next week Monday, and you will be the topic under discussion."

I stopped in my tracks. Dr. Wilmer was convinced I was a contemptible, magic-stealing sociopath and was convinced he would see me again in the Stygian. Being a mage himself, I thought he'd be more understanding. Had his magic ever been restricted with iridium? Maybe if it had been, he would have learned a bit of empathy.

The breath I took was ragged and tasted as bitter as betrayal. How much power and influence did Sumner wield? He and Dr. Wilmer were joining forces to get this menace off the street.

"I'm not going to use magic again," I promised. My voice was small and I could feel the color draining from my face.

"Good, that's a start. But I really think at your next appointment we should talk about the *incident*. You can't fight the demons if you pretend they aren't there."

Thank you, Dr. Cliché. Any more parting wisdom? What about a rolling stone never gathers moss? A bird in the hand is worth two in the bush?

On top of my current job, I was going to have to spend some time engineering a believable story to mollify him. Telling him I just didn't remember the *incident* wasn't going to work. It was true but would do more damage than good. A person who could take magic, and cause death when doing so, shouldn't be blacking out. That's what happened. Sort of. I think. For years, I've been trying to piece the fragments together to make some sense of that day.

Dr. Sumner spoke again. "I don't think you should be in the Stygian. I believe you can live a normal life, but I don't have a defense if you aren't even trying. You know Dr. Wilmer's stance on this; I don't share that belief."

"I'm going to fix this—fix me. I'll see you next week." I walked out more determined than ever to find a way to remove this curse. I wasn't going to be restricted. My magic wasn't going to be restricted. I had tried so many times and allowed it to discourage me. It wouldn't happen again.

CHAPTER 9

*W*ithin half an hour, the games had started and there wasn't much to see. If people knew they were on camera, they ignored it, with the exception of Asher. He looked at his cards, placed his bid, and the rest of the time his gaze stayed on the camera. I would have ignored him, but I had to keep an eye on the room, and each time my attention went to camera four, there he was, looking up at it.

He didn't look down at his hand or any card that was played or his growing pile of chips and two acquired items: another moon ring and a Glanin's claw. I had a claw. They weren't magical, just very useful when dealing with a shifter. It clamped around the arm, usually, although some were large enough to get around the ankle. A quick press of a button injected an unreasonable amount of silver into the wearer, preventing them from shifting. Even if shifters were mid-shift, the claw was strong enough to knock them right out of it. I could only afford one. A single-use product, I kept it as a last resort. And here these people were offering them up like they were trinkets.

In the time it took to move my gaze from one screen to another, everyone was frozen in their spot. Just as I suspected, there were two people involved and they were filling their bags like children grabbing Halloween candy. I did a quick check: Taser sheathed, 9mm with rubber bullets, another holstered at my left leg, and knife sheathed at my lower leg. I raced out of the surveillance room.

When I burst into the game room, the female's bright green eyes widened. A shock of red hair was pulled back into a high ponytail. Parchment skin flushed to just a few shades lighter than her hair. She wasn't able to dodge the rubber bullet. It hit her hard, knocking her on her ass. Distracted by whatever was in her hand that she was readying to lob at me, I didn't see the man who tackled me. His slim, coltish build felt denser than I expected. Struggling to get the upper hand, hammer pounding on his back, I felt him go for my gun. It was only a matter of time before he grabbed it. I smashed my head into his nose. It didn't break it but distracted him enough so I could toss him off me. Still on the floor, I blocked the blow from the redhead and countered with one that hit her squarely in the jaw. Her bleat, a shrill distressed sound, made it apparent she had never been punched before, used to having magic at her disposal. I reached for my 9mm, but it was gone. I scanned quickly and saw it sprawled several feet from us. When the man came to his knees, I grabbed the gun with the rubber bullets and shot him in the arm and her in the leg. She went down with a thud. Pulling myself to my feet, I grabbed the zip ties I'd lost and approached him.

Magic slammed into my back. I crashed to the ground and quickly rolled to my feet. My elbow caught the witch in the throat. As she gasped for breath, I noticed the chain around her neck. The charm on it explained her unlimited and powerful magic. I yanked it from her neck.

Her partner rushed me, moving so fast it took a moment to register his movement. The front kick landed in the middle of his chest, and the spin kick knocked him back to the floor.

Snatching up the zip ties again, I approached, ready to secure him. His red, furious eyes slipped in the redhead's direction. Something in his face made me realize she was the magic, he was the transportation, and no way was he leaving without her.

Without the enhancement charm, she didn't have an infinite pool of magic to pull from. Wynding in with her partner and rendering the players frozen would deplete even a powerful witch such as herself.

The man's eyes were still ablaze with anger but now they turned as black as the streaks in his brown hair. I stepped back, feeling a flood of magical energy pushing off him. I'd seen that wave of color before: Shifters had it right before they changed. What type of shifter could Wynd? My mind raced through the possibilities. New hybrid? Possible. He was a shifter and *what?* More magic, harder, tumultuous, rose from him. His body contorted, and black scales punctured his skin, rolling over his body, covering once-human arms as his body quadrupled in size. Before me, a black dragon with eyes just as dark as his scales emerged. His tail lashed at me and spun my other gun across the room. I flipped out of the way and grabbed the gun I had lost. I shot once, hitting him in the chest. He didn't budge, not even an inch. I shot again, hitting him in the temple. I was rewarded with a slight jerk of his head.

The woman was my only option. I turned quickly and shot her in the chest. The force sent her several feet backward into the wall. Her hand went up. I took the shot, hitting it. She wailed in pain. Magic shattered around us, everyone in the room moved, and simultaneously their eyes went to the dragon. A ball of flame formed in Kieran's hand. He flung it at the dragon. The creature moved away from the flames that landed at his feet, his tail striking the bar and destroying it. I made a note to stay the hell away from that tail. The massive wolf formally known as Alex didn't. He leapt at the dragon, sinking his teeth into him. He was huge but no match for a dragon. The dragon began to move, ignoring us, his tail whipping anything and anyone out of his way, his eyes fixed on the witch across the room, who was cradling her left hand. One claw grabbed a bag of stolen goods while he grabbed the witch by her shirt with his teeth. She looked like a rag doll in his mouth as he soared, using his body like a wrecking ball to slam through the ceiling, to get away.

"You don't see that every day," I said, watching him fly and trying to ignore the foolish urge to jump on his tail and follow him to his destination. I could do many things, but flying wasn't one of them, and I'd need that skill if he managed to knock me off.

"A dragon and a witch," Landon said, his voice a mix of incredulous amusement and disgust.

It wasn't just Mephisto's heightened anger that caught my attention, although he did look fit to burst with rage, but also the lure of his unique magic wafting from him. Even in his fury, he looked at me, and a devilish glint skated over his eyes as the edges of his mouth curled into an inviting smile.

Eventually he pulled his attention from me and shifted it to his guests, who were trying to piece the events together.

"When it comes to your parties, I can always find something interesting," Victoria said. She didn't seem angry; in fact, there was amusement in her voice. Probably because her items, which were in the bag the thieves left behind, had been returned to her.

Mephisto tried to ease his guests' frustrations by getting a list of the stolen items and assuring them that they would be retrieved and returned. Then he quickly and politely escorted them to Benton, who led them out. Only Landon stayed behind, and the two stood in the center of the room, looking at the dragon-sized hole in the ceiling.

"Well, if the folklore is right, your things are probably safe and not being sold on the black market," I said brightly, hoping to lighten the mood. It didn't help. Landon's dark eyes went to me and then to Mephisto, who brushed the dust from his suit and tugged on the arms and the hem of the jacket, straightening it. Even in the aftermath of a dragon attack, he couldn't bear to be anything other than meticulously dressed.

When Landon spoke, his tone was deep and edged with anger.

"I take it this will be handled rather quickly since we now know who the culprits are. I'm sure you will be providing me with more than just the items that were stolen—I'd also like a way to get in touch with *these people*."

Typical vampire. They wouldn't get their hands dirty or spend time finding the perpetrators, but they'd find ample opportunities to seek retribution.

"Your items will be returned to you," I said. I wasn't sure I was going to give him the information about the thieves. They deserved to be punished, but they probably didn't need Landon's brand of justice.

CHAPTER 8

*I*t had to be difficult for Mephisto to be even slightly indiscreet about the game, since his business and reputation relied on discretion.

His brand was the once-elusive purchaser of an amount of land large enough to have been a small neighborhood. People were intrigued by a person who required such space and privacy and gated himself away from most people. I just assumed he was a special type of self-indulgent jackass. I knew I wasn't wrong as I followed Mephisto's . . . butler? Alfred? Doorman—or door dude? Housesitter? Protector of the home? Home manager?—through the house to Mephisto's office. I never knew what title to give a person whose sole duty was to answer the door.

I trailed behind Benton, the middle-aged man whose skin had a healthy peach glow for someone who spent his days just answering the door and directing people to Mephisto. He was tall, and since answering doors didn't give him a lot of exercise, I suspected his fit build was a result of exercise—definitely weightlifting. Either I was wrong about his age or he was prematurely gray. Not salt and pepper, but a midnight ice.

Answerer of the door wasn't an exaggeration of his duties. I knew that once he had escorted me to the office, he'd retreat to one of the leather club chairs in the sitting room, with a book in hand and cup of tea on the table next to it. Hell of a way to get paid, but Benton seemed to enjoy it. I really couldn't blame him. He was essentially paid to drink tea and read.

I trailed him through the palatial French Provincial home that was heavily influenced by the Palace of Versailles. The ultra-modern interior was a design contradiction to the exterior. And in contrast to Mephisto's preference for dark clothes, his home was light-filled. There were marble floors throughout, walls bare except for a few metal works that added to the stark clean lines. Box chairs, metal tables, shocks of gray in some rooms. Occasionally a large plant added an earthy homey feel. Instead of being in the heart of suburban Illinois, this interior belonged in a Chicago or New York penthouse.

I liked Mephisto's home, but I'd never tell him. A person who built something as grandiose as this in the heart of suburbia was just inviting ridicule, and the first time I visited, I handed it out freely.

Despite the incongruity of the interior and exterior, the place suited him. A palpable mystique burnished each room. Mephisto at times was so feudal in his mannerisms that he seemed old world. If he weren't so arrogant, one might find it charming.

His magic was an anomaly of its own. Was it ancient or so new and uncharted that I'd never experienced it before? Those thoughts consumed my attention so much I nearly ran into Benton, who had stopped at the threshold of Mephisto's office. He opened the door, and I could see Mephisto looking out of the window that took up a significant part of the wall. Dressed in his typical black, this suit was a slimmer fit, showing off his leanness. He glanced at me with the same look of amused aloofness he had the first time I had visited his home with the expectation that he lived in a lair, or the suburban equivalent, then returned his gaze to whatever held his attention outside.

Perched on the edge of the dark-wood desk was a professionally dressed woman whose legs were crossed in a similar manner to the sleek legs of the desk. With the exception of the long swoop of asymmetrical bangs, her hair was short. Her skin was a deep umber color, and she was dressed in a black pencil skirt, garnet silk blouse, and red-bottomed three-inch black heels that would probably cover the cost of my office and my apartment for a couple of months, and if I included her jewelry, probably a year. Her lips slowly curled into a reserved welcoming smile that fit her rounded face. Her eagle-sharp nose that widened a tad too much at the tip made her seem sterner. When she stood, she possessed a powerful self-assurance that aged her at late thirties, early forties. Leather case in hand, she gave me another sweeping look.

"Mephisto updated the contract to add an NDA. You'll need to sign it before he shows you around."

I immediately looked at Mephisto, who, without looking from whatever had his attention outside, said, "You'll be given full access to my home. Privilege to rooms that most don't know of. I'd like a guarantee of privacy."

I rolled my eyes. "I promise not to disclose that you have a Life Saver or your love for superhero undies. However, I have an ethical obligation to disclose to the authorities where you keep the heads of your enemies." I shrugged. "But that's on you. Why on earth would you keep them in your home?"

The woman suppressed her laughter to a squeak.

Mephisto turned to look at me, fighting a grin. "Look over the papers. Ava will answer any questions. If you don't have any, sign it and I'll have you look over the room where the game will be, then take you to your final destination."

"Final destination?" That sounded ominous.

"Where you will be able to observe from afar. If magic is used, you won't be affected by it."

I nodded and reviewed the document. It started out like our typical arrangement, but he'd decreased his fee. There had to be a catch. Mephisto didn't strike me as someone whose altruism came without expectations. I continued to read and found his expectation of this assignment. *Not today, buddy, not today.*

My gaze snapped up to Mephisto, who had migrated to Ava. They were both standing watching me read over the document. There had to be something more interesting to do than watch me read a paper, but Mephisto seemed interested in just that. Ava watched him watch me with avid curiosity.

"I need a pen," I said.

Mephisto grabbed one off his desk and brought it to me before returning to his observation spot.

I huffed. "You don't have anything better to do than watch me?"

"I can't think of anything more interesting than watching you."

I made a show of standing, grabbing my bag of weapons, and moving over to the oversized chair across the room, angled to give a left-side view of the built-in library and an eclectic metal piece that was oddly serene. It reminded me of sunset and water. I'm not sure how twisted metal could do that, but knowing Mephisto, magic was involved.

The move earned me a chuckle from Ava.

No longer a specimen under a microscope, I refocused on the contract and started drawing lines through things that needed to be taken out. The main issue was revealing my sources and methods. This was new. It wasn't just that Mephisto gave me lucrative business, he didn't ask the "how," which kept our business relationship obscure enough to give me credibility. People knew I would rather lose a useless part of my body than disclose my sources and methods. Mephisto knew that as well. I just completed the job—and that was it. Unlike his employees, I didn't have to fill out a report or any other bureaucratic BS they had to deal with. It worked out well for me, for our relationship. So, I crossed out all of that in the contract. I left the nondisclosure stuff. It wasn't a big deal. Whatever weirdness or atrocities I was about to witness in his home, it was doubtful I hadn't seen it before. I hoped I had.

"She's not what I expected," Ava said in French. "She's younger and more unassuming. I expected someone more menacing. Especially after the stories you told me and what I heard in passing. I was looking forward to meeting her, but it feels anticlimactic. She's underwhelming."

Anticlimactic? Underwhelming? I came in with a bag of weapons and accessories; what else did she want? Me stomping into the room, a sword strapped to my back, blades sheathed on each leg, and dual wielding Glocks? Dark-blue jeans and a black long-sleeve shirt was a respectable outfit. It didn't scream total badass the way my leathers did, but I had no plans of being dragged across gravel today. Did she want me to mug her, growl like a rabid dog, hand out lollipops and slaps to everyone as I passed them? Maybe I wasn't her image of a retrieval specialist—I really did like that title—but I was far from *anticlimactic* and *underwhelming*.

I shrugged off her comments. I couldn't believe I cared what she thought. If I arrived in a fluffy sweater and a tutu, what did it matter as long as I got the job done?

I kept my face neutral so they wouldn't suspect I could understand them. Spending most of my childhood at Madison's home ensured I spoke French, although I wasn't as fluent as I would have liked. It became a private joke in the family, that the more French spoken, the thicker Madison's father's Irish brogue became. On several occasions, she would grin at her father and speak French with an Irish enunciation. That he didn't think it was as amusing as we did only increased our enjoyment.

"She's not a merc, she's a woman of many talents, but retrieval is her specialty," Mephisto said in French.

True, I did a little of everything. If it made me money, I would do it. But I couldn't put "I'll do anything for money" on a business card or website because the calls and responses would get lascivious pretty fast. Jack/Jane of all trades didn't work either because it cued more strange calls. People would be surprised what some considered a trade. So I kept it simple. Technically I was a bounty hunter. Merc sounded too ignoble. I operated in the many shades of gray of the human and supernatural system, but I didn't want to advertise it. You call yourself a merc and people assume you skated right past the gray areas and went wading in the dark. Sometimes I had to, but it was never my first choice.

"That's the beauty of her. She's not flashy. She's unassuming and her abilities make her tactics unique and noteworthy. That works in her favor. I assure you she's skilled and quite impressive. After all, at this moment she's pretending she doesn't understand us, when clearly she does."

My head stayed down looking at the paper, refusing to confirm his allegation. After several more minutes of looking over the contract, I looked up and feigned confusion over Ava's scrutiny of me. Ava's voice softened as she said something about her statements being rude before effortlessly slipping into another language that I couldn't place.

Once I'd finished marking up the corrections to the contract, I walked over to Ava, whose presence was pleasant, although her eyes held hints of displeasure at being underwhelmed by me.

Tough. I'm not here to entertain you with a dog and pony show.

They looked over the contract and the changes. Ava's

brow furrowed in inquiry and several weighted moments passed as Mephisto studied the paper and then me.

"This is a special situation, which is why I request full disclosure," he told me.

"Then find someone else to handle your special situation," I countered.

They spoke to each other in the unidentifiable language. There wasn't a point to such an extensive discussion. People would be in his home in less than two hours. Was he going to cancel? Doubtful. It was just a matter of whether his ego would get in the way. He knew it, I knew it, and if Ava had dealt with him for any amount of time, she knew it, too.

Finally, he nodded at Ava. She pulled out her computer, powered it up, and started typing. As she worked, Mephisto pulled me aside.

"We really need to establish more trust between us," he whispered.

"Of course. My name's Erin Katherine Jensen. What's yours?"

His jaws clenched as if he was afraid his secret would escape. "You know my name."

"Is it like a Rumpelstiltskin situation?"

He chuckled. "Erin, you are not so removed from magic to not know the importance of a name. And blood. Why don't you just ask for a vial of my blood?"

"Sure, can I get a vial of blood along with your name?"

Releasing an exasperated breath, he moved to Ava, who had finished the contract and was looking it over. She handed it to him, he scribbled his signature, and handed it to me. It took longer for me to sign, because I wasn't going to until I was sure they had made the changes and hadn't slipped in any new requests. Ignoring Mephisto's periodic deeps sighs, I finished reading and signed.

I might not have met Ava's expectations, but she seemed to like me. When I handed her the contract, she smiled.

"It was Setswana," she said softly.

"What?"

"The language we were speaking."

I repeated it, to commit it to memory.

"Thank you."

Mephisto had apparently grown impatient waiting and left. I headed for the door while Ava gathered her things.

"You're nicer than I expected." She spoke in French.

I'd been discovered and there wasn't any use denying it, so I responded back in French. "I'm not some rogue vigilante."

"I hear just rogue," she teased, smiling.

Mephisto was just outside the door, one hand shoved in his pocket. He was a little over five inches taller than me, and I had to speed up to keep pace with him. We went to the front of the house, where he had someone positioned, as well as at the side and back entrances.

"They aren't going to come or go through the front door. You have three shifters. They don't possess magic. How do you think they'll stop someone who's using magic to get in and out?" I asked.

"They have incredible speed, sense of smell, and protective senses. They'll know the moment the person is on the property."

"Unless they do what they did before and just Wynd in, do their spell, and pop out with their stolen goodies."

"You're here to stop that, and the shifters will be good with the assist."

I inhaled sharply as I looked at the entertainment room that Mephisto had transformed for the game. I wasn't expecting anything less than extravagance, and that was exactly what he'd delivered.

I'd seen the room in passing on a few occasions but had only got a glimpse of the bar, which effortlessly fit in with the rest of the home. Dark-wood cabinets and frosted glass concealed some bottles while others sat in front of the frosted sky-blue backsplash. A wine cooler displayed an extensive collection of white wines and a rack of red. It was nice for a home and wouldn't be out of place at a bar, especially if it came with the bartender behind it.

Instead of art decorating the walls, they were textured, which provided a modern elegance that fit the relaxed atmosphere. Heavy curtains filtered out light, but not for Landon's benefit, because vampires his age could walk in the daylight.

In keeping with the décor of the rest of the house, all the furniture in the room was dark.

"How many people did you invite?" I asked, looking over at the bartender and the two uniformed servers standing at the bar.

"You said to invite enough to make an impressive showing. I invited eight."

"Eight?"

He finally smiled. "I can assure you that the offerings of my guests will be tempting enough."

"I'm sure they'll be quite impressive. Why do you have servers for only eight people? Are these people too good to get off their asses and walk a few feet to get themselves a drink?"

His chuckle was melodic. "I promise you they aren't used to it."

"Well, perhaps you can do them and the community a favor and make them."

"Are they coming here to receive a lecture on etiquette and their sense of entitlement, or to be pawns in your little plan, Erin?"

He nearly sang my name. I wasn't thinking devil, or servant of the devil, although the devilishly wicked grin he gave me should have led me to that. I looked away from his deeply commanding eyes, which had a reddish glow rolling over them. That was new, too. Each meeting made him more comfortable with showing me the many facets of his magic. Or maybe he was using them to draw me in. Leaving out breadcrumbs to the house—to him.

While I continued to take inventory of the room, Mephisto went to the bar to get a drink, then retreated to an unobtrusive corner in the room to observe his guests. When people started to arrive, the servers greeted them, taking their drink order.

"I know you lied about never having had a problem managing your magic before," Mephisto accused me softly, once I was next to him.

"I'm no fool. I don't doubt you know everything there is to know about me."

"You make me curious. I have a feeling you're a little curious about me, too. I've never been a donor for a death mage, and it intrigues me. What does it feel like?"

"I wouldn't know, I've never almost died."

His face was close to mine, his warm breath feathered over my lips, and his eyes were lively. As his Scotch-laced breath wisped against me, I wondered if it was just my magic that had him interested.

"Most people aren't really curious about death," I pointed out.

"Then you don't get this offer often, do you? You should consider taking me up on it. Test my magic and what you can do with it. It might be quite interesting."

I closed my eyes. It wasn't just curiosity on my part, it was the addiction, that surge I got when I first absorbed the magic. It was a high that never got old.

The inconsistency of my magic was that people responded differently to it being taken. Cory could sustain a place between life and death for nearly an hour without crossing over. He could resist the seduction of the other side that would give him peace from the disturbing void. He'd said it wasn't painful, just a feeling of overwhelming emptiness, which he said was worse because he craved feeling something, anything. I wasn't sure how much truth there was in this description. Everyone always had a grimace etched on their faces, their mouths parted ever so slightly as in a state of shock, as they were ushered into a liminal state between life and death.

Mephisto remained rooted in his position, and the intensity of his gaze didn't fade. His magic was becoming more difficult to deny. Sensing my wavering abnegation, he inched even closer. I moved in, sliding my hand up the nape of his neck and then grabbing his head. People always jerked away when it started. No matter how much they prepared for it, life slipping out of their grasp was shocking. Impulse and fight or flight kicked in, the desire to get away paramount. I only had to be close—our lips didn't have to touch—but I wanted to let mine touch Mephisto's. I wanted the connection. His magic tempted me on a carnal level. It elicited a desire that made me forget the reckless behavior of my youth, the trail of bodies, the long nights of withdrawal, the small rooms with white walls, the disappointment of my parents.

I forgot the control I'd worked so hard to master. I didn't want to be responsible and strong. I wanted to be weak and careless. I grasped his hair even tighter, slowly inhaling the power, breathing it in, waiting for the typical reaction. But I didn't get it from Mephisto. He welcomed the darkness and was so easily willing to claim death. He wanted it. I could sense his desire. I'd never felt anything like it before. I would give him a good death.

"Am I interrupting something?" Kieran asked. "I'm a little early."

I thanked the universe that he had. Madison was right, I needed to do something else. At the very least, stay as far away from Mephisto as possible. Kieran's eyes bounced between us.

"No," I said, moving away from Mephisto. "You're right on time."

Mephisto forced a thin smile.

"No, you're just in time," I repeated. And he was. He'd prevented me from making a big mistake.

Mephisto extended his hand to Kieran and they exchanged insincere greetings and small talk as I rushed to get more distance between me and Mephisto. Dammit. What the hell was I thinking?

I moved toward the bar, the arrivals giving me a once-over and dismissing me, probably assuming I was there for gaming oversight. In the time I'd spent with Mephisto, several guests had arrived. I stared at the assortment of bottles. Tequila. I needed tequila. Nope. The last thing I needed was to be less inhibited. As soon as I ordered it, I canceled it.

"You always struck me as a bourbon type of woman," said the deep, smooth baritone voice behind me. A blush of anger spread along my cheeks and bridge of my nose as I resisted the urge to move away. Asher sidled up to the bar a few feet from me and ordered whiskey.

I kept my hands balled tight into fists at my sides because if I didn't, he would have been wearing the whiskey, not drinking it.

He took a sip and when he pulled the glass away, his lips furled into a crooked smirk. Silver eyes sparked. The low growl that came from me surprised me and amused him.

My nails dug into my palms the tighter I balled my fists. I shouldn't let him get to me. He gathered too much joy from it. He shifted his weight to his left foot, once again giving me a better view of him. Why did it always look like he was posing for me? He took bigger sips from his glass, finally emptying it and placing the glass on the counter.

"Erin, it's always a pleasure to see you." He drawled my name with the excitement and familiarity of an old friend. My mood lightened at the thought of the Taser sheathed in my belt, near my lower back, concealed by my shirt.

I smiled. Welcomed him closer. *Come closer.* Flashes of him jerking on the floor, flopping around like a fish out of water, brought an even wider smile to my face.

"It's always a pleasure seeing you as well, Asher," I said, my tone just as bright and friendly as his. I hoped the menace didn't show in my eyes.

He looked at me, eyes skeptical and assessing. "If I didn't know any better, I'd think all was forgiven."

"Of course, it was just business, right? You got there first, it was your find." No, it wasn't. *You cheated.* He had anticipated all my moves and had specific details about my whereabouts. I was careful, so how did he know?

"That's a very mature and professional way to look at it. All's fair," he said.

He was close but not close enough for me to lunge at him before he could react. He had the advantage of shifter speed and agility and was adept with it. The movement of a predator on the hunt—even in a casual setting. I needed him closer. His gaze dropped from mine to look at my hand that was inching around to my back. Then I stopped abruptly. Compromising this job and possibly ruining my reputation, for what? Him? I wouldn't do that. The best way to get back at him was to beat him at his own game. Find out what he wanted most of all and ensure that I got it first. What did someone like Asher want most of all?

He moved closer and noticeably inhaled the air, closing his eyes and making a light noise, a beat. The steady metronome of sound kept increasing in pace. It was just too easy now to grab my Taser and zap him. The potential sweetness of that revenge lingered on my palate. I hated that I couldn't indulge the idea. He opened his eyes and fixed me with a look, and I knew he was mimicking the beat of my heart as it increased with his proximity. My gaze narrowed on him.

He grabbed his refilled glass off the bar and leaned toward me. "You're a hunter. Good at what you do, but you're still *just* a hunter. I'm an apex predator. I will always be one step ahead of you."

Screw it. I was going to wipe that smirk off his face even if I made a scene. I didn't care. They knew he was a jackass. It might just increase my credibility. People may applaud me for daring to live the dream. Living my best life and putting the wolf in his place. My hand was slipping down my waist toward the weapon when Mephisto eased between us.

"Erin," he said smoothly, invading my space so much it forced me to move back and distance myself from him and essentially Asher. Drink in hand, Asher sauntered away, past me, the smug vulpine look on his face making everything in me desperate to wipe it off.

"I need to show you where you will be stationed," he said, heading for the exit. I followed, looking straight ahead, aware that if I looked back at Asher, I would react badly.

We hadn't made it to the door when Benton approached, escorting a woman. She didn't need any introduction. Victoria Kelsey, the owner of Kelsey's, was the center of attention wherever she was. Her movements were a fluid glide with an air of confidence that managed to be both captivating and off-putting. Despite her petite stature, she had a commanding presence. The lilac blouse with oversized bow complemented her warm, fawn-colored skin, and the fitted beige pants highlighted her toned form. Once in the middle of the room, she shrugged off the jacket she had resting over her shoulders. Narrowed midnight eyes gave the room another sweeping look. Bowed lips pressed into a tight delicate line; she was unimpressed.

Her attention went to Mephisto, leveling him with a look

that could only be interpreted as "I expected more." Amusement flitted along her heart-shaped face as she watched me studying her. Then her face faded to neutral and I knew any questions I may have had about her, she had no intentions of answering.

"This is quaint," she said. The melodious tone didn't soften her barb.

Mephisto approached her with the casual confidence of a person who cared so little of what others thought that insults rolled off him as if he were Teflon. Taking her hand in his, he kissed it and she nodded in appreciation.

"Of course, Victoria. When you are in a room, all things pale in comparison. Everything becomes quaint."

Seriously?

Minutes were spent blandishing each other, stroking egos that didn't need it. I looked around at the guests. With the exception of Landon, Kieran, Alex, and Asher, I didn't recognize anyone. If there were any humans present, I couldn't tell because of the strong magic that inundated the room. It was always better when I didn't focus on it, actively ignored it. Madison was right: Why did I keep doing this to myself? *Because I can handle it.* It was usually the euphoric feel of the magic that got to me. Now it was a little harder because there were waves of magic, with Mephisto's overpowering it all. The odd difference in his magic snagged me again. Then there were the low notes of Victoria's, which was another lure I wasn't familiar with. I took it all in, and for a brief moment regretted taking this contract and considered Madison's job offer, where I'd avoid most of this.

I can handle it. I whispered the mantra over and over, my gaze moving over the room, taking it and the people in. It stopped for a moment on Asher. Doing so evoked the same anger as earlier, but it was better than fixating on the magic surrounding me.

"Erin." Mephisto's tone was light and easy but still

commanding as he redirected my attention back to him. "Let me show you where you'll be set up."

Drink in one hand, he used the other to nudge me to turn around. I didn't leave the area without giving Asher a final baleful glare. He kissed the air and mouthed a goodbye.

Mephisto guided me out, his imposing body close to me like a bodyguard.

"I see you two ex-lovers still have some unresolved feelings. May I suggest you deal with them later and not while you are working for me?"

"I'm not working *for* you. It's a contract I got from you. And Asher and I aren't ex-lovers." My voice was dagger sharp with irritation, but instead of adding to my denial, the tone held the edge of a lover scorned. I understood why Mephisto looked unconvinced.

With a light airy chuckle, he whispered, "Passion is often misdirected, Ms. Jensen. You may intertwine it with your anger, but it doesn't cover its existence. I suspect there is more than just anger between you two." My scowl earned me another laugh. "I could be wrong, but I rarely am in matters like this." His dark gaze roved over me slowly. "Just like, no matter how you deny it, you are curious about me, and I am about you. I admit mine. I'm not sure why you continue to deny yours. It's just curiosity, nothing more, unless you choose to . . ." He let the rest of the sentence linger.

After moments of silence, he added, "Such denial can't be good for the soul," his tone teasing and dark.

He wasn't wrong. I was curious, and knowing that he shared in that curiosity complicated things. *He named himself after the devil's servant,* I reminded myself.

"Stop worrying about my soul, Satan," I blurted.

His laughter rumbled throughout the room. It was too friendly, disarming. It sent out alarms. I considered declining the job, returning the retainer, and going on my merry way. Sever my relationship with him. Take the job Madison suggested and live my boring life. I wouldn't be happy, but it would make my mother and Madison happier.

But then my curiosity and desire to experience his magic blazed up again. He seemed willing to let me. Did he realize how dangerous a game he was playing? His curiosity could be the end of him, and mine could be the end of the life I knew.

He opened the door to the room just a few inches, leaving enough space for me to enter sideways and causing us to be face to face.

"I trust no harm will come to me," he said with breezy confidence.

Pulling my gaze from his, I walked in and took in the surveillance system. It was highly unlikely it had been installed upon my request for the game. Two large screens took up one entire wall. Dropping down into the large executive chair, I kicked my legs up on the desk, looking at the screens that gave me a panoramic view of the room I'd just left. On the wall to the right was a view of the entire house, each room on a separate screen. I tapped a few keys to change the view in each room.

"Do your visitors know that they are on video?"

"There aren't any cameras in my bedroom, or any of the bedrooms, if that's what you are worried about."

"That's good. No one wants to see what goes on with that chicken and goat in your bedroom," I countered.

He gave a deep chuckle, half turning to give me a look over his shoulder. "Chicken? Goat?"

"I don't claim to know what your deal is with the devil to keep him from claiming your soul, *Mephisto*. I assume there's a weird dance, chanting, and an animal sacrifice."

He moved so sleek and fast, I sucked in a sharp breath when I found him leaning over the desk, his intense, inquiring eyes fixed on mine.

"I'm confused. Do you consider me Satan or his servant?" he asked.

"Only you would know that. Are you Mephistopheles as seen in the works of Faust or are you the devil himself?"

His answer didn't come immediately. How hard a question was it: Are you Satan or his servant? I knew he was neither, but I wanted to know his name and had been reduced to juvenile antics to try and get it. I wished I was above it.

His real name. The complexity and absurdity of people's nature is that denial heightens longing. Upright now, he took slow, measured steps backward, away from me. Amusement played over his features. "I'm no one's servant," he said before turning to look back at the screens.

It was ridiculous calling him Mephisto. He seemed to know far more about me and my kind than I had thought, and I didn't know the first thing about him. It was bugging me. With a name, I could begin to investigate. *Just give me a name.*

"Is it working?" he finally asked.

"What?"

"All the effort you make trying to make me seem so undesirable? Have you succeeded?"

His dark eyes appraised me intensely for several moments. "If it hasn't, know that the offer stands. Perhaps you will enjoy that devil's playground." As if to drive home his words, I heard the faint sound of The Rigs's song "Devil's Playground." I was now convinced that he chose Mephisto for the numerous songs about the devil at his disposal. I remembered our first meeting, when I made a comment about working for the devil; on my next visit, I was met with the song "Sinnerman" by Nina Simone. It played at a low volume during the entirety of the meeting.

My rebuttal was not nearly as well thought out as I'd like. Mephisto flustered me.

"I have no interest in what happens in your bedroom because I'll never be one of the women in it. Your magic makes me curious and yes, I want to know what it feels like, but not enough to risk having anything more than what we have now. The tall, dark, and mysterious shtick doesn't intrigue me the way you think it does."

"Hmm," he mused, "if you believe any of that to be true, then good for you." He was out the door, giving me a quick, "Be careful with the job."

Be careful. It was the platitude I hated the most. Most people tried to be careful. What was the alternative—be reckless?

CHAPTER 10

"*I* need help finding a dragon."

Cory stopped me at the door to his apartment and pointed at my shoes. It was a wonder we managed to remain friends. His home was a tribute to his type A personality. Everything had a place, including my shoes, which I dutifully placed next to his where they were lined along the wall.

Each picture was perfectly aligned on the walls. The decorative pillows were placed neatly on the sofa. The coffee table was exactly positioned—I didn't doubt that he'd used a ruler to make sure it was an equal distance from each end of said sofa. The color scheme throughout the house was tan, in contrast to mine, which featured vibrant colors. I thought the military would have made him crave color, but instead he wanted more uniformity and structure. The muted walls sometimes reminded me of being in the Stygian—institutionalized and lacking control. For a brief moment, I thought of Mephisto.

"A dragon?" Cory asked, his brows arched in disbelief. He plopped down next to me on the sofa.

"Yep, a dragon *and* a witch."

"Cool. I'm looking for a unicorn."

I laughed before recounting everything that had taken place at Mephisto's.

His eyes widened. "Well, finding a dragon should be easy."

"Really? I've lived here all my life, and not one time have I ever seen a dragon. He's a shifter. They love their animal form. I should have seen him at least once."

I ran my hands through my hair, then pushed my bangs from my face.

"If he's like other shifters, he'll have to change during the full moon. I guess we can try to track him then," Cory suggested.

I wasn't sure if shifter rules applied to large flying reptiles. And he would have to live someplace large enough to allow his dragon form to roam unseen. I tried to think of secluded housing in the area. But when you flew over the Midwest, you could see that it was full of places that could be easily hidden. Homes overshadowed by thick trees or acres of farmland.

"*Do* dragon shifters have to change during the full moon?" I asked Cory.

His lips twisted to the side in thought before he shrugged. "I don't know. But if he went through a wall, it's doubtful he did it without injury. He probably left blood behind. Blood, like a name, can be used for a tracking spell."

"How important is the name?" I knew names could be used for spells, but I hadn't seen Cory do one or learned it in magical school during my brief stint there. Cory had said it so many times I hadn't really considered it of any consequence until now. Mephisto guarded his name for a reason.

"It's important. But not to the extent that it can have total power over you. Depending on how strong the spell caster is, they can call the person. However, specification is your friend in this situation. If you want to do a spell to target all Corys, you're going to be in a world of trouble. But if you call

Cory Keats, how many are there? Maybe three or four. With a combination of a real name and blood, you can do damage. But it's limited to others of the magical world. Our names hold power."

"Maybe that's what Mephisto is afraid of."

"Nah, he's just going for that whole hot and mysterious brand. After all, if he told you his name was Henry Joe Smith, you wouldn't be here thinking about him, now would you?" A brow arched as he studied me and a flicker of amusement curled his lips. "The thing about a name and blood—you have to wield some serious power for them to be of any use to you."

"Power like yours," I noted.

"Oh shucks, you flatter me." He grinned, exposing his bright and perfectly aligned teeth.

I winked at him. "You need to be flattered. Who else is willing to be a donor to a misfit like me?"

"Oh stop gushing. I can only take so much. If not me, there would have been someone else. Not nearly as handsome as me though, probably a trollish-looking guy that you'd have to suck face with for all of eternity."

"You know I don't have to actually touch my lips to the person. I did in the beginning because it's easier."

He laughed. "Yeah, I wasn't happy about that part at all."

I rolled my eyes. Cory hadn't come out yet, although I wished he would. Once he was ready, he would. Even if I was wrong about it and he wasn't gay, our friendship was platonic. But Mephisto . . . what had happened between us was different, and I didn't like it. I preferred it when I had an aversion to him.

"I don't possess the level of magic necessary to be a threat to Mephisto, so I don't understand why he won't tell me his name."

"For this very reason. You're supposed to be looking for two thieves but instead you're here, fixated on Mr.

McBroody because he refuses to give you his real name. Even without the name issue, he'd be on your mind."

"And why is that?"

Cory fixed me with a look, his lips lifted into a half smirk. "Because you have a type and he's it." Before I could offer a rebuttal, he said, "Speaking of dark, sexy, and mysterious, we need to pay him a visit. If he has some dragon blood, we can track that critter and get us some money." Cory got to his feet.

"Us?"

"Of course. You can't do this without my talents, and I don't work for free." His hands swept over his jeans and the t-shirt that molded around his muscular chest. "This costs money to upkeep. Grocers refuse to take a smile as currency, despite how spectacular it is." As illustration, he flashed me a dazzler and started toward the door.

"Your modesty is the most endearing thing about you."

"I know. I'm lovable."

"Of course, and no one ever has to tell you because you already know."

"It's still nice to hear it every once in a while." He came to an abrupt stop and I slammed into his back. He didn't budge when I gave him a little nudge. "I'm waiting," he informed me.

I did an eye roll he couldn't see. "You're wonderful, lovable, and I'm a better person for knowing you. The birds only sing and the sun only rises because you wake in the morning."

"How sweet. I wasn't expecting such flattery."

I scoffed and gave him a playful shove. "Move, we can't stand here all day and bask in your glory."

It was entertaining watching Cory take in his surroundings as Benton escorted us to Mephisto. If I didn't know any better, I'd assume he hadn't moved since I left. The room looked no different than it had a couple of hours earlier. Splinters of wood from the destroyed bar peppered the floor, which was still wet from the broken bottles of alcohol. I picked my way around the shattered glass.

Face twisted in disgust, Mephisto's eyes skated over the destruction before looking at me, ignoring Cory, who stayed at my side.

"This is a mess. I hope you have something for me," he said.

"Maybe," I offered, "if he left any blood behind."

He nodded slowly, but it took him a moment to drag his eyes from mine, and when he finally did, he walked over to a pile of debris, pulled out a broken shingle, and handed it to me. There was just a small speck of blood on it. How had he found it so quickly? The magic drifting from him was thick and intoxicating. It was getting harder to be around it and even harder to ignore my desire to feel it, touch it, enjoy it. A wicked grin crossed his face. Apparently I hadn't successfully hidden my yearning.

"Erin." Cory's voice was insistent, and I refocused. He took the shingle from me. Mephisto eyes narrowed and bounced between the two of us.

Even Mephisto looked at him in quiet awe as Cory performed a locating spell. Cory's magic was more than simply calling forward his powers to perform a task. It was an elegant show of power, control, and beauty. Vibrant colors skipped around him before enclosing him in thick vines of teal, peach, white, and crimson, obscuring our ability to see what he was doing. That wasn't a big deal because we were fixated on the color show unfolding before us. The melodious sounds of his incantation filled the room.

Watching him was a reminder of how much better I was.

I shuddered, remembering those dark years where my restraint was so tenuous that it was difficult to be around anyone who possessed magic. My eyes slipped in Mephisto's direction: He was watching me. I gave him a weak smile, my wanton need to try his magic finally doused. I was thankful for that.

Mephisto moved closer to me, and as his hand pressed against my back, warmth wrapped around me. He leaned down, slightly angled so he could continue to watch Cory's impressive display of magic. "Erin"—he spoke my name as he would to a lover, deep and breathy—"are you okay?"

Discreetly, I inched away. "Yes, just a little distracted. I need to finish this job"—I gave him a wry smile—"or you might never hire me again."

I got the impression he was ready to close the distance I'd put between us when Cory said, "I got it." Once the colorful cocoon around him had dropped, he pulled out his phone and started tapping. Seconds later, my phone buzzed with an address.

"May I have it as well?"

I hesitated but went ahead and sent it to Mephisto. "For your information only," I said. His nod was a tacit agreement that he wouldn't disclose it to anyone else. I was sure he wanted it for more than sending repair bills; my request for compliance came with an ulterior motive. Trust. I would trust him with this information and eventually he'd trust me with his name.

CHAPTER 11

*C*ory parked the car. I looked around at the miles of fallow land, surprised not only by the desolate area but also by the presence of Kieran and Alex. The more the merrier, as long as they didn't think their assistance would result in a reduction in my fee. They'd agreed to allowing Cory to cast a mind sweep, so I wouldn't have to worry about them telling Landon the location. I didn't mind Kieran; a fire-throwing mage might be exactly what we needed. But shapeshifters weren't known for playing nicely with others, and one of Alex's status would be even harder to rein in.

Before opening the car door, I turned to Cory.

"Are you sure this is the place?"

He nodded. I surveyed the area again before getting out of the car. I ushered a smile on my face and greeted Kieran and Alex.

"I'm glad to have the assistance," I said in a spritely voice, "but I'm the lead and we move on my command." Alex's eyes narrowed as he gave me a lingering once-over and then responded with a grunt. He might as well have said, "We'll see." Kieran's defiance was subtler; he gave me a crooked smile and a dismissive shrug. *Maybe the more isn't merrier.*

Alex inhaled. "Yeah, there's magic here. Recently spilled blood, too." It was definitely a good idea, or at least not a bad idea, to have a shapeshifter with us, even if he was insolent.

Cory stepped a few feet to the right, running his hand over something I didn't see.

"This should be fun," he said.

Fun meant *hard as hell*. When he pulled out a knife and ran it over his hand, we were past fun and into strong magic territory. Blood magic was the strongest.

"It's a ward. I can bring it down, but once I do, I won't be able to use magic for a while."

Now I was more than happy to have the ill-tempered shapeshifter and fire mage to draw from. If needed, I'd even borrow magic from the witch if she was there.

A stream of blood came from Cory's hand, and he let it fall. Words spilled from his lips, and the ward pulsed and undulated. The more power he poured into it, the deeper the dips became, thinning the barrier until eventually it ripped, allowing us entrance.

Cory didn't look like he could stand upright for much longer. Alex supported him as we walked into the miles and miles of open space, dotted with large trees that stretched to a clear blue sky. This was a world where dragons had space to roam freely.

I heard the powerful whipping sound before I saw two dragons soaring through the air. I looked around for more. One was substantially smaller than the other and a brownish color, the other black—the thief from earlier. He could crash through a house, lose blood, and still be able to play in the sky.

"I'll stay with Cory until he can be of some use," Alex said.

I nodded, and Kieran and I headed for the only house around, several feet away. I continued to listen for the dragons, making sure they were still in the air. For thieves, their locks weren't impressive. I broke through them in less than five minutes—but they lived in a land no one knew existed. Why did they need locks at all?

As we walked through the door, the witch looked up from the sofa where she was sitting, cradling her injured arm. She jumped to her feet, but before she could do anything, a ring of fire encircled her. It danced around her, increasing in height and intensity every time she attempted to breach it. She performed a spell, and the fire breezed closer. A spark jumped to her, flicked on her skin. She screamed.

"Don't move. You have something of mine. I want it back. Either you can tell me where it is, or this fire might get a little out of control. Don't make me burn a witch. It's such a cliché." Kieran gave her one of his dashing smiles, and if he wasn't in a position to burn her to death, I was sure she'd be swooning over it.

Her lips tightened into a defiant scowl.

He shrugged, and with a gentle gesture of his hand, the fire performed for him. It dipped in, burned her uninjured arm, and she howled in pain. I looked away. I wasn't ready to see someone burn to death, and based on her insolent expression, that was exactly what was about to happen.

I left, searching the house, going through the bedrooms. There were two that looked lived in. Beyond the bedrooms was another small room. I opened the door and was met with a narrow pathway between several feet of items, presumably stolen. Statues, paintings, expensive-looking swords, gold, jewelry, and rows and rows of priceless arti-facts. Apparently, dragon shifters weren't any different than the average dragon in their desire to hoard. In the far corner was a collection of expensive liquor, handbags, and electron-ics. I started to walk farther into the room, resigned to the fact that I had my work cut out for me, but stopped mid-stride. They most likely wanted their newest acquisitions closest to them. To my right, on top of a large wooden chest, was another smaller chest. I opened it, and there was the dagger, gleaming; next to it was the stone. When I moved them, tucked in the corner was the ring. I placed them all in the little over-the-chest pack I'd brought with me. Their haul from the poker game the night before hadn't been unloaded yet. I grabbed it, too.

There wasn't any way I'd be able to commit everything in the room to memory, so with my phone, I took pictures. A lot of pictures. They had a storage system, but I couldn't quite figure it out. Chronological? Perceived worth? Location of acquisition? I suspected it was chronological and perhaps perceived worth, which explained the positioning of the retrieved items. Limited on time, I couldn't spend any more trying to decipher their system. The longer Kieran was with the witch, the higher the chances of finding her burned.

Kieran was still putting on a show for her.

"I have them," I said.

He nodded and let the fire fall from around her. Her eyes were as fiery as the blaze that had just surrounded her. Her hair was scorched, and there were burns on her arms, mostly first and second degree. She didn't seem too badly injured but was clearly damaged enough to remember her run-in with the pissed-off fire mage.

We walked out to find Alex riding the smaller dragon. It twisted, speeding up and rolling, trying to throw off the shifter, who had his massive arms clamped around its neck. The black dragon was on the ground and attacking Cory, who kept flicking increasingly less effective magic at him. When the dragon lunged at him again, I took out my Ruger LC9 and shot. The bullet grazed its side, but the scales provided some protection. Three more shots and the dragon whipped around in my direction. He thrashed the ground with its powerful tail, making the earth rumble and shake and throwing me off balance. When the tail came swinging in my direction again, I yanked my knife from its sheath and jammed it into the beast. The dragon made a shrill, furious noise and started hurtling toward me. I jumped out of his way, whirled, and grabbed my knife from its tail as he passed.

He padded toward me, lunging and baring his teeth, moving to the side to swipe at me with his tail. I flipped back, and it barely missed me. Three sharp strikes with the knife and he wailed in pain. The other dragon made a sharp, spiraling dive to the ground, then flipped so it could land on its back and crush Alex, who jumped off and rolled out of the way. The dragon I was dealing with was becoming increasingly irritated.

"Well that's enough of that," Kieran said as the small ball of fire that he played with in his hand became a massive orb. He extended his hand back as though throwing a baseball and flung it into the house. It caught on fire, and the dragons raced to the house, transitioning to their human forms as they moved. Their distraction let us make it back to the entrance, which was sealed. *Fuck.*

Cory pulled out his knife, barely able to stand.

"You're not going to be able to do it." I said, laying a hand on his arm. I turned to Kieran. *Yeah, this is going to be easy.*

"I need to use your magic. You won't be able to take the ward down. I can once I have access to magic. To borrow it, I need . . ."

I was sure he knew what I was about to say: I needed to borrow his magic. I took a deep breath. If I were him, I would say no. We could probably wait until Cory was rested enough to do it, but we ran the risk of having to deal with two angry dragons again and an even angrier witch.

"Okay," he agreed quickly. Too quickly. I narrowed my eyes at him. "Like Mephisto, I, too, am curious."

What the hell is wrong with them? Not once had I ever wondered what it would be like to be suspended between life and death.

"It won't take long." I looked at Alex. "You'll have to carry him out when I'm done."

Hesitantly, I moved closer to Kieran, who welcomed my approach with a small smile. Just a few inches from him, I whispered the spell, the power in it flowing through me. The only words of power that I possessed, and they caused death. They captured Kieran's breath, slowly pulling his life from him. His magic coiled around me, prickling over my skin, then settled on me, familiar and welcomed. It was when I felt it that I became intimate with the hunger I denied constantly, the need I ignored, the cravings I left unfulfilled daily. It was flavorful and satisfied me in a way that nothing else ever did. Kieran collapsed. I was too caught in the throes of having my addiction satisfied to notice him falling. I blinked myself into the moment as Alex moved past me and caught Kieran before he hit the ground. I had to get used to the difference from Cory's magic. This was new. New was always good. Better. Different.

"Do the spell, Erin," Cory commanded in a stern voice.

I nodded. Magic melted over me, the energy and connection with death, the soothing and intoxicating feeling of it, the thrum of magic. I stared at the glow of fire that rolled off my fingers and danced over my hand. I should have been screaming in pain, but I felt nothing except the glorious power of being able to control fire. Mesmerized by the flickers of oranges, reds, and little idyllic blues, I watched them engulf my hand.

"Erin." Cory said my name with force, rough and hard. I dragged my gaze from the flames to him. I nodded again and extinguished the flames. I walked closer to where we'd entered, feeling the pulsating magic that came off the ward and secured it. I whispered the incantation that Cory had used earlier. The magic felt familiar, as if it were my own. I concentrated on the ward and Kieran's life that was held in the liminal state between life and death, making sure I returned it to him before he crossed over. The same thoughts passed my mind that always did when I appropriated another's magic. How long would it last in me if I let him cross to the other side? Consequences. I forced the images into my head. The counselors, cells, treatment, my mother's disappointed face. I checked my desires, buried them deep, and completed the spell.

Alex carried Kieran over the threshold, then helped Cory over. I was just about to step through when I was hit hard from the side, a ball of magic melting into my skin. I rolled and attempted to stand and was thrashed with another. When I finally got to my feet, the witch's angry glare was fixed on me. A wave of her hand and she tossed me back again. I threw magic back at her when she stumbled and then mashed my hands to the ground with flames corralled around them, setting the grass ablaze. I pushed it toward her with a gust of magic. I might not have exhibited the pageantry and skill of Kieran, but anyone who saw magic raging toward them was going to retreat.

It had taken too long. A shadow eclipsed my mood. Bleakness moved into my chest and settled. It was death's whisper right before the tingling of my skin that let me know that death was about to claim my host. Claim Kieran. I had to get to him. I bolted toward the entrance and threw myself through it, sealing the ward. Kieran was on the ground. I knelt next to him. His face had relaxed into a state of somnolent calm, ready to accept the fate of death. Any thought of keeping his magic vanished. I didn't hesitate. I leaned over him, exhaling death and restoring his magic. He lurched up with a gasp, his eyes hazy and distant. He blinked several times before he reached for me. I jerked back from his attempt to kiss me. It always happened, no matter who it was; they were drawn to me, the giver of life. It was as if they'd forgotten I'd taken it from them in the first place.

He looked startled by his own response. "Sorry," he whispered.

"It always happens," I said with a small shrug. It took a

minute for him to stand, but not before he tested his magic. I stood just a few feet away, longing for it—and hating myself for that. But I clung to the joy of knowing I'd stopped. I hadn't hesitated before restoring him. I was getting better. Much better.

"You're up," I whispered to Cory.

Realization swept over Alex's and Kieran's faces. I'd explained to them that the mind sweep was necessary to protect my business, and they'd been agreeable at the time. People always agreed, but when the time came, they'd usually come up with a number of excuses as to why they had to retract their consent.

"You agreed," I reminded them. Both of their jaws clenched, but their original agreement was all that was needed for the spell. And the sample of blood they willingly gave. I'd let them come because having a big-ass wolf and elemental mage wasn't a bad thing when going up against a dragon and a powerful witch. And I wasn't wrong. But I didn't want them coming back administering their vigilante justice either. There were tons of treasures in the dragon trove, and I suspected I might need to try to establish a business relationship with the dragons and witch. They'd be more amenable if none of the victims of their thefts showed up to deliver their own vigilante justice. With the mind sweep, Alex and Kieran would remember the location but not the reason they were there.

CHAPTER 12

*H*umans don't get nearly enough credit for their brand of pseudo magic, I thought as my chest pounded from the thrum of pulsing music at Tryst. The club was loud, crowded, and overwhelming. It was exactly what I needed. After the adrenaline high of earlier and borrowing Kieran's magic—new magic—I needed a reprieve. Trading real magic for the eclectic pseudo magic that humans offered was a satisfactory deal.

Supernaturals often had disparaging things to say about humans because their magic was imperceptive compared to what they possessed, and they thought humans had nothing to offer. That couldn't be further from the truth. *They have much to offer,* I thought, feeling the avalanche of hedonism, rampant joy, and flagrant, unrepressed joy of indulging in the moment. It created an energy that couldn't be replicated and was as intoxicating as a drink, weed, or narcotic. It was an acceptable substitute.

The room was blisteringly hot from the bodies thrashing, grinding, and gyrating on the dance floor in intemperate expression. I took it all in, navigating through the crowd, moving in where I could without a definitive partner. I just moved, swayed, gyrated, rocked to the music, allowing the human energy to carry me to a place of relief. Music washed over me and I let it, refusing to stay in one place, finding different people to dance with.

The five-mile run earlier hadn't quelled my desire to experience Kieran's magic once more. It was the unfortunate quandary of my life: I kept telling myself that once I felt it—experienced it, used it—the desire for it would go away. It was a big damn lie. The desire wasn't squelched at all. Except when it came to Cory. If I made a mistake, someone died. I refused to allow a mistake of mine to be paid with Cory's life. I didn't feel the same way about others. I should have—I knew I should have. I wanted to; I just didn't know how. I didn't think "what if I hurt them." No, my mind immediately went to "how could I keep from being found out." Magic over life. The only thing I knew was—it was wrong to feel that way. I'd yet to learn how to stop feeling that way.

The more I thought about it, the harder I danced, the wilder my movements, the more engulfed I became in the music. It needed to be my escape.

An arm slinked around me from behind and I turned to face a tall blonde. Her straight hair matted with sweat, her smile brilliant in the low lights, and her hands at my waist. The navy-blue dress that ended at the top of her thighs didn't allow a lot of movement without compromising modesty I wasn't sure she had. She danced with abandon, allowing the music to overtake her, too, getting into the hypnotic sound of the pulsing bass and the wild lyrics of the crooning man. It was a different kind of high and I was enjoying every moment.

Wash over me, invade my thoughts, take away the thirst, I commanded the music and the humans, demanding more of the music than it could ever give. I continued to move as if my life depended on it, pushing away thoughts of Kieran—not him, his magic—trying to forget the look in his eyes that told me he'd let me borrow his magic whenever I wanted. For a brief moment, I considered what it would be like to use it, play with it for a while, spend a day getting to know it. And then he'd be dead, I scolded myself. *If you did that, he would die,* I thought. That should have been enough to deter me, but it wasn't.

The pretty blonde moved closer. "What?" she whispered. Her light-brown eyes studied me. Obviously she hadn't noticed my lack of interest.

"Nothing."

Whatever minute space existed between us, she closed with a quick movement. Her body hummed with energy. Human energy. That's what I loved about clubs. It could never totally replace my desire for magic—it just couldn't—but the raw energy of people dancing, drinking, partaking in whatever indulgence necessary to have a good time offered a temporary fix. It was fleeting but it helped. Sex was a close second, and when I felt like this, I tended to do anything to prolong the euphoria—stave off the desire. So, I usually indulged in both.

"You seem to be enjoying yourself," she murmured into my ear. Her voice was low, sensual, and melodic. Pleasing to the ear. As pleasing as her face. She was aware of it.

"I just needed to dance—work off excess energy. Get my mind off things."

"Hmm."

She moved back just enough to study me. I hadn't taken nearly as much care as she had in getting ready. Fitted jeans, blush-colored sleeveless shirt with an asymmetric neck, and, because my intentions were to just dance, flat ballet shoes. To give the illusion of more effort than the fifteen minutes it took to get dressed, I had put on a bracelet and earrings, thick coat of mascara, and pale-pink lipstick, both of which were applied in the parking lot. My hair was upswept to keep it off my neck and with a quick twirl of the curling iron on a few strands, dressed up enough to be passable. From the looks I was getting from my new dance partner, it was more than passable.

Her eyes lingered on my face for an exceptionally long time. Without my hair framing it, the sharp angles and oval face that no makeup trick or hairstyle could round out were more obvious. Her eyes traced the lines of my lips that garnered accusations of visits to Dr. Full Lip Maker. I figured that any accusations of surgical alterations would be for my nose, with its narrowed sharp points that looked like a surgeon got a little scalpel-happy.

"I'm about to get a drink. Care to join me?"

I smiled. Shallow enough to be flattered whenever a hot person hit on me, I wasn't interested.

"Maybe another time."

Once again, she leaned in, warm breath breezing against my skin, and with a quick sleight of hand, she slipped something into my pocket. A card, I was sure, with her number.

"Maybe another time, Erin. Give me a call sometime."

My heart dropped to the pit of my stomach and I stepped back, not nearly as gracefully as she had in her five-inch heels. This wasn't a casual meeting. When had she noticed me? The moment I walked in? I'd seen that look she gave me in other people. She was a Grup—humans drawn to supernatural beings. But these special kind of maladroits weren't just drawn to any supernaturals, just the ones that others considered badly behaved. Usually vampires got the brunt of their attention. Grups were drawn to the creatures of the night, which was a misnomer, because although vampires preferred the night, they didn't have a problem going out in the day if the hunger hit them. Grups were especially fixated on shapeshifters, new ones, who struggled to control their animal half and form the symbiotic relationship necessary to function. It was seen in the younger shifters or newly changed shifters.

The least sought after were mages, witches, and fae who enjoyed their magic too much, who bucked at the rules and were a danger to themselves and anyone around them. Grups liked them, but apparently they weren't dangerous enough. They didn't make the Grups feel like they were living on a razor-sharp edge between life and death, the way dealing with vampires or shifters did.

Were they adrenaline junkies, whackadoodles, or products of the need to just feel something, even if it was immense fear?

Her easy smile and gaze remained on me as I looked at the card.

"I will, Ann."

I likely had a small following of miscreants who were drawn to me. After all, my arrest and trial made the local news. My kisses were deadly, and that fact was sensationalized for all it was worth. Even though I wasn't a threat to humans, there was that murky draw for the sort of people who fall for prisoners and marry them while they're incarcerated. I didn't like being among the infamous. I preferred anonymity. Once again, I found myself contemplating moving. But my family, business connections, and friends were here. I'd be leaving too much behind and wasn't sure I'd be able to reestablish myself.

Moving was still on my mind when I took a seat at the bar and ordered a drink. A strong one. A double vodka neat. Whatever was on my face, the bartender asked if I wanted to keep them coming. I declined but I wasn't sure how long that would hold up. Kieran ran through my mind. The feel of his magic. Exhilarating, strong, and *different*. It was the difference of it that I'd liked. It didn't have strings attached, the way Cory's did.

I blew a curse into my drink. *This can't be happening.* I could sense the newly familiar magic. It pricked at my skin and heightened my desire. There was a reason I had chosen a bar mostly populated by humans: My resolve was low. I was doing what I was supposed to do, taking myself away from temptation, so how was this happening? It's not as though bars weren't integrated; they were. Supernaturals weren't forbidden from going to human bars any more than humans were barred from going to bars populated by supes. But no one wanted to be around an irritated shapeshifter whining about a weak drink because his high metabolism burned off the alcohol too fast. Or their penchant for stripping down in front of the club, leaving their clothes near a building, and using their animal form to get home as opposed to calling a ride share like everyone else. Either way, a naked group of people or a pack of wolves can't be good for business if most of your clients are human. Or vampires griping about them not carrying some obscure and unaffordable wine or the crimson martinis that were only made at Kelsey's. Many bars had attempted to replicate the popular drink, but whatever Victoria put in hers couldn't be copied, and the vampires were quick to let the attempting bartender know. Or fae and their glamours and antics with the weather, or their failed bar tricks of ripping fabrics between the worlds. They do that once and they aren't being invited back. Mages and witches seemed to be the only ones who could walk effortlessly between the supernatural and human worlds. With the exception of me. I didn't—couldn't—walk seamlessly anywhere.

The pulse of Kieran's magic teased me as soon as he walked through the door with two other men. One was a vampire and the other a witch or mage, I couldn't figure out which.

"Erin." His raised voice was silky and laden with the unintentional intimacy that came with sharing magic. A coupling that linked us. A tall man moved, trying to get out of Kieran's way, but ended up blocking him. Obscured for a moment, I took the opportunity to head in the opposite direction, planning to take the circuitous way out to avoid seeing him. Someone caught me by the arm then let his hand slide to my hand. I turned to find his warm fingers grazing along my hands before he took my hand in his. I looked down and snatched my hand away as if it had erupted in flames.

"Are you leaving?" Kieran asked.

"Yes."

His fingers brushed against my hand. "Can I convince you to stay and have a drink with me?" Sensing my hesitation, he added, "And my friends." He gave me one of his devastating smiles. "I promise, they can be quite entertaining."

My gaze flicked over to the vampire at the bar, who was whispering something to the bartender. With a nod, the bartender departed. His witch or mage friend had made his way onto the dance floor, doing exactly what I was doing earlier, dancing partner-less, the entire floor his domain.

"Well, Sanders is fun for a dance or two. On the dance floor is where he'll be most of the time."

Kieran hadn't lied. I wasn't sure about the vampire, but Sanders was quite entertaining. Unapologetically a rhythmless juggernaut having the time of his life. I liked him. He moved as if he'd just gotten new limbs that morning and was testing their range of movement, but his smile was so bright and approachable, he quickly became the draw of a group of women on the floor.

"I guess he's the fun one." My gaze drifted back to the vampire, now sipping from a wine glass filled with sanguineous liquid that had been brought out to him in a special case. He assessed it carefully before giving the bartender a nod of approval. Pretentious much?

"He's the less fun one," Kieran admitted, dryly.

"*He* can be just as fun and has excellent hearing as well."

Vampires. He rose. His graceful fluidity of movement was an immediate reminder, if I had forgotten, that he was a vampire. Warm, deep-umber skin looked even more flawless up close. Deep-midnight eyes were a bottomless pit of intensity as he assessed me. Hints of amusement dwelled in them. The edges of his fangs showed when he flashed a bright smile in greeting.

Kieran jerked his thumb in his vampire friend's direction. "The bartender's nightmare is Dallas."

He didn't look like a Dallas. Not that a Dallas would have a particular look, but the name did evoke cowboy boots, jeans, and a nice crisp white button down. The image of a man wearing a dark three-piece designer suit just to have drinks at a bar didn't come to mind. But there he was. Dallas brings to mind a fun night out on the town, whereas this guy probably considered forgoing a tie and leaving the first two buttons of his shirt undone gallivanting on the wild side. I glanced at Sanders, in a button down and slacks, obviously dancing to the music in his head because nothing about his movements coincided with the beats blasting from the speakers.

Kieran had kept things as simple as I had, although it looked like he had put more effort into his slightly mussed hair than the dark-blue soft-looking t-shirt that lay pleasingly over his chest muscles. My gaze dropped lower. His jeans fit tightly enough to show developed quads, I assumed from running.

They seemed like an unlikely group of friends and it made me even more curious about Kieran's inquiring gaze and mischievous smile.

"So, what is it with vampires being so particular about their alcohol?" I asked Dallas. When he tilted his head, it was the first time he didn't seem quite human. An oddly graceful,

109

slow, serpentine movement. The lack of a moving chest to breathe didn't bother me, but most found it off-putting. I found it more disturbing when they attempted to breathe like humans. That never seemed natural. It was abrupt and shallow and only occurred when they remembered to do what was vital for human existence.

Dallas's wicked smile slowly emerged again. Like most vampires, he was too handsome. Not in the "he's too handsome to be with me" self-deprecating way but in a celestial way. He was too handsome—that was it.

"Would you like to try it?" he asked, exhibiting preternatural movement that had him suddenly close to me. In reaction, my hand shot to my side, where I usually kept a weapon. The space was empty because I couldn't get into the club with it. I exhaled the breath held.

"Sorry," he whispered. He took a step back, keeping his dark gaze on me. This guy was trouble. Dallas's voice was still low, melodic, and honey sweet, as if we were having a cozy conversation and there wasn't anyone around but us.

"Dallas, bring it down a notch. In fact, turn it off. Not just down. Off." I waved my hand over his face and down his body. A body that was still closer than I'd like. "Switch it all off, the whole ewweee vampire-y stuff." I made a silly face to break the effect he was having on me. I wasn't immune to it. And it wasn't unique to me. I'm sure whatever he was doing, although subtle, was indiscriminate. At that moment, I was just some random person on the receiving end of a vampire's seduction. For them, it was a way of acquiring food for the evening—and a little more. I was on edge, in need of staving off the urges in me, and I was trying to find better alternatives than being vampire vittles. If I didn't get away from him, I was in danger of that happening.

His brow hitched up before he roared a laugh. "'Ewweee vampire-y stuff'? Priceless." He cleared his voice, no longer a sultry, entrancing whisper but normal. Well, his normal. He'd probably been doing this so long that it was harder not to be the embodiment of seduction and promise of a sensuous night a person wasn't likely to forget. After all, his life depended on him being beguiling enough for people to allow him to feed or he'd be reduced to the synthetic stuff and, apparently, they didn't like it.

"We're picky about our wines because some of them serve a dual purpose. They are a pleasure to drink and they—" He lightly bit into his lips, embarrassed. He didn't have to finish. I guessed it tasted like blood. Alcohol-infused blood, which was why there were select ones that they liked. They commanded a high price, and apparently, if ordered ahead or provided to the bar, they were available.

"How did you know they'd have it?" I studied the liquid in his glass.

"Places that I frequent often, I have arrangements with the manager." The space he'd put between us disappeared and he was standing next to me again, tilting the glass in my direction. It didn't look like red wine anymore. It looked like thinned blood. My curiosity dwindled fast.

I shook my head. He took another sip, then before my mind could fully grasp it, he was back at the bar, relaxed in the chair, his movements languid as he used his foot to move the chair in a semicircle to get a better view of the club and the people in it.

Kieran had been watching me watch Dallas. I could feel the weight of his gaze on me. I dragged my eyes from Dallas to Sanders.

"Would you like to get that drink now, or go on the dance floor with Sanders?" Kieran teased. Sanders was out of the question. I was afraid of getting pummeled by one of those wayward arms.

"He's enjoying himself." I defended Sanders. He might have looked ridiculous, but unlike the other people on the floor who seemed to be performing for a nonexistent audience, Sanders was living in the moment and dancing to his own drum. Literally.

"He is." Kieran nudged his head toward an empty table at the other end of the club, farther away from Dallas, Sanders, and the dance floor.

Erin, go home. Nothing good can come from this.

I ignored myself and followed him to the small table in the corner. He got the attention of one of the servers, who seemed to already know what he was going to drink so only asked about mine. I shouldn't have ordered another drink, but I did.

He leaned over the table, his eyes dancing. "Today was quite interesting," he mused.

"Yeah, I'm glad we were able to get your things back. I guess there won't be any more contests to see who's got the biggest man parts." I grinned at him.

"It wasn't a pissing contest, as you so eloquently put it. It was just a fun game among friends. But you know I wasn't talking about getting our things back, although that was fun, too. The . . ." He paused. "What happened between us."

"Between us?"

"What you did. Have you ever had it done to you?"

"I can't have it done to me. We can't do that to each other." I knew that for a fact because I tried it with one of the death mages before they dropped out of school. "I don't really have magic to take," I admitted, grateful for the distraction of the server bringing our drinks. It pulled me from the intensity of his eyes. When my attention moved back, he was still staring.

"I think I should leave. You're dangerous for me," I said.

He removed the glass from his lips and placed it on the table. "Me? Dangerous to you?" He looked as bewitched as if I'd cast a spell over him. His finger ran lazily along the rim of the glass, then he eased it into the amber liquid, igniting flames with his finger. With an easy wave, he extinguishing them. My desire for his magic rekindled.

"I try not to borrow magic. It's not good when I do." I hoped he'd understand. He looked as if he wanted to relive that moment, and I was ready to let him. I remembered the dossier I'd established about him. "You like to be in dangerous situations. You're an adrenaline junkie and that's a hindrance to your mother's political career."

He leaned into the table, flashing a wicked look. His voice was husky as he asked, "What makes you think that?"

I relaxed back in the chair, letting my eyes drift over the patrons of the club. I didn't have to worry about Ann, who'd found Dallas. The way she was leaning in to talk to him, she was falling for his seductive promise. She'd get her Grup-fix. It would be even better if he gave her a life-changing experience that would cure her of her fixation. Giving them another passing look, I knew that wouldn't be the case. He'd probably found a donor for as long as he'd like it.

"How was your climb on Annapurna?" I asked.

"I'm here, aren't I?"

"You're very lucky, too. It has the highest fatality rate of all mountains climbed," I informed him, an edge of censure in my voice.

He pursed his lips. His finger dipped into his drink, rekindling the flames. They became bigger and brighter and were reflected in his eyes.

"I'm sure it was an adrenaline rush you needed," I went on. "Probably more than the six street races you were involved in this year. One ended with you in front of a judge. Mom couldn't make that one go away, could she?"

He blew out a rough breath. "You got me. I like to have fun."

And I was the next dangerous mountain he wanted to climb, the next street race he needed to win, the next skydiving excursion, the next hike through Hoia-Baciu. Very few people were indifferent about me, but most possessed a caustic fear and abhorrence or a morbid and aberrant curiosity. Kieran was the latter. An interest that bordered on masochism.

"What you call fun, most people call a death wish. Today wasn't merely interesting, and I suspect you liked it. A little too much, which is why you are dangerous to me," I said.

"Am I alone in thinking we could have a fun arrangement? I don't mind you borrowing the magic, and you could use it."

I took a long draw from my drink while I considered his proposition. There were spells I wanted to try and magic I needed to test. He was willing to be a donor and…. My mind drifted to darker places, indulgences that I wanted to believe didn't still exist. If I had an accident, who would know? With his reckless past, I could hide a mistake easily. Make it look like an accident. I cursed under my breath. The ideas were a runaway train, and I was having a hard time controlling them.

He said, "I admit to having bouts of ennui. I think you're the fix to that."

"Ennui? You're having bouts of pretention if you're using words like that so casually."

Laughing, he brought the flaming glass close to his face and blew on it, killing the flames and causing crystals of ice to form. I looked away. This was a magical seduction and I was falling for it.

"Most elementals don't have control of both."

"I know," he whispered, arching one eyebrow.

Delving into the unfairness of my kind being cursed to possess magic and cause the death of someone else was something I tried not to pine over. They were the cards I was dealt, but sitting across from so much power made me sulk about the unfairness of it.

I finished off the contents of my glass and slipped out of my chair.

"Good night, Kieran."

I ignored him calling after me. Ignored him calling my name. I stopped at the bar to settle my bill and then headed out of the club, grateful for the cool night. It bristled against my skin, the fresh breeze and open space clearing my head. I was offered and I declined. This was in the win column for me.

CHAPTER 13

J couldn't tell if Madison had been waiting long. Her face was unreadable, but at least she didn't look irritated. Our weekly meetings at the coffee house were something I enjoyed—when I knew there wasn't an impending lecture.

She was smiling in a pleasant, plaintive way. Taking a detour to the counter, I ordered coffee and pastries, taking longer than needed to gather my defense as to why I hadn't applied for the office job. It wasn't her intention to be the annoying older sister. She'd been thrust into the position by our parents. I wondered if she despised the role and wished she had been an only child instead of being saddled with a responsibility that wasn't a birth obligation. My role as the screw-up younger sister wasn't helping. As they prepared my drink, I stole a look in her direction. She looked pensive. Guilt made me want to concede and take the job, surrender to a dull existence. Make life easier for her and remove the stress from my parents.

Coffee and muffin in hand, I handed her the bag I had brought in. She hesitated before opening the bag, then choked back a gasp. She bent, examining the contents more closely: three objects on the STF list, coded black—the highest urgency, with the largest bounty for their return. Two of the objects, I couldn't remember their uses, but the Anastasis gem was used for resurrection. It wasn't bad in itself, but when paired with the fact that anyone could use it, the danger increased. Not all magic wielders were responsible, but when it came to resurrection, they tended to exercise a healthy level of discretion and restraint. Humans, on the other hand, well, they tended to lose all restraint when they got an opportunity to perform magic. Common sense and logic were overridden in favor of the thrill of sharing in something that wasn't usually available to them. Reckless behavior usually followed, which was why retrieval of the objects was so important.

"Thank you," she breathed in relief. "You'll have to fill out the reward paperwork to claim the bounty."

I shook my head. "I don't want the bounty. It'll be quite impressive at the end of the fiscal year when you've acquired these things without your budget taking the hit."

Seeing her face brighten made it all worthwhile. This was the relationship we were supposed to have. Madison closed the bag and tucked it closer to her. Her hand ran thoughtfully along the plate her muffin was on. Moments ticked by in silence. Her face twisted.

"Do I want to know how you got them?" she asked, pinching a piece of muffin off and absently placing it in her mouth, chewing only occasionally. At the speed she ate, it was unlikely she'd ever finish whatever food she was eating.

I gave the question long consideration. She was STF, legally bound to uphold the law. Things were black and white, which is why it was a perfect job for her. My jobs tended to submerge me in innumerable shades of gray. My silence implied that she didn't want to know. It hadn't been the dragon's property, either. If you take from a thief, is it theft? I don't think so. And I was making sure the items didn't fall into the wrong hands. It was the right thing to do.

"Does it have anything to do with Mephisto?"

I nodded once. "I found them while working on a job for him."

"Erin," she chastised in a hiss. "You need to stop working for him."

"I'm not going to stop," I asserted with new clarity. It wasn't an act of rebellion. I liked working for him. The payoff was worth it. "If I hadn't taken the job, you wouldn't have those." My gaze slid to the bag that she periodically touched in a protective gesture. "I'm sure if I stop taking jobs from him, gifts like that will come less frequently."

Each acquisition would improve her standing with the STF. Unfortunately, her reputation took a significant hit whenever she helped me, although she'd never admit it.

"There's absolutely nothing about Mephisto anywhere. He shows up five years ago without any significant paper trail, and everything is in the name of his corporation." She frowned. A blush ran along her cheeks and nose at the admission that she'd checked on him.

She made a face that was a combination of a frown and a scowl, scrunching her nose like a child disgusted by the request to eat vegetables. "Mephisto," she croaked.

I wanted to go into detail about his room, how easily he discovered the bloodstained shingle, and his peculiar magic. The discussion of his otherworldly movements and the odd glow to his eyes that I'd never seen before needed to be explored more. But mentioning it now would just lead to her investigating him more deeply and making more appeals to me to stop working with him.

Closing her eyes, she inhaled a long, measured breath as she committed to whatever she was contemplating.

"It has to be hard not having your own magic. Your entire childhood, I watched you struggle with it. I really wish there was something I could do to make it better for you." The sorrow in her voice made my heart wrench.

"I know you do. I wish there was something that could be done, too. I'm sure it seems like I'm being needlessly defiant by ignoring your pleas to stop using magic. I try to. But I can't. I go through life with a void that can't be filled by anything other than magic. At my last appointment with Sumner, I described it as being in a perpetual state of dehydration . . . maybe that's not the best way to describe it. Taking myself out of the situation, sitting in an office with humans, and never being around magic just isn't realistic. It doesn't stop when I'm around you, your parents, and Cory. I'm just always trying to manage it."

She nodded in understanding. My mother was a different story. If I didn't know she possessed magic, I wouldn't know from being around her. It was a weak pulse that never tempted me. Perhaps I ignored it so I wouldn't be tempted.

Madison looked past me, her eyes intense with concentration, lips puckered, and brows inched together. "You can't use external sources of magic, like the Crelic, Mavin, Keystone, and the ilk, correct?"

I knew I couldn't use the Crelic. I'd proved that when I apprehended Grayson. My assumption was that it would be the same with the Keystone and Mavin Stone. I could absorb the magic but nothing else. It wasn't usable.

Madison had stopped pinching at her food and had taken out a notepad and pencil. She scribbled a few notes and zoned out past me with a look in her eyes similar to when she was planning a sting operation.

"What spells have you tried to keep a person's magic and keep them alive?" she asked.

It didn't make any sense to deny it. When the *incident* happened, I had borrowed his magic to perform several spells, hoping to remove the raven's curse, or at the very least modify it so people wouldn't die. It was something I had been doing for years—trying to fix who and what I was. I started telling her.

Seeing the list of failed attempts take up two pages of her notepad was discouraging. Madison deliberated over each spell, making notes at the side. Before I questioned her notes, she asked, "When you shifted, what animal did you shift to and how long were you able to sustain it?"

"A cat. I was able to hold the form for ten minutes." I was surprised at her line of questioning, which was like nothing in the past. Before, it centered around her determining how much I borrowed, what spells I used it for, and justification of the need. This was different and it made me apprehensive.

The pen tapped absently against the table.

"Madison, what's going on?"

Ignoring my question, she asked, "Domestic or big cat?" She made more notes on a different page.

"Maddie!" I said, pulling her out of her thoughts enough for her to give me a scathing glare. I snorted a laugh at her response, amused that a simple nickname could evoke such contempt. I liked the name.

"Madison," I amended. Her face relaxed, but her eyes were still pools of intensity like nothing I'd seen before. "What are you doing?"

"Helping you." She placed her pen on the table and slouched back in her chair. A frown downturned her lips. "Yesterday, I got a call about a class five object and decided to investigate it myself." She shrugged. "I love my position, but I miss being in the field. It's more fulfilling than administrative stuff. I should have at least put a team together or had backup, but it was just a lead and the suspects were human. I didn't think it was a big risk." A flush of embarrassment moved along her cheeks, spreading to her neck. "It was a successful lead and I retrieved the object, but it wasn't without incident. One of those bastards injected me with an iron-laced substance." She frowned. "It just got out of my system today. I was without magic for over twenty-four hours. *Twenty-four hours.*" She pushed the words out through tightly clenched teeth. Her eyes softened when they looked back at me. "I can't say that I understand what you feel or what it's like to be—well, you, because let's face it, you're not like most. Having an iron brace placed on me, like they did in school and the STF academy, was a different experience. I knew that once it came off, my magic would be restored. Feeling the magic in me, knowing I should have access to it but not being able to use it felt terrible. Empty. That's how I felt the entire day. Empty and wrong."

Snatching the pen up, she reviewed her notes again. "We need to exhaust all resources and see if we can lift the curse, get you access to magic. Something."

Smiling, I wondered if that's what Dr. Wilmer needed to experience to eventually show empathy—to understand me and my struggle.

"Domestic. I turned into a domestic cat."

Resting back in the seat, Madison studied me, her brows furrowed in concentration. "Erin, your magic is so unlike other mages'. Shifting to a cat can be done with so many different spells. It's just a transformation spell and it can't be done with large animals. That's strictly shifter magic, and I don't think you have that type of magic in you. When you have access to magic, it mirrors all the denizens' magic *except* the type that shifters have."

I wasn't sure how this would help. It was just another piece in the puzzle. Scribbling more marks on the paper, she started to group the different spells in categories. Then she turned the paper to me.

"These"—she pointed to one group—"are *Curatio* or healing spells. They didn't work. No need to do any more in that group. You've done *Ablatio* spells"—she tapped her pen on another group—"removal spells aren't going to work, and these are *Opsaepio* spells, which I'm assuming you were using to try to block the donor from slipping into death's sleep?"

I nodded. She tapped on the table with her pen, splitting her attention between the notes and me. "These are good spells and a good approach."

Her approval meant a lot, and in that moment, it seemed like the frayed bond between us was mending.

"That's everything. The strongest spells and they didn't work." My voice stayed even, hiding my growing feeling of desolation.

"I don't know." She sighed. Her despondent look made me less hopeful.

We both gave in to silence, and for several long moments our pastries seemed to be the most important thing.

"There's the Mystic Souls book. If we can get our hands on that, there could be spells in there we can try," she suggested with a confidence that shouldn't have existed when talking about Mystic Souls.

Suggesting Mystic Souls was about as realistic as promising a child a unicorn ride for their birthday. It wasn't going to happen. The book was a myth, an unsubstantiated legend. It gave hope to the hopeless, promise to the disillusioned, and filled magic wielders full of what-ifs. Mystic Souls was a book of spells that contained the answer to everything—or so it was rumored. No one had ever actually seen the book, and yet the legacy of its existence continued. It reminded me of how people were so adamant about the existence of Big Foot or the Loch Ness monster. Just when the rumors of its existence threatened to die, there'd be a sighting or a so-called reliable lead, and hope was renewed.

"Do you really believe it exists?"

"They. Books. It's rumored there are two of them. I do," she admitted, earnest. "And if anyone is able to find them, I think it would be you. If there is a way to fix your magic, it won't be in the new books. I believe there are so few of you because the magic is archaic, so it's reasonable that only archaic spells would work—spells that might be found in Mystic Souls."

Mystic Souls. I'd settled on it being a fable, but Madison's suggestion gave me hope. I could fix this.

CHAPTER 14

Cory's finger drummed against the side of the door at a steady rhythm, something that he'd been doing for the past twenty minutes.

"How was the concert?" I asked.

He shrugged. "It was okay." The elation in his tone said otherwise.

"Did Alex enjoy it?" I was surprised when Cory told me that Alex had invited him to a jazz concert in the park. It was even more shocking that Cory accepted because he didn't like jazz.

"He said he enjoyed the company more than the concert," Cory admitted shyly. *Is he blushing?* I had to yank my gaze away from the rose color creeping up his cheeks and back to the road.

"Tell me about it," I urged. Cory wasn't discreet about much and we didn't have any secrets, but for some reason he was distracted and unwilling to spill the details. Between terse responses to my questions, his fingers continued to drum on the car door.

"Ask it," I huffed out.

"Okay. Are we this desperate?"

Considering all the comments I'd made and warnings I'd given about staying away from the Woman in Black, it was understandable that he might think I was desperate. Maybe I was.

The past two days had been spent talking to sources, no matter how obscure, about leads regarding the Mystic Souls. Our questions garnered the looks of pity one would give an adult who still believed in the Easter Bunny, or astonishment that I would take on such a daunting task. Hours and hours spent without discovering anything that would lead me in any direction. Desperate, I found myself going through all the pictures of the shapeshifting dragon's lair on the off chance that it could be there. It was a long shot, but their horde was the most impressive that I'd seen in years. It was worth the look.

"You always said dealing with the Woman in Black was the worst thing a person could do," Cory reminded me.

It wasn't necessarily the worst thing. Being a demon host or helot, which was a blood servant to a vampire, were the worst. They both destroyed the person's life. Helots were different than someone who chose to donate occasionally or even frequently. Helots were used more callously, and at times cruelly, usually as punishment for a perceived slight against a Master Vampire. I'd rescued my share of those people. It was illegal to keep helots, but people with extensive funds and years of experience hiding their reprehensible behavior, along with the ability to compel, made finding the helot and capturing the vampire problematic. I solved the problem because I couldn't be compelled. Anyone with magic couldn't be compelled; it was surprising that despite having inactive magic, I possessed the same immunity.

Demon hosts left the body just as broken. If the mind wasn't destroyed after their use, the body often was. Demons were very powerful, and if the person survived being a host, they were handsomely rewarded. I never understood what offer could be good enough to entice one to deal with them, but there was no shortage of people willing to do so.

I shook my head and refocused on Cory. "I based that comment on the stories of others, not my own experience. I've never dealt with her."

"Stories of people visiting her for a favor and losing their sight, becoming mute, losing their magical ability. She took away a shifter's ability to shift! You really need to experience it firsthand?"

"First, we should put it in perspective. They chose to give those things up in return for a favor. That isn't a secret. All the stories are the same." I knew this because I'd been hired several times to connect the debtor of the WIB with someone who could reverse the spell she'd cast on them. Her spells couldn't be reversed. From what I'd seen, they could only be minimized. Debts weren't always severe—like a body part, for example. Cash, jewelry, or a favor were often requested as payment. I was hoping for the latter. From my understanding, she informed the requester of the payment she was willing to accept. For all I knew, she'd want my grandma's oatmeal cookie recipe or for me to wash her car, although I'd heard of her making really obscure requests as well. She was clearly an eccentric and unorthodox magic wielder. It wasn't unusual to find that the stronger the practitioner, the more eccentric they tended to be.

It was rumored that she was a fae, but the fae denied it adamantly. The only thing the mages and the witches ever agreed on was that her magic was too menacing and grim to be their brand of magic. All magic could be menacing and grim—it depended on the wielder.

"Make me a promise. No deals with her today. We just talk and see what she wants and then we think about it. Okay?"

I nodded. I didn't have any plans to make a deal with her

today. If the stories were correct, her help came with a side of mischief and unexpected consequences.

We drove up the dirt road and stopped where it ended and the narrow dirt path began.

"This is where she lives." I offered the unnecessary information, stalling.

The glow of the sun faded behind the expanse of trees that flanked the dirt trail, making it darker. But the mid-day sun could only be subdued, not cloaked. We both exhaled loudly and opened the car doors. Cory walked next to me along the narrowed path. The farther we walked, the less dense the trees became, eventually thinning out into a vast area of lush well-maintained grass edged by an assortment of violet, blue, white, and yellow alpine and tropical plants.

"This is beautiful," Cory said, taking in what could easily be considered a botanical garden. The vibrancy and soothing mood that often accompanied being surrounded by nature and beauty settled over me. Despite my best efforts, the sweet, aromatic air made it difficult to stay on high alert and overly cautious. Cory and I looked around for a house, but there was nothing but trees. I knew she didn't live in the forest. Cory pointed to the right where two massive trees formed an archway over a concrete pathway.

We followed the unnecessary labyrinth, which spat us out in the same place we would have ended up if we hadn't taken the unwieldy detour. Perhaps it was for our benefit, to give us time to reconsider our visit. We looked at each other and kept going.

The bridge over a pond led to the rust brick-colored exterior of the ranch home. It looked as if she was going for a log cabin look but her eccentricities wouldn't allow her to create something so mundane, so she framed it with wood, including the pillars to the entrance. From the distance, I could see chairs on the porch and a flower garden as beautiful as the garden at the entrance. There seemed to be a small vegetable garden at the back and to the right of it an apple tree and vine of berries. My imagination had gotten the best of me and I'd expected a dark home, with isolated rain pouring down on it and crows cawing from a distance warning us to stay away. This wasn't at all what I expected.

"I'm getting a fairytale vibe," Cory admitted.

"I feel you, Hansel. If she offers us cookies, decline the hell out of them."

"You got it, Gretel."

Just before we could get to the entrance, colored fish in the pond jumped higher, gaping their mouths to expose abnormally placed teeth. Smoke erupted in front of us, and when it cleared, a reddish imp dressed in slacks, a vest, and a turquoise tie that contrasted terribly with his coloring appeared. His imperious look didn't stop the bark of laughter that came from me. He looked comical. Rough leathery fingers pushed the wire, rectangular glasses up the bridge of his narrow, sharp nose. Even the miniature bark-colored horns on his head stood erect with an air of self-importance.

"Is it just me, or is he simply adorable?" Cory asked in a hushed voice.

"It's not you," I assured him, my eyes rooted on the creature before us. The requisite smile the imp gave in greeting quickly vanished. If he were taller, he would have been looking down at us. But since he was just shy of four feet, he looked down his nose at our legs.

"Are you two finished?" he asked in a patrician English accent. It was so stilted and prim that we sobered and stood a little taller. After moments of silence, he darted forward, something silver in his hand, and a sharp prick caught me on my leg. I crouched to get a look and found my skin had been punctured, and so had Cory's.

The imp was standing in his original position, a small

slim sword in his hand, which he made a show of making disappear. The natural reaction was to protect and respond in kind, and I reached for my taser, which was missing. With haughty indignation, the imp revealed my taser and the knife I'd sheathed on the opposite leg. He made them disappear, too.

"They will be returned to you on your exit," he informed me, then he shifted his attention to Cory. "So will your magic."

A blaze of frustration and anger moved over Cory's features and made his scowl look vengeful. He waved his hand in the direction of the imp. Nothing. Barely concealed panic rose in him.

"I give you my word, the restrictions will be lifted. It's only temporary." The prick wasn't a punishment but to invoke a spell on Cory. Was the imp the Woman in Black? No, that definitely would have been part of the stories. "Hey, the Woman in Black isn't actually a witch, mage, or fae, but a persnickety imp."

"I take it you are here to see the mistress of the house?" the imp asked.

"No, we just thought it was a good day to get stabbed, have our magic and weapons confiscated, and hang out with an uppity imp." Cory glared at the leathery man. Usually easy-going, Cory quickly became harsh and irritable when someone messed with his magic, a quality most magic wielders shared.

"Yes, we're here to see the mistress," I responded in a softer, amiable tone. It was probably a good idea to refrain from calling her the Woman in Black, because I wasn't sure if that was actually her preferred title.

"You'll be allowed to pass and speak with her if you can answer these three riddles."

I should have known it wouldn't be that easy to get to her. After all, why would a person who peddled in nefarious spells be welcoming? "Come one, come all to the land of misrepresented spells. You ask for immortality; I grant it to you but ensure that you are weak and sickly your entire time —or I make you into an immortal beaver."

"Are you kidding me? You treat us like this and now we have to play a silly game?" Cory was furious. I really wished he'd decided to stay home because if he didn't get a handle on his temper, he was going to make things worse. I placed my hand on his arm and gave him a look that gently told him to cut it out. His head moved marginally into a nod of agreement. Reluctant agreement. The hard stare he wore confirmed that.

"What happens if we don't answer them all correctly? What if we only get two out of three?" I said it with a hint of levity to lighten the heavy atmosphere, partly since the imp hadn't made an effort to smile or offer any hint of geniality since his initial smile.

"All three riddles need to be answered correctly. If they aren't, you will be escorted out." He lodged a sharp look in Cory's direction. "With everything confiscated from you returned. The mistress of the house is a woman of her word and I am held to it."

I suspected he was held to it because obviously the magic he used was hers. Did he have a magical bond that allowed him to share her magic, or had she taught him the spell used to divest Cory of his magic? Did he move that fast on his own, or was it a result of magic? The questions I had were endless. Hopefully, I'd have the opportunity to ask her.

"Go ahead with your questions," Cory said.

"Riddles," the imp corrected.

My eye roll mirrored Cory's. Weren't riddles just tough questions?

"Riddles," Cory amended with a heavy sigh.

The imp maintained his haughty look as he took off his spectacles and withdrew a handkerchief from his vest to clean them. When he replaced them on the bridge of his nose, I saw the sharp claws that looked similar to hands when first seen. It could have been his claws that pricked us.

"No conferring with each other and you have only one chance to answer each question, do you understand?"

We nodded.

"First riddle," he said studiously, his gaze bouncing between me and Cory. "Which creature walks on four legs in the morning, two legs in the afternoon, and three legs in the evening?"

Keeping my face neutral, I looked at Cory. I was pretty sure that, like me, he was hoping all the riddles were as easy as this one. How could we not get the infamous riddle of the sphinx?

"Man. He crawls on all fours as a baby, walks on two feet as an adult, and walks with a cane as an old man." I blurted it too quickly. I should have taken longer moments of pause, to give him the impression that it was difficult so he would give us easier ones.

He nodded, face expressionless. Even his dark abysmal eyes held no decipherable expression of whether he was surprised or expectant at how quickly we answered the question.

"Correct."

After several moments of silence, he scrutinized us with narrowed eyes, honing in on me. "This is for the embittered man," he said. Then he gave Cory his full attention. I almost laughed because there had been several variations of the scowl on his face since his magic had been pilfered.

"Ask." Cory attempted to sound just as aloof as the imp but failed miserably. He was irritated and nervous.

"Second riddle: Turn me on my side and I am everything. Cut me in half and I am nothing. What am I?"

Cory's eyes narrowed in concentration. He rolled his thumb and forefinger together. He didn't want to be the reason I didn't get to see the Woman in Black and that would lead him to overanalyze everything.

After two minutes had passed, the imp said, "Tick. Tick. Tick," in a low beat.

"I can do without the sound effects," Cory snapped.

It was the first emotion the imp had shown since our greeting. A self-indulgent smile showed overly bright teeth with extended and sharp canines. Cory's hesitation ignited his personality. Our discomfort and anxiety fed his enjoyment.

The imp made a display of bringing his blue-black tongue to his teeth to start his effects again, when Cory blurted, "The number eight. On its side, it looks like the infinity symbol, and when you cut it in half, it looks like two zeros."

"Correct." The imp's glow of pleasure faded quickly. He shoved his hands into his pockets and looked in our direction before pacing a few feet. It was apparent that he had a substantial number of riddles memorized and was sifting through them to find one that couldn't be answered. I'd committed to seeing the Woman in Black by any means, even if it meant punting the imp out of my way. It had seemed like an easier feat when I first considered it, before he'd stabbed us and stolen our magic and weapons in a blink of an eye. But it was still an option.

Becoming increasingly impatient with his rumination, I bit my tongue to keep from telling him exactly how I felt. Although it didn't seem like we had been there long, the sun had receded behind the trees. The air cooled and the area had a dim, ominous appearance. I wasn't sure of the extent of his magic. Elemental mages could control the weather and so could some fae.

Finally he stopped, and a whisper of a smile flitted across his lips.

"Third riddle. Feed me and I live, yet give me a drink and I die."

"Fire."

His eyes widened and he opened and closed his mouth several times, like a fish out of water, revealing his disturbingly colored tongue.

"Incorrect," he stated with the unearned arrogance of someone who was right. He wasn't. I knew that was the answer.

"Then what is the answer?"

"I do not owe you that."

"You do!" I shouted, unable to contain my anger. Blistering at his cheating, handling this amicably wasn't even an option anymore. "You owe me that because there isn't possibly another answer and you know it."

"I owed you an audience and a means to get to the mistress of the house. You failed."

"So much for honor. Do you have any plans to return our weapons and magic?" My gaze drifted to the bridge just a few feet away. It was so close. I had every intention of kicking the red cheater clear across the forest and heading for the bridge. Cory beat me to it. He reached into his pocket and returned with a closed hand. Then he lobbed whatever was in his fist at the imp's face. White and tan particles dusted the air and got into his eyes. It distracted him. Cory punched the imp hard enough for him to retreat. A right hook made the imp airborne for a few seconds, and he crashed back to the ground. Cory hovered over the imp, his hand pressed into his chest, fastening him to the ground.

"What are you waiting for? Go."

I ran toward the bridge, hearing the imp's words carried by the light breeze of wind. My face smashed into a barrier and waves of magic pulsed through me like a little electrical shock. It traveled from my nose, which hit the border first, to my toes. Numbness came after. I ignored it, directing my attention to the painful grunt coming from Cory's direction. He'd moved away from the imp and was shaking his hand the way one did when they touch something sharp. The imp whipped to his feet, heaving breaths, lips moving feverishly as he spat out more words.

Cory and I both backed away as the imp's small body began to expand and stretch. His breaths mutated to something between a bark and a growl. Maybe even a strangled hiss. Sharp sounds of clothes ripping tore through the air. His skin tore and stretched to accommodate the growing body, the bones breaking and reassembling. His small horns extended and curved like a ram's. The body stretched to ten times its original size, including the claws on his hand, which now looked like they could rip through flesh. His movements had slowed, though, and that was our only advantage as he came at us. His footsteps pounded into the earth, making it reverberate with each step. He advanced, slashing his claws back and forth like machetes cutting through a forest.

We turned and raced for the exit. The pounding steps came faster and harder. He might not have been fast with his massive new form, but he was fast enough that we could feel him behind us, his frame casting an ominous shadow, dimming the fading light. Refusing to risk slowing down by looking back, we just kept running. Saving ourselves to fight another day. Or that's what I tried to convince myself. Clawed hands grabbed me by the leg, roughly hauling me up and dangling me upside down. I could see Cory had received the same treatment. Pitching forward into a V, I made a futile attempt to claw at the leathery skin to get the imp to release me. The grip tightened and he continued in the direction we had been running.

He tossed us out into the middle of the forest. My weapons crashed on the ground around me. The imp on roids took obvious pleasure in piercing Cory's skin and whispering a spell as he turned around—returning his magic. Cory worked his fingers, conjuring up a lively ball of energy.

"Do you want him to come back?" I asked softly, feeling a little lightheaded from being dangled upside down.

Collapsing on the grass, I took a cleansing breath, inhaling the floral scent that lingered and the oaky smells, hoping it would relax me.

"So," Cory started slowly, "what's plan B?"

CHAPTER 15

I wish I had a plan B. It would have lifted my spirits as I limped around my apartment the next day. Cory used magic to heal the cuts, but witch magic wasn't really as effective on soft tissue damage. My body ached. I'd have to deal with it for a few days and just ice it until it was better. It didn't help that Cory tried to use his magic so soon after it was taken. After being laced with iridium, it took a few moments for the magic to return to full strength. There had to be a similar effect when someone took it. It seemed to be the case when I borrowed magic. Some recovered faster. It could be a minute or as long as an hour. The longer I kept the magic, the longer the recovery. Cory remained an anomaly when it came to the effects, as he recovered faster and I was able to use it for longer.

The copious amount of cream and peppermint syrup in my coffee didn't improve its bitterness. It was probably the taste of defeat that tasted bad. I dumped the coffee, made another cup, and mixed it with Kahlua. It wasn't as bitter and gave me a nice buzz. Something I didn't need at ten o'clock in the morning but still welcomed.

Not one story I'd heard about dealing with the WIB

ended with the person being unceremoniously thrown out. Why were we so special? Why didn't she want to see us? It wasn't the most strategically executed plan, granted, but I'd had no idea what to expect since the stories of meeting her varied greatly. The only thing that seemed to be the same was there was always a cost. Nothing was free when it came to her. But I couldn't even see her to find out if the cost was too high.

Frustrated, I didn't immediately answer the door when I heard the knock. I wasn't expecting anyone, and I wasn't in the mood for unexpected guests. My frown was automatic when I looked through the peephole. I definitely wasn't in the mood for this guest. *Asher.* I ground my teeth together. After that imp, the last thing I wanted to deal with was another asshat who didn't know the meaning of rules and propriety.

When I didn't answer, he knocked again. The hard, arrhythmic rap seemed to hold a hint of arrogant amusement. A silver-gray eye glinted through the peephole and the shifter eyes, a light glow, seemed more pronounced. I was committed to letting him stay right there smirking at the peephole, while I thought of ways to wipe it off his face.

"I know you're home. I can hear you breathing. And your heartbeat," his deep smooth voice pointed out.

I held my breath. A robust laugh roared behind the door. A vibrant lively sound of pure amusement. "Surely you don't believe holding your breath will stop your heartbeat. Erin," he entreated. "I come bearing gifts. I want to make amends."

It took a few moments for me to get ready for his entry.

"It's open."

Throwing open the door, he was met with the barrel of a tranq gun pointing directly at him.

He looked at the weapon, his eyes gleaming. "It seems like you are just as anxious to end our little tussle. It has to be quite exhausting directing so much energy into hating me."

"It's pretty easy. I see you, and the feelings just spark like fireworks on the fourth of July. I don't have to do anything. Your smug face and voice are enough to ignite it."

"Most women enjoy seeing my face," he said, a small smile playing at his lips.

"Probably not nearly as much as you enjoy seeing your face," I snarked back.

Was modesty a lost attribute? He was strangely relaxed for a person with a weapon pointed in his direction, which only irritated me more. Why couldn't he display the wide-eyed fear of a predator realizing he was the prey? Perhaps I should have had a gun, but unless the gun had silver in it, the tranq was more harmful to him. The bullets would hurt, but a tranq would knock him out. Shapeshifters freaked out at the very thought of losing volition. I suppose when you are forced to change once a month, losing any control is discomforting.

Making a show of it, he placed the bag he was holding on the coffee table. He backed away from it and raised his hands to show they were empty. Shrugging off his suit jacket, he laid it across the arm of the chair. Bringing his arms up, so I could see them, he slowly did a three-hundred-sixty spin. I was sure it wasn't to show he didn't have a weapon but to showcase his nicely proportioned body. He grinned at the sharp glare I shot at him.

"I am weaponless and at your mercy. Totally harmless," he said, his tongue sliding over his teeth. Then he gripped his lips with his teeth, a less than subtle reminder how that could change at any moment. I'd witnessed him change into a huge chocolate-colored wolf in under thirty seconds. If the size of the wolf didn't scare you, the menace in his movements would have.

He appraised me as I relaxed the gun to my side, my finger still close to the trigger. I'm sure I wasn't a sight to look at. I wished I'd spent the day meditating, to calm the emotions that were running rampant. At the idea of visiting the WIB, I'd allowed myself to dream, to consider that I'd be able to borrow magic without consequence. To indulge in the various aspects of it without penalty. That dream now seemed so far away.

"Why are you here?" I asked, exasperated and sure he could smell the Kahlua. I wasn't drunk, but I probably shouldn't have been handling firearms.

"Like I said, I want to make amends. How can we be friends again?"

"Friends," I scoffed. "You can contact Webster or Oxford and ask them to consider changing the definition."

"I'd like to try something a little more plausible." His confidence that his betrayal could be forgiven with a little gift annoyed me. The arrogance of a shifter was only exceeded by that of a vampire, or maybe Mephisto. "Come on, Erin, you want to end this war between us or you wouldn't have let me in."

"I didn't want you to disturb my neighbor. She gets irritated if Judge Judy gets interrupted."

In hindsight, I should have left him out there with his loud obnoxious laugh and let her give him a tongue lashing he'd never forget. Maybe she'd poke him with that cane she didn't seem to need. I thought it was a prop she used for her helpless, hard-of-hearing act to get out of standing too long chatting with the neighbors.

"Ms. Harp? You said she has no fucks to give. Those were your exact words about her. You think she would care about me loitering in the hall?"

He wasn't wrong. All the primetime comedies hadn't prepared me for my elderly neighbor. Teaching me that my black-haired seventy-something-year-old neighbor would be overly friendly, nosy, and want my company all the time. She couldn't care less about me. She acted like I was bothering her when I introduced myself when I first moved in, and was polite because it was the Midwestern thing to do. Helping her with her groceries earned me a thank-you, nothing more or less. I wasn't going to see her peeking out her door to see who my gentleman caller was, and her hearing aid, which must've been a special invisible one that couldn't be detected by the naked eye because I had never seen it, was always too low or missing. Conversations were quickly dismissed by a shake of her head and a finger pointing to her empty ear.

Plus, her cane moved in double time when trying to get away from the neighbors upstairs, whom she referred to as the "chatty ones." If they managed to get close enough, she abandoned the cane and did a geriatric jog.

"Unless the Salem Stone is in that big bag, we won't be mending anything."

His jaw clenched. "I think you'll like your gift better. You couldn't do anything with the stone anyway. It's only of use to witches, fae, and mages."

"Then why do you want it?" I countered roughly. There was no way he was getting out of explaining it that easily.

He ignored the question, pulled out the expensive-looking wooden box from the bag, and presented the contents to me. I placed the tranq on the chair behind me, close enough to retrieve quickly if needed, and picked up the dagger. It was an exquisite weapon. My fingers traced the intricate and beautiful patterns of interlocking shapes that decorated the black mother of pearl handle. Pulling a dagger like that out would definitely let someone know I meant business. The blade was the work of true talent and crafts-manship. It was too beautiful to consider using for work and could never replace my weapon of choice—the double-edged karambit, which was battle worn.

Each breath I took was measured in an effort to suppress any show of appreciation. He would have to work harder than that for my forgiveness. I took a few steps away and tested the dagger with several jabs and slices through the air.

Again, I examined the razor-sharp blade and closed the distance between me and Asher. I turned, extending it in front of me. Asher was just a few inches from the tip.

"Nice blade. Why did you take the Salem Stone?" I asked, my tone arctic cold and punctuating each word for emphasis.

His eyes fixed on mine as he inched closer until the tip of the blade was pressed against his chest. His lips spread into a challenging smirk. I wanted to apply just a little pressure. Not to injure him but to meet his challenge. Who was I kidding? Injuring him would have been a bonus. His close distance goaded me, daring me to do something. His confidence that I wouldn't hurt him frustrated me. Just a little nick into the skin of the Alpha of the Northwest Wolf Pack would surely wipe that smile off his face. Just a small prick with the blade would allow me to watch with satisfaction as his shirt turned crimson. Who was I kidding? "Nick" and "poke" were just niceties for stabbing. I was considering stabbing him. Logic reared its dream-killing head and reminded me that he was an Alpha. *What the hell is wrong with me?* Yet thirst for retribution seemed to override logic—he deserved it.

Asher's head canted to the side and the smirk became a vulpine smile as if he could see my desire and my quandary.

I knew why logic wasn't driving my actions—Asher had betrayed me and I was hurt. Admitting it felt weird, but that was the case. I'd enjoyed working for and with him. He paid well, was easygoing, displayed confident assurance—which now that I was on the receiving end of was quite annoying—and his tolerance of the gray lines I straddled made navigating the supernatural world easier. He'd discarded it, our occasional partnership and our trust.

"The markings on the handle can be spelled so the weapon can't be used against you," he offered, ignoring my question.

I repeated my question. Examining the blade for several

minutes, I placed it back in the box and closed it. "I needed the Salem Stone. You knew I'd been tracking it for months for a client." My voice sharpened to a blade's edge, feeling the betrayal anew.

"I told you I wanted it and told you to stop your search. I even offered to buy the contract. You were the one who continued to pursue it."

"It was a job!"

"A job you could have declined."

As if my reputation and my record wouldn't have suffered from doing that. I was glad I'd put the weapon down; my fingers might have listened to my anger and not my logic.

"I paid you for it. Triple your rate."

I was reminded of the smug look he gave me from the jeep as he passed me traveling in the opposite direction. Away from my destination. Before I even got to the cave in South Dakota, I had a feeling it was going to be empty. All I found was a pissed-off troll.

Asher shoved his fingers through his hair. "I gave you a heads-up," he said. "I wanted it and told you to end your search. Your words were 'game on.'" He shrugged dismissively. "The game was on and I won. Isn't it time you let it go?"

"You won because you cheated." The serrated edge to my voice was lost when I said the rest. I wasn't sure how, but my gut was yelling that he did. He was always one effortless step ahead of me, which seemed odd. Somehow, he was spying on me.

"It's on the STF's list. You would have been inclined to give it to them, or tell of its location. I don't feel obliged to do such a thing," he admitted.

That wasn't necessarily true. I used my judgment with that. I didn't follow the STF recommendations blindly since they erred on the side of extreme caution and put items on the list that I didn't agree with. It was the source of many lively debates between me and Madison. If they considered that an object could be used to injure or for evil, it was put on the list. With that logic, someone could poke someone's eye out with a lollipop and it should be put on the list. I wouldn't let Asher know that, though.

"They're the government, why don't you want them to have it?"

His jaw clenched and his lips tightened.

"You wanted the Salem Stone because it has something to do with your pack, doesn't it?" Speak to any shifter and the moment the conversation steered in the direction of their pack, they adopted the same posturing. Tension as if they were afraid to spill any of their secrets, of which they tended to have more than most. Maybe not more, but unlike the witch's coven, the fae courts, the mage's consortiums, and the vampire families, the packs seemed a little different: more rules and definitely more confidences.

I understood their discretion and even their apprehension about the human, governmental, and supernatural worlds. Shapeshifters' outing wasn't welcomed with the same level of acceptance as others. I still wasn't sure what it was about some human thought processes. People who could control the weather—cool. Supernaturals who lived for centuries and subsisted on blood—not a problem. People who could do spells that changed the world as they knew it— what's not to love about that? Wynding in and out of a space —fun times. But shifting into an animal was where they drew their obscure line.

Pack challenges didn't just bother humans, they were repudiated by the supernatural community. It bothered people that a position was acquired or lost by death. I had a feeling it bothered a lot of shapeshifters, too, which might explain their easy concession for it to be considered a crime. Now, challenges were to submission.

Maybe it wasn't the shifting that bothered humans, or the

nebulous magic that allowed that to happen. It was the shifters themselves. They were off-putting in an intrinsic way. Midwesterners appreciated modesty and manners, whereas shifters tended to ignore and reject both. Outing themselves had grandma clutching her pearls when she encountered a werewolf shifter who had changed to his human form and was strolling down the street with his man berries on show as if it was just a normal thing to do. And their keen observational skills came off as rude since they had no qualms about calling people out on their lies. People were polite but not necessarily honest.

They could seamlessly deal with humans if they wanted—but part of me felt they didn't want humans to find them attractive. Despite what they might want, most humans did find them attractive, but in an ethereal way. Showing the world that they not only had to shift to their animal form during the full moon but could do it at will simultaneously intrigued and repulsed people.

Their coming out wasn't without incident and significant compromise. A lot of that had to do with the packs' lawyers, who were more vicious than any animal they could turn into. Because of them, if they shifted in public, rendering them nude when they shifted back to human, it was a fine instead of arrest.

They came out and the packs went corporate. There were four in each state, headed by one Alpha who was also like the CEO of their chosen area. Standing in my living room trying to negotiate with me was the CEO of Northwest Wolf Pack. Although all the canidae fell under its rule. It was the same with the cats, but they went by Northwest Lion Pack. I guess lion and wolf sounded more menacing than fox and ocelot. The other species had their ancillary packs but didn't mind being part of the larger packs for political and financial purposes, giving up some of their independence to benefit from the luxuries afforded them by the hard-fought battles won by their legal teams. The combination of eye rolls, anxiety, and annoyance was palpable when they entered any room in the fire jet formation: the lead lawyer in front, two associates on the side, and three presumed paralegals or assistants. An intentional formation that forced people to move out of their way.

I studied Asher for a moment, the glint of amusement that danced in his eyes and the plume of shifter energy that formed around me.

He plopped down on my sofa, legs stretched out and hands clasped behind his head, stretching his fitted dress shirt over the lean muscles of his chest. Everything he did had a hint of deviance and arrogance, right down to the little lift to his crooked smile. Looking up at my ceiling, he seemed at ease, not like an unwanted guest of a woman who wasn't very fond of him and had access to sharp things and firearms.

"Emotions—fear, anger, frustration—they all have a distinctive smell, a noticeable physiological change." The languid lilt to his voice matched the way he sat on my sofa. He sighed, his voice cloying—annoyingly sweet. "How can I mend the rift in our friendship?" he asked.

"First we would have to have a friendship. We were never friends and never will be. I don't trust you."

"And that breaks my heart," he purred. "Tell me how to get that trust?" It had a hint of mockery to it, and I knew he didn't care that I didn't like him. This was just another challenge. It was obvious he thrived on them.

"How did you do it?"

"I'm a predator. I follow the footprints and scents. It's what I do."

"Does that mean you followed my digital footprints?" Had that asshole hacked my computer?

He leaned forward, his face pensive, and for a brief moment, I thought maybe I was mistaken. Maybe he was being serious about repairing the rift between us. The people I dealt with daily had made me cynical. Then it dawned on me. When it came to shifters, it all came down to protecting the pack. Adding "corp" behind their pack name didn't change their dedication and priorities.

"Why did you need it?" The Salem Stone was a magic connector that allowed the user to siphon magic from others and strengthen the borrower's magic. It wasn't as malicious as it sounded. A person had to willingly sacrifice their magic by invoking that spell. Contrary to how dramatic and portentous the STF made it sound, it wasn't as if a person carrying the stone could rip magic from people and become an overpowered, unstoppable magic wielder. It had limitations. It also required magic to use it, something that shifters didn't possess.

"How does it affect your pack? What's going on?" I asked pointedly.

His casual smile faltered. "What goes on with my pack, stays with my pack. Are you interested in being part of it?" he asked in a cool challenge. His brown eyes flickered. Slowly, measuredly, very intentionally, his features shifted. Skin stretched, the carved lines of his jaw relaxed, allowing the jaw to elongate. The narrow slope of his nose extended and reshaped, as did a partial facial shift into his wolf counterpart. It stopped mid-transition, to give me a look at his canine, and before it could fully register, he shifted back to human form. I expected a sheen of perspiration, panting, increased heart rate, rapid breathing, or some sign of distress. Nothing. He'd donned and doffed his wolf half with the ease of someone changing a shirt.

"If that creepy performance was a true recruitment effort, you need to work on it."

His laughter filled the room, and for a fleeting moment, I wondered if I could actually be changed and how shifter magic would affect my magic. Was becoming a shifter even

146

an option? Would it take away my desire for magic since I'd have a different type of magic working through me? I didn't let the idea linger too long—especially in front of someone as perceptive as Asher.

"Then you know I can't tell you anything. I needed it and now I have it," he said bluntly. "Now, my goal is to make recompense." He seemed earnest, someone a less cynical person would believe. If someone could tell when someone else was lying, it gave them the necessary tools to be a good liar, too.

"Are you really sorry?" I asked.

He nodded. "Not for what I did. I'd do it all over again in a heartbeat if I needed to. I'm sorry that you got screwed over."

Direct but honest. I could work with that.

"Get me the Mystic Souls," I blurted. "Then we'll be even. No more bad blood between us."

I didn't have to be a shapeshifter to see the change in his mood. His tension was palpable, and he sat up and eyed me, his interest kindled.

"Mystic Souls," he repeated, his voice grim. "You know it is rumored that only two copies exist in the entire world, right?"

"I only need one." He wasn't going to be able to get it, but it was worth the shot.

His hands washed over his face and then scrubbed along the shadow of beard that accentuated his jawline. For a while, he seemed to contemplate my request. I needed the Mystic Souls book and if he could get it, I'd mend our pseudo friendship.

"If you are asking me for this, you really need it, don't you?" The arrogance and playfulness had melted from his face and words. Whatever he was doing with his eyes, I didn't like it. The intensity of his gaze was hard to hold. I nodded. Standing, he straightened the sleeves and nodded.

"Okay, give me two weeks."

Okay, give me two weeks? What the actual fuck? I'd like a unicorn, a zero-calorie Snickers, and snow on my birthday in July, too.

Hiding my shock, I just nodded again. Of course, it would only take a couple of weeks to find one of the rarest books in the world. I swallowed hard with my hands balled at my sides as I kept my breathing normal, trying not to show my excitement. In a couple of weeks, my life was going to change. Or was it? I snuffed the excitement. He would probably come back with some knockoff consolation prize, one of the spell books I already had or had access to. I didn't allow myself to hope too hard.

Stopping at the threshold of the door, he looked over his shoulder and smiled. "You'll get your book."

"Okay." I loved that I sounded so nonchalant. *Whatever, Mr. CEO, Alpha Man, just drop off the book whenever. It's no big deal.*

Madison believed the book contained a spell that could remove my curse and give me access to magic, and I wanted to believe it, too. I wanted to believe it so much.

CHAPTER 16

The knock at the door pulled me from my thoughts. I figured it was Asher wanting to negotiate another solution after realizing he couldn't deliver. It had to be humbling for him to admit it. I opened the door, prepared to find Asher, and instead saw Mephisto.

He had an envelope in hand but waited patiently for me to invite him in before handing it to me. Setting the new cup of Kahlua-free coffee on the table, I took it from him. The anticipation of getting the Mystic Souls had me so distracted, the coffee cooled and had to be refreshed several times.

Magic enveloped me as soon as Mephisto entered the room. He was no longer subduing it, instead letting it cloak him like a second skin. The urge to taste it came back with a vengeance. By the look on his face, he knew. I wouldn't miss this feeling and the aggrieved feeling that followed when my desire couldn't be satisfied.

Mephisto took in the desk and chair in the corner that I used as my home office. I rarely used the space, preferring to meet clients at my office. The corner was the only possible place to put my desk since I'd converted my other bedroom —if you could call the tiny room that—into a meditation room. It was my everything room, allowing me to escape the heaviness of magic that lingered even after I was no longer near the person. The scent from the vanilla candle that I always kept burning wafted into the living room.

He stood in the middle of the room and did a complete turn, giving the space another once-over.

"If you worked for me, you could afford better."

He was right. My two-bedroom apartment could easily fit in his living room. It was small, but it was mine, and it fit me to a T. The tiny kitchen was all I needed since most of my meals were just a sandwich or peanut butter and apples. The quaint living room was just big enough to hold my multicolored sofa and a small tan accent chair. I had a TV on the wall.

"I don't want better. I like what I have."

He looked around doubtfully, then said, "Landon said you returned his items."

As of this morning, Mephisto hadn't paid me, so I suspected he had a check and planned to use it as an introduction to inviting me to be an employee, with the promise of more consistent checks. I didn't need the consistency because anytime he contacted me for a job, it paid more than enough.

"Did you get my payment?"

"No, not as of this morning." I grabbed my phone off the little nook near the kitchen, pulled up my bank app, and looked. I raised a brow at the amount. "You didn't take out your fee." I'd expected him to, as well as subtract the cost of the repairs. Either way, the amount was more for one job than I'd make for half the year. It was more than enough.

"Alex and Kieran helped. Surely they weren't okay with paying full price."

"My fees aren't negotiable. Alex and Kieran wanted their things back. Honestly, them helping was for them more than you. The two sent a clear message not to take anything from them again."

Kieran and Alex must not have told him that their memories had been wiped. Maybe agreeing to the memory sweep was something they regretted and weren't in a rush to disclose.

I hesitated before speaking. "There are dragons and a witch living near the city. You know this and also that we just retrieved some objects from them. Once they nurse their wounds, the dragons will be back to their antics and terrorizing the 'good folks' of the city."

He gave me a lazy smile. "Ah, of course. I'm sure they will have the good sense not to steal from Kieran, Alex, Landon, or me again." And then he shrugged. "*But* you are right, they will continue with their thefts, and people will come to me—to us—because we will become known for quickly and efficiently retrieving those goods. It seems like a win-win to me."

I sucked in a breath, and my eyes sharpened on him. I didn't want to be part of his dubious plans and decided I would give the information to Madison. Drawn into my plans to circumvent Mephisto's, I hadn't noticed that he was now just inches from me, invading my space. I turned my thoughts from my plans to his magic—his unique, dark, bewitching magic. The aura of it seemed even more enchanting than before. I tried hard to deny it, but I didn't move. I stayed planted as he inched even closer, taking away any distance between us.

"We were interrupted before, weren't we?" he said in a low voice.

Taking a big step back, I looked at him. *Satan.* I kept saying it over and over, a reminder that he was the devil. You never made deals with the devil. But that was just something I'd made up from a name he'd adopted. He was still a man I didn't know, with a name he wouldn't provide, with magic stronger, more unique, and darker than any I'd felt before. I stepped back farther. The contrast in our appearances was stark. He was dressed all in black again, slacks and a button-down shirt. His eyes were molten lava as he looked at me. They made their way from my bare feet to my white leggings and slowly from the edge of my shirt, over my white tank top and unconfined breasts, to my throat. They lingered there. I focused on my meditation room, channeling the feeling of tranquility that it brought. Once I'd found that calm, I returned my eyes to his.

"There is a cruel beauty to your magic," he said gently. "Death can be a gift. It doesn't have to be a curse."

I should have stepped away. Run like a knife-wielding psycho was after me, but I didn't. I was an alcoholic being offered a drink, a drug addict being seduced into her next fix.

"Let me make it easy for you." His lips covered mine. It was second nature—my nature. I said my incantation, pulled his magic to me, felt it coil around me, bathe me in power. Windows and doors opened to something strong, enchanting, all-consuming. I slipped my fingers through his hair and pulled him closer. I felt him stiffen and eventually slip to the ground.

I stood rooted in space, the room hazy but pleasant, my body languid and relaxed. The magic continued to course through me. It was my drug of choice, and it was like experiencing it for the first time. I could hear my own soft pants. My hands glowed, and when I waved them, sparks of color flitted around the space. I let the magic carry me to places full of wonder, moving from door to door and reveling in each new experience it brought me. I walked through one door and into a thick, lush forest with vibrant flowering trees. The smell of honeysuckle inundated the air. I looked for signs of human life—none. A few animals off to the side: deer, rabbits, a giraffe, a lion, and farther out, a bison. I stared at the odd assortment and pondered how some should have been prey and the others predators, but they remained in a state of harmonious interaction.

Before I could explore it any longer, I blinked and was swept away. The magic was still strong, feathering over me, stretching around me, cradling me. It wasn't ominous, the way it felt as it wafted off Mephisto, but it wasn't similar to anything I'd felt before. I waded through sparkling blue water that rose to my waist. Hints of the setting sun peeked over large mountains. I looked off to a waterfall and the rainbow just a few inches away. And winged dragons . . . no, humans, wings expanding, filling the clear sky. The wings were as varied in color as the naked bodies they were connected to. I kept my eyes open, afraid that if I blinked, if I glanced away for just a second, I would be swept away again.

It didn't stop it from happening. The new world I entered was bleak, absent of sun, and the moon gave off just a hint of light. Stretches of dark, uncultivated earth as far as I could see. Animals skulked behind trees. All I could see of them were their eyes, which glowed with feral curiosity and menace. I locked eyes with one of them. I should have felt fear or a sense of dread being in a place so dark and dreary, but I had the same comforting feeling as in the place of beauty. Mephisto's magic found comfort, strength, and contentment in all places. Nothing was foreign or scary to him. My curiosity welled even more. What creature could possess such wonderful magic? Covetous desire rose in me in uncontrollable waves. I tried to push the thoughts away. *Think about jail, the clinic, Madison, Mother's disappointment; think logically; remember that the magic would be fleeting.* Once the body was dead and I'd exhausted the residual magic, this would be gone. Would it be worth it to have him dead, to send my life into havoc once again for a few days, months, a year?

What made the desire to possess this magic even stronger? Even the doors that opened to something dark didn't elicit fear, just ignited my curiosity. It wasn't only the fantastical worlds his magic revealed to me. I understood

Mephisto's arrogance; I felt omnipotent. Stronger than ever. Braver. All self-doubt and worries melted away. It was peace and torment. I'd never experience this again. If I were to, I'd be at Mephisto's mercy and his willingness to share. He'd be in control, and I wasn't willing to give him that much control over me. But if I kept it . . . how long would it last? It was so much stronger than anyone else's. I'd conceded to keeping it. I would have it for as long as it lasted. I resisted when my conscience urged me to look at him. I remembered the counselors trying to force me to have feelings of remorse, which were needed to override my desire to possess magic. But remorse was a learned behavior for me, not intrinsic. I had learned it and needed to make myself act on it.

I turned around to look at him. His body had been placed into a state of in-between, and seeing it would prompt me to do the right thing. But he wasn't on the floor. He was standing, studying me with a slight smile and intense curiosity and pleasure, as if he'd found a sordid satisfaction in watching me enjoy the many facets of his magic. He moved toward me and leaned down, his lips covering mine. They were warm and commanding as he laced his fingers into my hair, crushing my body against his hard chest. His tongue teased mine before he pulled his magic from me, not as gentle and seductive as when he gave it to me. The kiss lasted longer, becoming more heated with each moment, and then he pulled away. My ragged breathing and the sound of my racing heart filled the air. I leaned into him, the way others did with me, wanting to taste his lips again. I wanted to be bonded to his magic, and if the trade-off was being tied to him as well, I'd do it.

I closed my eyes, trying to hold on to the sensation and committing it to memory, hoping that would be enough. *Memories were enough, right?*

He kept me at bay, maintaining the small distance he'd placed between us.

154

"Beautiful curse . . . let me be the one who lifts it. You help me, and I will help you. You *can* have it both ways."

With that, he went out the door, leaving me staring at it, wondering what the hell he was. And how was I going to help him?

I was frozen in my spot for several moments. He hadn't died. I could borrow magic from him without any repercussions. Even if I didn't get my hands on the Mystic Souls, *he* was an option. Not the best option, I knew that. Making a deal with Mephisto might accumulate a debt I wasn't ready to pay, but I needed more. In my bare feet, I ran out the door in time to see his black Maserati Quattroporte drive off. As soon as I got back to my apartment, I called him. He didn't answer, but I received a text telling me we'd talk tomorrow.

"We need to talk now," I responded.

"Tomorrow morning."

Twenty minutes and ten texts sent to him without any response. I was being managed.

I didn't like being managed, especially by him.

CHAPTER 17

*T*he code used to get past the front gate to Mephisto's no longer worked, and I had to be allowed into his community, or rather the acres of land his one house took up that made up the community. Benton's professionally eloquent voice answered and he opened the gate for me. Shelving my emotion and agitation was becoming increasingly difficult as I drove up the driveway to the house. My aggravation at being managed was also increasing. Mephisto had shown me something life altering, left a few enticing crumbs, and walked away. Who does that? Someone like him, that's who.

Benton greeted me with a thin smile. He'd probably been warned that I wouldn't be in the best of moods.

"Erin, Mr. Mephisto is expecting you," he said, holding the door open and ignoring my brusque greeting. "Please follow me."

Coffee in hand, Mephisto was seated in front of a large bay window that gave a scenic view through the few but lush trees of the man-made lake, framed by colorful wide-petaled flowers I'd never seen before in the Midwest. The tropical appearance seemed like it would require a great deal of maintenance, which I was sure was the point.

Steel gray was his alternative to black and the color of the suit he was wearing. Crisp, fitted shirt and matching slacks. The cuffs of his shirt were rolled mid-forearm and he had on socks. Printed socks that seemed so off-brand for the prince of darkness. Satan's little helper. Seeing where my attention fell, his lips kinked into a small smirk before quickly fading.

"Waffle or omelet?" he asked, once I was within a couple of feet of him. "Or would you prefer something else?"

"What?"

"What would you like for breakfast? I assume you are joining me. I'm having a Western omelet. You had waffles at the restaurant, would you like that or something else?"

"I want answers, not food."

My stomach betrayed me by growling. Self-righteous anger wasn't enough to keep my stomach full. As soon as I thought it was a reasonable time to storm someone's home, I did. And I had come prepared. His amused gaze took inventory of the collection of weapons I had on me. First, his eyes went to the dagger sheathed at my left thigh, drew up to the blade at my left waist and then to my right, where I holstered the double-edged karambit. He studied my face, where I'm sure he saw the signs of sleep deprivation. I hadn't bothered to try to hide them with concealer. My hair was piled on my head in a disheveled bun. Something, based on the faint smile that breezed over his lips, amused him.

"You didn't die," I whispered.

"I'm aware, Erin. After all, I was there." Several more moments of silence passed between us before he spoke again. His voice was low but commanding. "I'm going to ask that you disarm yourself and join me for coffee, breakfast if you'd like."

Removal of the weapons was just a polite suggestion since a

tall woman, who had me by nearly six inches, sidled up next to me. Lean muscle, lissome grace, and predatory alertness were demonstrated in her slightest movement. She moved with the stealth of a feline. I checked her eyes to confirm. Shifter. Her height didn't bother me. Her solid build gave me pause because with faster reflexes, strength, and speed, she would have me at a disadvantage. Another person entered, a broad man, hair skull short and a glower as sharp and unforgiving as his clenched jaw. The severe look he shot in my direction challenged me to disregard the request. It only heightened my determination to do just that. Mephisto grinned at my display of defiance.

"How delightful, breakfast and a show," he said, lounging back and slowly rocking the swivel chair from side to side in a slow rhythm as his gaze moved between me and the two shifters.

I removed each weapon at a snail's pace, gathering a puerile enjoyment from their frustration at having to stand there and wait. My eyes locked with Mephisto, who was also forced to wait. His ego wouldn't allow his gaze to drop from mine the entire time. His subtle fidgeting just made the situation better for me.

He looked at the pile of weapons and stood. Still keeping his gaze fixed on mine, Mephisto positioned himself directly in front of me, shifting his attention to my hair. His lips twisted in inquiry.

"There's nothing in my hair."

"Show me."

I huffed, snatching off the ponytail holder that secured the messy bun and letting my hair fall.

"Satisfied?" I asked through clenched teeth.

"Of course. But I'd be more satisfied if you were comfortable coming to see me unarmed. We definitely need to work on our trust issues if we are going to work together." He nodded in the shifters' direction, dismissing them.

"It's not about trust. I like to be prepared," I said, gathering my hair and putting it back in the bun, not caring how it looked. Based on the way Mephisto eyed it, the style was presentable.

"You have security now?" I asked, taking a seat at the large table.

"I have plans later. They will be joining me, and since you came armed as if you were planning a coup, I guess it's good that they were here." A mischievous glint flickered over his eyes.

"Plans with the 'fine people of the city.'"

"There's an auction I will be attending, and it is good that I don't leave it alone." His gaze roved over me lazily. "Would you be interested in joining me? They are quite the experience."

"I'm not sure I'm interested in an auction that requires a security detail." So many things about the auction piqued my interest but there were more pressing issues. "You didn't die," I repeated, grabbing his attention from the view outside where it had gone.

"I'm aware. I was there, remember?"

He turned from the view to face me, a slight curl in his lips. *Oh no, he thought his comment was funny!*

"Because you're Satan?" I asked breezily, although part of me was serious. What was the explanation for his ability? Magic that not only unlocked magic to me, but worlds.

He leaned toward me, his dark eyes an abyss. "I'll be whatever you want me to be," he said softly, intimately. His voice was low and seductive. I cursed the flush of warmth that moved over my face because it widened the smile on his face.

"I want your magic," I blurted, getting straight to business. Getting his magic was my main objective and there wasn't any need to be coy or evasive.

Before he could answer, a young man interrupted to ask me what I wanted for breakfast. To make things simple, I

159

told him to give me whatever Mephisto was eating. He waited for a moment as if he expected me to change my mind. He didn't realize that most of the time, my breakfast consisted of a makeshift grilled cheese sandwich, with toasted bread and a few seconds in the microwave to warm the cheese. My omelets had to be eaten out of the pan, to which they were stuck. Unburnt omelet was going to make my day.

"Your magic, how do I get it?"

"No dinner, wine, wooing. Just straight to it."

"I'm not here to play games. Do you understand what happened between us? Did you know that would happen?" Hope fluttered in me at the possibilities. Mephisto's magic could be a temporary solution until I had the Mystic Souls. If the spell book didn't provide a solution, he could be a permanent one. Linked to him and his magic wasn't a bad compromise. I'd have magic. It was worth the cost.

"I speculated but wasn't positive. I've met many Raven Cursed, but you are stronger than most. I felt it the first time I met you. Like standing next to a live wire. Invigorating."

"Standing next to a live wire is invigorating," thought no one —ever.

"How much do you want?"

He choked out a laugh. "I don't want money. As I stated before, you help me and I will help you."

"Help you do what?" I wanted clarity—a lot of clarity because I knew exactly who I was dealing with. Specificity would be necessary at all times.

He dismissed my question with a wave of his hand. "A conversation for another day," he said.

"No." I needed an answer.

His brow lifted. A feeling of drowning overtook me, gulping at water trying to stay afloat as waves of failure washed over me. And I hated that he was the source of it. That he'd somehow weaseled a hold over me.

He continued to regard me with interest. When he shifted in his seat, it brought him closer. A slight change in my position put me even closer—really close. His magic was so strong, making me desire it even more. Whispering the words of power, I watched his face flash with the initial shock when the donor knew they were about to be swept under. Magical euphoria was the precursor, easing them into the state where they'd stay until I chose to bring them back. If I chose to bring them back. But Mephisto didn't have to worry about being brought back—and neither did I. The elation of freedom took over.

The cool, refreshing feeling of magic inching over me was like the first dip in a pool on a smoldering day. It felt right. My thirst would be slaked.

The wall hit with a fierce blow; my head snapped back. Pain throbbed and my vision blurred. Mephisto's eyes were alight with energy that shone bright and then faded. Magic continued to strum off him like a violent wave. Pain didn't squelch my desire to possess his magic by any means. This was bad.

"Sinclair," Mephisto's voice raised slightly. The male shifter returned.

"Yes."

Mephisto's eyes were arctic and his demeanor crisp.

"Ms. Jensen will be leaving. Make sure you return her weapons to her once she is outside," he instructed.

What? I was about to be thrown out of his home? The throbbing in my head subsided, leaving me with more questions. He'd prevented me from taking his magic. How in the hell had he done that? Desperation makes people illogical, and logic had taken a leave from my body. I considered clamping my fingers around the sides of the chair and refusing to leave. The tension in Sinclair's jaw negated that option. Sensing my reluctance, the shifter woman appeared beside him. I was too angry to be embarrassed.

Mephisto, in an aloof sign of dismissal, swiveled his chair away, returning to appreciating the view outside.

"Are you serious?" I hissed through gritted teeth. I was in the wrong, though I'd never admit it to him. He hadn't agreed to donating his magic. I took it. Seeing the set of his jaw and the determination, I knew he was resolute. I hated dealing with stubborn people, because I was one myself. I cursed my poor self-control. I'd ruined things. What were my options? Leave and risk him never discussing an arrangement to keep the magic permanently, or shelve my pride and acknowledge I hadn't made the right choice? His smug profile made apologizing difficult.

"I shouldn't have done that," I admitted. It wasn't quite an apology, but I had confessed to wrongdoing. That had to count for something, right?

Mephisto relaxed, turning slowly in his chair. Empathy eased onto his hardened features. Linking his fingers over his stomach, once again I was the recipient of his undivided attention.

Then his eyes dropped from mine and silence stretched for several moments. "We can discuss things over breakfast," he said.

Compromise was good. This negotiation could go in my favor after all.

With the exception of the slight sounds coming from the kitchen, the faint songs of birds in the garden, wind easing through the trees, and occasional expectant looks from the squirrels outside, which led me to believe he fed them, there was silence.

"Do you like it?" he asked when I took a sip of coffee.

"It's very smooth and rich." The banality of the conversation was going to drive me crazy.

"It's Kopi luwak, civet coffee." He took an indulgent sniff before sipping. "I always considered the fondness for it was the result of elaborate branding and marketing. Nothing more that catering to the whims of decadent needs. I'm pleased to be wrong."

We were talking like friends and we weren't friends and weren't going to be. I wanted to get to business. Make a deal —and get the magic.

After several more minutes of colorless conversation about me, the flowers in the garden, me, coffee, nature, me, music, and me, he asked if I had plans for the weekend. That was the final straw.

"Mephisto, this isn't a date. You said we can help each other. We know how you can help me, how can I help you?"

"If I asked you out on one, would you go?"

Yeah, address that and not the real reason I'm here.

"I'd say no."

"You don't mix business with pleasure. Admirable."

Everything had to be on his terms. That's what this was all about, although, I thought, maybe I was just as bad in that regard.

"Not at all. I'm not interested in anything but your magic. Either discuss the agreement..." The rest of the sentence lingered.

I watched a thoughtful expression slowly eclipse his face; his assessing gaze traveled over me. Silence swelled. His chair moved in small movements from side to side in perfect time as if following the beats of a metronome. Anger rose in me as he took his sweet time. One kiss, one touch, one whisper of my words of power and magic could be mine. I'd never feel that hunger again. My desire would be sated. And the person standing between that life and this one was handling it with casual indifference.

"You're being an ass," I told him.

He nodded his head slowly, in consideration.

Is he wondering if he is being an ass? Who puts that much thought into it? Either you're an ass or not. Let me help you out— trust me, you're being an ass.

163

His lips beveled into a half smile. "Perhaps I am. I suppose impertinent as well. Now, can we discuss your behavior? Why not have breakfast and discuss things?"

Several times I looked at the exit and considered just walking out and putting all my hope in the Mystic Souls basket, but watching this opportunity slip away out of stubbornness wasn't a good idea.

In the time I had made my demand and considered leaving, the food had unobtrusively been placed on the table.

"We need each other, so let's eat and discuss it," he said, placing a napkin on his lap.

Either way, he was in a stronger position. He knew I needed to talk to him to find out what he needed from me, and he had magic. Curiosity and desire and temper burned in me. My ego was a petulant child, urging me to walk out to make a statement: That'll show him.

My ego was an ass, too.

I slipped back into the chair, placed the napkin in my lap, picked up my fork and knife and started to eat. With each bite, I was acutely aware of Mephisto's gaze that kept slipping in my direction.

He took a few bites of his omelet and spoke. "You can go into the Veil," he said. "The other Ravens couldn't see the entrance. You can see it and travel through it easily. That's a rarity."

He put his fork down and stared at me.

"The Veil separates the two worlds," I said to confirm.

He nodded. "Like here, there are places of beauty and some that it's best to stay away from. The inhabitants are different. The magic, shifters, vampires are the attenuated version of what you will see and experience behind the Veil."

"Do they choose to live there because it's better?"

"No, not at all. Not better, just different. Simply the difference between cities, states, and countries. They have their own laws, rules, social norms, and everything you have

164

here. There are parts that are breathtakingly beautiful, but you have that here, too." His voice had become wistful.

"Me being able to go into the Veil means what?"

"If you can move through the Veil with ease, and if that's true for most of the places there, you can retrieve something that was taken from me."

"Why can't you do it?"

"I've been restricted from entering by the person who took my possession." His face flushed and his eyes darkened, cutting to slants.

"You used to live in the Veil, didn't you?"

He nodded.

"So, Satan's not from the underworld but inside the Veil," I teased.

He flashed a smile. "I ruled it for a while, but I find I have far more challenges here—especially when dealing with a particular retrieval specialist."

Did he escape, choose to leave, or was he expelled? What was stolen from him?

"What do you need me to get?"

"A box."

"Pandora's?" It wasn't unreasonable to think that he was in the market for it.

He chuckled. "No, I know where Pandora's box is. You know it's not a box but a jar, right? Poor translation." He frowned. "Humans now perpetuate the misinformation."

"Box works better," I offered.

"But a jar is safer."

"Is it really?" *Erin, seriously, are you having this conversation right now?* I cast off further urges to debate the issue. "So, there's a box and you need it?"

He nodded. I stopped eating. There was more to this than me just going into the Veil, getting a box, and returning it to him.

"What's in the box?"

165

"The contents are irrelevant. I just need it out of the Veil and returned to me."

"It's very relevant. What's in the box?" My eyes narrowed at the tension in the curve of his jaw.

He shook his head. "It's not a danger to you or anyone else. But the content is something I won't share."

"Why not?"

"Because it's my secret to keep," he offered tersely.

The box wasn't a danger, that's all I needed to know. Or was it?

"I'd never heard of the Veil before this," I admitted.

"That's understandable. It's arcane and only accessible by some magic. Even those who possess magic only believe in that which can be seen. If they can't see it with their magic, then it doesn't exist. And so few can do it."

"I get the box and then you give your magic to me, and we are done."

"If you want to be done with me, then yes, we are done. But I want you to know, it's not as simple as you seem to think it is."

He took an extended time to gather his thoughts and I'm sure to give me as little information as possible. Enough to get me to agree to doing it but limiting information on the contents—the very thing that now had my undivided attention. Knowing what it contained would give me insight to who Mephisto really was.

I was finished with breakfast and my coffee by the time he spoke again.

"I need to find the location and then you can retrieve my item."

"Why don't I just Veil hop throughout it? Search until I find what you're looking for. Do you have a picture of it? I can do it now and get it over with."

I tamped down the excitement that rose at the thought and gulped a breath. The sharp breath that he inhaled made

166

me straighten up and scrutinize him. Face unreadable, eyes darkened to a midnight shadow.

"That can't be done," he said.

After several beats of time passed and he hadn't elaborated, I asked, "Why can't it be done?"

"Your presence is known now. It's safer to be specific about the location."

"I could die?" No need to beat around the bush.

"All jobs come with the risk of injury or death. I got the impression that is what draws you to most jobs."

"I don't want to die."

"I didn't say you did, but you've never shied away from danger. In fact, you strike me as the type of woman who seems drawn to it more than most."

He tossed his napkin on the plate, pushed it away, and relaxed back in his chair to watch me.

"Danger I don't have a problem with, but if this is a no-win situation, there's no way I'm agreeing to it."

"No situation is ever a no-win. It's about the odds and whether they're in your favor enough to take the risk."

"Are they in my favor enough for me to take the risk?"

"I believe so, but you have time to decide. Are the benefits worth the risk? That's something you should think about."

He stood, his refilled coffee in hand, and went to the window, staring out of it again. For a man who draped himself in darkness, he seemed entranced by the beauty of the light. He remained silent.

I guess this meeting is over. It would have been nice to say, "Bye," "Meeting over," "Let's chat later," or something.

Taking another sip from my cup, I then stood and headed for the door.

He stirred and spoke. "I suspect Ms. Kelsey will be calling you in the near future. She was quite interested in your services. I spoke highly of your skills...of you." Before I could exit, I heard him say, "If you work for her, I will not be taking my fee. This is fully your job."

"Why, is she too demanding?"

He sighed. "She is quite delightful, but working with her should be rewarded with a bonus. It is only fair."

It was Mephisto's way of saying she was so high maintenance that a healthy incentive was required.

CHAPTER 18

Working for myself had its benefits. Forward my calls to my phone and when someone wanted to contact me for work, I was at home. Instead of engaging in typical daily activities—watching TV, cooking, or cleaning—I was meditating. Or rather trying to. My mind was firmly on Mephisto, his job, and the many facets of him and his magic. Four hours had been spent searching Google and all the magic and magic history books I owned. I had borrowed magic from many people, and they had all responded similarly. Not knowing what he was put me at a disadvantage. He couldn't be the only one of his kind. If he could loan me magic and survive, more than likely they could, too. This opened limitless possibilities to me.

I sat in my pale-yellow room, candle burning, seated on a yoga cushion, trying desperately to forget the brush of his magic against my skin. It could be mine but at a cost. Was the cost too high? I wasn't convinced there was a price I'd perceive as too high.

Interrogating him would be a start. Find out exactly what the chances and risks were and if they were in my favor.

What would be an acceptable success-to-failure rate for me to take the job? Forty percent? Thirty? Ten?

Then there was the Mystic Souls, if Asher came through, but that was just speculation and wistful expectations. The book might have a spell that would work—but it might not. Mephisto was definitive.

I was about to text Mephisto again, to request another meeting, when my business phone rang.

"Phoenix Consultants," I said in my administrative voice. I'm not sure why I did it. I wasn't fooling anyone. This was a one-woman operation. There wasn't an assistant, partners, or employees. Janus Consultants was my operation born out of need six years ago when I realized that a regular nine-to-five didn't work for me. My year in the Stygian, which led to the failure of that business, gave the new business name, chosen initially for my love of the mythological bird, more meaning.

I kept my thriving business small with minimal operating expenses. The only reason there was an office was because I dealt with questionable people that I didn't want in my home. Mephisto and other undesirables knew my address, which was why I was saving up to buy a home. Someplace I wouldn't be easily found. Something outside of the city, probably in a rural area. I wasn't opposed to living on a farm. A place where I could have some anonymity.

Speaking of questionable people, one was on the line. I recognized the soft, refined, mesmeric cadence the moment she said my name.

"Erin, this is Victoria."

"Yes. What can I do for you?"

"Do you have any meetings with clients today?"

"Is there something you need?" I asked, evading the question and giving myself room to decline if necessary without lying.

Taking that as an indicator that I was free, she said, "My driver will pick you up in thirty minutes."

Rarely did I allow clients' drivers to pick me up. One, because most of the people I dealt with treated laws like mere suggestions and were often in need of someone to handle things that weren't technically illegal but would probably need to be defended with counsel. They paid a really good price for it. There weren't many jobs that I declined, but the rare times that I did, I wanted the option to drive away and not be subjected to their tantrums or refusal to bring me home. Occasionally I was called to a penthouse in one of the homes overlooking the city—those rides, I took. I hated driving in the city.

"I can meet you at my office," I suggested.

"I'd prefer you meet me at my home. I have a pet I can't leave alone and I have no one to care for her."

Yeah, right. It was a power play, something I dealt with a lot.

"It is urgent that we meet as soon as possible." Her voice didn't sound urgent, but even if a building was on fire, she'd likely never crack her calm façade.

"What's your address?"

"It would be best—"

"If it is in fact urgent, then you will be fine with my conditions. I drive to you. I don't need an escort."

Her exasperation wasn't hard to miss when she exhaled into the phone.

"Fine."

Slowly navigating the winding roads of her subdivision, I found myself asking the same question: How many homes did a community need to be considered a subdivision? Based on my count in Victoria's community, five. My Camry looked totally out of place. A wrought-iron gate opened when I eased toward it. The metallic-painted brick exterior gave way to beautiful gray-and-silvery stone at the peaks of the home, which was surrounded by stretches of manicured lush lawn and willow trees. Hues of burgundy, gold, and sienna shrubbery flanked the building. The air was rich with the scent of flowers in the garden a few feet away. I made my way up the entrance and the door opened. A woman dressed in a black-and-white uniform greeted me.

Just as I suspected, someone to care for her pet.

"Erin, I presume."

I nodded. She smiled. It was a welcoming one that I appreciated. It provided the warmth the stark home desperately needed. I stood in the marble-floored foyer, looking around. Rows of expensive-looking crystal in large cases. Stairs with decorative iron rails spiraled up from the foyer. The houseplants, flowers, and earth tones added a personal, welcoming touch to the home. The place was a contradiction to Victoria's persona.

"Please follow me," the woman directed as she led me to a room not far from the entrance. I appreciated that the meeting was in a professional setting. Victoria kept me waiting for nearly fifteen minutes. I started off seated in the oversized chair in the corner but quickly became restless and walked around the office that was half the size of my apartment.

The light-peach walls were complemented by a cream-colored oversized chair and sofa and in contrast to the deep-cherrywood executive desk and comfortable-looking leather chair. A built-in bookcase lined one wall, and the various first editions of classic books might be the reason for the glass doors on them because my first instinct was to flip through the pages. My gaze immediately went to the small bar on one side of the room and the coffee station on the other. I chuckled at the idea of walking into an office and having to decide between coffee or whiskey.

"My office amuses you?" Victoria inquired in that sultry purr that I realized wasn't an act. The way it coiled around each word made everything she said seem teasing and cozy. I would have answered if my attention hadn't immediately fallen to the snow leopard at her side. One that I quickly noticed wasn't on a leash.

Increasing the distance between me and the cat, I kept my gaze firmly on it, my hand on the Taser at my waist.

"You won't need that, silly. My kitten is harmless." She knelt and it placed a large paw on her shoulder and licked her face. It certainly behaved as if it thought it was a kitten and not a hundred-pound predator. If watching a predaceous beast wasn't enough of a distraction, Victoria was dressed in an off-white suit, its opening revealing a printed chemise, an obvious effort to match her "kitten."

Victoria stood with Murder Kitty at her side, her appearance the embodiment of her exclusive establishment. I didn't get the appeal of Kelsey's. It was advertised as a restaurant, but it was more of a bar with nicer seating and fancy-schmancy food and drinks. Perhaps I wasn't urbane enough to appreciate the appeal. People flocked to the place like they were selling ambrosia. It was one of the few bars that actively catered to both humans and supernaturals. Not that any place discriminated, but based on advertising and branding, it was always apparent who they wanted as their clientele. At Kelsey's, if you could afford their overpriced drinks and food for the simple pleasure of listening to the short list of elite performers, they didn't care if lasers shot from your eyes; you were welcome. During their grand opening, it only took two drinks, an appetizer, and the three-figure bill for me to recognize that I wasn't their clientele.

Victoria exuded the same level of luxury and exclusivity in her home. Waving her hand in the direction of the chair where I'd been sitting, she invited me to sit again. I couldn't. Instead, rooted in position, my eyes ran over the animal, looking for any magical marks, runes, or medallions that force a shifter to remain in its animal form. Then I looked at its eyes.

"It's not a shifter," Victoria said. "That's illegal and frankly cruel. This is my pet. She wandered into our campground when she was just a kitten. Poor little thing. Her mother had been killed. She was so tiny. Look at her now, she's still petite. She'd never have survived in the wild."

Victoria needed to search for the words "petite" and "kitten" because she obviously wasn't familiar with the words. The tight smile on my face was making my jaw ache.

Victoria studied me for a moment, then gave a small sigh and clipped the leash in her hand to the animal's collar. I highly doubted that she could control it if the animal became aggressive. I kept my hand close to the Taser and mentally checked my concealed weapons before taking a seat. I didn't want to hurt the animal, but nor was I going to be mauled.

Victoria sat in a chair across from me. "Pearl," she whispered, signaling her leopard to sit at her feet. She offered me a drink but I declined. This wasn't a social visit and I wanted to keep my reflexes sharp.

"Your handling of the objects that were stolen from us was quite impressive," she began slowly, choosing her words carefully. "And I find your reputation equally remarkable." She smirked. "All of it."

She was alluding to my stint in the system. My reputation either made me appear as though I had a way of manipulating the system, so if I was caught I wouldn't be penalized, or that I was innocent and had taken the fall for someone else, so I was loyal. It gave me street credibility to the ones who believed I was guilty. None of the assumptions about me were correct, but I never put them right, which was a double-edged sword that sometimes came back to bite me. Like now. Whatever she was about to ask of me wasn't going to be good.

"Running a business in this city is hard. There's so much competition, so it's always good to have an edge. Something that makes it special, draws people in. The drinks, the ambiance, the fun had by those that come into my establishment requires . . ." Victoria thought for a moment. "Maintenance. Urging."

"Victoria, let's not be coy, there isn't much I haven't heard." My patience was thinning as she issued her soliloquy of an excuse. All that needed to be said was "I did a bad thing, now I need help fixing it."

"I trust that anything said at this point stays between us. It would be quite unfortunate if others found out about this, especially someone from the STF," she said darkly.

Why didn't people just use the gangster colloquialism and say "snitches get stitches"? I wasn't stupid. I knew where I stood.

"Yes, this will be handled discreetly."

"Good." She nodded in approval. "I think it will be good for both of us." Ugh, another poorly veiled threat. She cleared her throat delicately. "I called on the assistance of a D'Siren to help with my business."

My eyes narrowed on her. "You don't just call on the assistance of a D'Siren. It takes complicated magic to get one to do your bidding."

There wasn't anything innocent about the stone she used to maintain her business. It manipulated the minds of the people exposed to it in the subtlest way.

Victoria didn't have the moral depth to be ashamed. Instead her little nose lifted in indignation.

"It's not deceptive. I offer wonderful things at my restaurant. The D'Siren just allows my patrons to appreciate them more."

Part of what she was saying was true. It did heighten the experience. If you liked the drink, it was ambrosia on your tongue. If the music spoke to you, it became the siren call you were willing to die for. If the food was just okay, it became the cuisine of gods.

"It's not illegal, either," she pointed out.

"No, it's not illegal, but it is deceptive." *And cheating and frankly freaking immoral.* I rarely climbed on the moral high horse, but at that moment I was clomping around on it.

"Have you been to my restaurant?"

I nodded.

"Have you returned?"

"I'm not your target market," I admitted. "I don't think I've ever had a drink I'm willing to pay fifty dollars for."

"Exactly. People come to my restaurant because they enjoy the feeling. I'm not forcing them there, simply offering a service."

She walked to her desk, her cat languidly moving behind her, picked up the paper on her desk, and handed to me. "If you take the job, this is the payment."

Accompanying the piece of paper was an envelope with half of the payment. I looked at the high five-figure amount and my censure and disapproval softened a bit. The frown remained.

"I must reiterate the importance of discretion," she said. "Your expenses will be covered. I plan to open another restaurant and would like to acquire another D'Siren. I have it on good authority that there is one in the possession of a man named Collin Evers, in Nevada." She bent to stroke Pearl. If her intention was to look like a Bond supervillain, she succeeded.

"I'll look into it."

"I know you will." She smiled. She was so sure that I was about to rob Mr. Evers. I wasn't. I was either going to make a deal with dragons, or rob them, because in the trove of stolen goods, they had a D'Siren.

CHAPTER 19

*W*atching Cory pace back and forth was just as frustrating as trying to run out the clock with Dr. Sumner earlier. Telling the good doctor that I was closer to finding a cure to my curse only led to more questioning and techniques to manage the urges. There was nothing new, only variations of things that didn't work. Unconvinced of their ineffectiveness, he suggested consistency. Consistency was the key—to break the curse, slay the urges, and make me a normal functioning person.

Once I'd satisfied my arrangement with Mephisto and had magic at my disposal and rid myself of the cravings, Dr. Sumner would write a book praising his psychological acumen that enabled him to cure the incurable and bring me back from the brink of destruction.

When I'd first arrived at Cory's home, he was drinking from a bottle of water. Now he was squeezing the bottle, making annoying crackling sounds. I had just given him the Cliff Notes version of the past few days. I edited out the bit about Mephisto stopping me from taking his magic. That was embarrassing.

Cory's long legs ate up the length of his apartment as he

paced back and forth, his fingers moving nervously over his short hair, eyes sharp with concentration.

"He didn't go into death's sleep, you're sure? No slipping into the in-between?" he abruptly asked. He cursed under his breath. "You've borrowed magic from a fae, witch, and mage, right?"

"And hybrid witch/mage combination."

"Fae/witch hybrid, too, right?"

In magical school, they'd explored all true bloods and hybrids to determine who'd survive best from a death mage's kiss, but it was consistent—especially with me. Cory's face was twisting into a painful-looking scowl.

"I know." My shoulders sagged as I let out a heavy sigh. I reviewed the genealogy of each species. "Shifters are said to be descended from Vicis, fae from Decis witches, and mages from Ameritis—"

"Witches from Verne and mages from Prae," Cory injected proudly. My sidelong glance at him stood as my response. The same look I'd given him on several occasions and during numerous debates.

Mage: elemental, spell weavers, earth, and dark. The exact same terms were used for witches, with the exception of elementals. Witches who could control elements called themselves weather weavers. Just a fancy-schmancy word for elemental. Their gifts weren't any different, and once they accepted that, they could stop being a pain in everyone else's ass each time they belabored the point that they were distinguishably different. They were as different as a skillet and a frying pan, and I still couldn't tell the difference and both burned my food.

For now, I simply placated Cory with a smile and an occasional nod as he persisted with his tale of the history of witches that ironically mirrored the history of mages.

"Yep," Cory said. "You took magic from a vampire, too."

"His magic was stolen, so I don't think it really counts,

and I wasn't able to use it. I can't borrow magic from vampires or shifters."

Vampires had magic; it was the reason behind their immortality, their ability to compel and Wynd. Although Wynding was a gift only a few possessed.

"Shifters." Cory rolled his eyes, exhibiting the same prejudice as most of the magical community. Shifter magic was such an anomaly, most people had a difficult time grasping that their magic was limited to shapeshifting and nothing more. The peculiarity of it didn't stop there. It was the most potent single-targeted magic seen. It overrode all other magic. If a human mated with a shifter, they were having shifter children. The same was true with fae, witch, and mage. At one point, I suspected they were experimenting with breeding to see what happened. Rolling the dice came up with one thing: shifter. No hybrids, just shifter. It was hard to believe magic that strong couldn't do anything more than change them to an animal. But it remained the case.

"Elf?" Cory speculated.

It was possible, but if Mephisto was an elf, he would be one of the very few. People said they existed, but no one had ever seen one. If I were one, I'd hide the fact, too. Their lives would change drastically, becoming a spectacle as people gathered to get a look at a descendent of Dryada. Many claimed that elves were extinct. Could Mephisto be one? I stored it for further consideration. I thought about calling Madison, as that was her area of expertise. She loved the history of magic and supernaturals and was familiar with the intricacies of origins, myth versus truth, and the kernels of truth found in the most obscure myth—because there were always some.

I made a mental note to wear my palladium bracelet. When I found it on a job, I thought it would be useless since elves were the only supernaturals affected by it.

"Demon?" I offered. Mephisto being a demon didn't seem so unreasonable.

"A demon would have to be summoned," Cory said.

"But they can inhabit a human's body for short periods of time."

"Yeah, but they can't perform magic while in the body."

"Then he wouldn't have been able to stop me from taking his magic, or take it back when I tried to keep it," I remarked absently.

It wasn't until I felt the intensity of Cory's disappointed gaze on me that I realized what I had admitted. I lifted my eyes to meet his.

"What happened, Erin?" he inquired in a low, measured voice. The muscles of his arms and chest bunched with tension. "Erin." He took a seat on the large ottoman in front of the sofa, and bent forward with his hands clasped and resting on his knees. The look of consternation and scrutiny made me feel like I was right back in Dr. Sumner's office. "Tell me what happened."

"When he loaned it to me to go into the Veil, I, uh, I tried to keep it and he was able to take it back." I sucked in a breath and held it.

Cory stood, walked a few paces, and returned to his place on the ottoman. I guess he needed me to see his frown of disappointment. His mouth was open, brows pinched so close together it forced his nose to flare. It took several moments for the strain on his face to relax even a little. "Erin," he breathed out.

"I know. I'm not proud of it."

It was the right thing to say, but I wasn't sure if I was embarrassed that I tried or that it failed. Placing my drink on the table, I pushed my hand through my hair and gripped it so tight, I felt the tug on the roots. Cory would take my response as shame and would drop the subject. Actually, it was contemplation. I *should* feel shame. After all, I attempted to steal Mephisto's magic and keep it. The test I took in the Stygian was right. Something was wrong with a person who'd do something like that.

"He was unaffected by it and I just let that drive my actions." My voice had dropped several measures lower.

"How often are you seeing Sumner?"

"You know how often," I snapped, knowing where this was going. Madison was the only person who constantly urged me to increase the visits. "I'm seeing Sumner for one reason only. I don't control my magic well. But if I have it, there's nothing to control. I'll be fine. My life..." I sighed. "My life will be normal." Maybe not completely normal, but somewhat normal. Something I thought it would never be.

Cory scrubbed his hand over his shadow of beard. "You're going because you killed someone, Erin," he reminded me softly.

"You think I don't remember why I'm going?" The heat of my irritation suffused my voice.

He covered my hand with his and gave it a little squeeze before getting to his feet.

"Demons don't smell like expensive cologne and cedar," he said, providing a much-needed topic change. It was the reason we were such good friends. We understood each other.

"True."

Once again, the room faded into silence.

"It seems like you're going to have to make nice with Mephisto," Cory finally said.

"I always make nice," I said, indignant.

"Do you? The first time you met him, you said, 'What's up, Satan?'"

"Who chooses the name Mephisto? He was asking for that. That's on him."

Cory smirked. "No, he got exactly what he wanted from choosing that name. He's getting what he wants from you. If you're fixating on the name, you're fixating on the man with it. I'm sure it doesn't help that he might have the name of a devil but the face of a god."

I choked out a gag. "You know I can't unhear that. You've made more work for yourself, Mr. Spell Weaver. Make a spell to turn back to a time I never heard you say that. No, rewind it to the time right before you say that. Save us both the trouble."

His lips slipped into a sideways grin. "I may have said it, but you've thought it a time or two."

"I have *not*." *The woman doth protest too much.*

"Okay, well tell that to your lingering, salacious eyes that ogle him when you think no one's looking."

I dismissed him with a wave of my hand. And he went back to leisurely walking around his living room, busying himself with straightening things that didn't need straightening, including my shoes next to his near the door. He moved the pillows on the chair around, then moved them around again. He stopped to shake his head and laughed, but it was without a hint of amusement or mirth.

"In the span of two days, after we had our asses handed to us by an imp—side note, I hate imps. Maybe not all imps, but I sure as hell hate that cheating little red bastard. The answer was fire!" He huffed. It wasn't about the imp cheating—he took Cory's magic. A magic wielder would rather lose a limb than be divested of their magic. With power just a wave of their finger away, they relied heavily on it.

Cory shook his head and continued. "Not only did you find out that Mephisto can loan you magic, without consequences—"

"I'm sure there are some consequences, but they aren't as severe as death," I said.

"Okay, without dying." He rolled his eyes at my correction. "Asher is going to get you a copy of Mystic Souls because . . . well, when you're the Alpha of the Northwest

Pack, I guess you can just find rare books on a whim." His words dripped with sarcasm. Then he started fluffing a pillow, too aggressively. "Last but definitely not least, you've been offered close to six figures to steal a D'Siren from Collin Evers, but apparently you have the brilliant idea to try to strike a deal with the dragons—whom you robbed—for the one they have."

"I didn't rob them. If you're going to be pedantic, I burgled them."

"You set the witch's hair on fire!"

"No, that was Kieran. And it still doesn't make it a robbery. It's still categorized as burglary. There's a clear distinction."

"Are we seriously having *this* conversation?"

Seeing his face flush red from frustration, I bit my lips. Cory definitely tipped the scale toward handsome rather than cute, but his ruddy coloring and full bowed lips and single dimple that indented when he pursed his lips made him look youthful. And cute. Two things that would earn me an acerbic response and sneer if I told him.

"That's beside the point. This is what has happened to you in the past three days." He made a snort of disbelieving amusement.

"When you put it like that, my life seems more amazing than complicated, right?"

"Amazing? What part of this seems remotely amazing? We have no idea what Mephisto is, and I was content not knowing, but now we know your magic doesn't affect him . . . things just got real. And then there's Asher. You're lovely"— he made a face indicating that he was taking creative license with that statement—"but being friends with you isn't Mystic Souls fabulous. You went from not having any options, to two. Two apocalyptic, terrible, probably deadly options."

Cory was being overly dramatic.

"It's not that bad. It's just complicated." I wasn't underestimating the seriousness of the situation, but I needed to stop him worrying needlessly and spiraling.

"It's more than just 'complicated.' Do you seriously think that Asher, Mr. Cunning and Dangerous, doesn't have a motive? You'll be indebted to him—to the Northwest Pack. I don't think that's something you want." Tossing the pillow onto the sofa, he started to walk away but couldn't until he adjusted the askew placement, then he was back to pacing and stopped only to give me a stern look. "And Mephisto. Don't think for one moment that Hot and Broody isn't setting you up for something so dangerous you might not survive. What do you think he's going to have you do, pick strawberries at a pumpkin patch?"

"Why would I pick strawberries at a pumpkin patch? Wouldn't I pick pumpkins at a patch and strawberries at a strawberry farm? Is there such a thing as a strawberry farm? I bet you'd go to an orchard."

Cory was a beautiful shade of magenta and his eyes were ablaze. "This isn't a joking matter. How does Madison feel about it?" A slightly less threatening rendition of "I'm going to call your mother."

"I told you it was Madison who suggested the Mystic Souls."

"Yes, but I'm sure she would have been a lot more cautious if she knew you were getting it from Asher." He rubbed at the crease between his brows without any success.

"It's not like I won't have a choice whether to turn down the debt," I said more confidently. It was basic knowledge that it was better to live your life without any debts to the pack, and it was my plan to follow that rule. I lived in a world with many shades of gray—from dove to charcoal—but when it came to dealing with the pack, I stayed in the white zone. No debts to the pack. "He screwed me over and is trying to make amends."

"Asher screws everyone over. If it were an Olympic event,

he'd bring home gold every time. He has a PhD in it. He has no qualms about doing it, especially if it involves his pack. They come first and always will. So whatever dark strings and shady dealings he would have to engage in to get your book, I'm sure he's going to pass it on to you as a debt."

"He probably won't be able to get it." Seeing Cory's distress made me hope he wouldn't. Reluctantly I had to admit that I hadn't given it as much thought as I should have. What would happen if there wasn't anything in the book that could help? There wouldn't be any kind of "if you aren't satisfied" policy.

"And you can't think dealing with Mephisto is better."

Cory flinched at my noncommittal shrug. It couldn't be worse.

When I washed my hands over my face, Cory knew that was the sign I was getting frustrated. Like Madison, he wasn't trying to be a pain; it was born out of concern, but now I was overwhelmed. I needed time to figure things out.

He walked to the sideboard and pulled out a bottle of whiskey—the good stuff—and brought two glasses over to the sofa. He handed one to me and sat next to me. I looked at the clock across the room and arched a brow at him. It was just eleven o'clock.

"What else do we have to do?" he asked.

"I wanted to go see the dragons today."

He took a long drink from his glass and set it on the table next to him. He rested back on the sofa, fingers clasped behind his head.

"Tomorrow," he urged. "Today we discuss Asher, Mephisto, and your absurd plan for getting the D'Siren from the dragons, and tomorrow we do it, so *we* can get the remainder of the payment."

Of course there was a *we* because he was my partner and the reason, or so he claimed, he worked as needed as a physical therapy assistant was because I needed him—which most times was true; his magic came in handy. He failed to point out that the payment for jobs like this one matched what he made for a month or more. I didn't doubt he enjoyed the jobs and used my need for his assistance as reason for not going back to school to become a physical therapist. In the human world, where he worked, using his magic to treat people was frowned upon. A powerful witch was reduced to healing the old-fashioned way.

Cory hadn't taken another drink after his initial sip. Despite many attempts, Cory still didn't like whiskey. He kept it for my benefit. The small wire rack on his counter was filled with his favorite wines.

"We could avoid all of this if you could make a spell that would compel Mephisto to loan me his magic."

Cory's eyes bulged in disbelief. "If he's strong enough to withstand death's kiss, do you seriously think there is any spell I can weave that would work against him?"

"The dragon's witch partner was able to," I reminded him.

"Yes, with a magic-boosting charm."

"I can get you one."

"Erin." His voice was ringing with disappointment and censure. "I won't do anything like that."

Sometimes I wished that, as powerful as he was, he'd be a little more renegade. It was wishful thinking to expect him to suggest weaving a spell that would force Mephisto to hand over his magic. That would never happen with Cory.

Oh well, I'd just do it the right way. Looked like I was going to have to make a deal with the devil.

CHAPTER 20

The ward was an impressive mirage of tall grass and trees, enclosed by a gate. Passersby wouldn't think anything of the view: a nondescript cluster of forestry. But the magical illusion that hid the dragon's home blended with the other trees on the opposite side, the magic coming from the illusion and the ward the only indication that there was more to it.

Cory had pulled his lips into a tight line. His eyes were heavy with doubt as he moved his hand over the ward. It was stronger than before. Picking a ward and bringing one down are very different. We wanted the element of surprise, but after our last visit we no longer had that. I was sure there were alarms on the ward, which left Cory with the option of picking it, which required the same level of fine motor precision and adroitness as picking an actual lock.

Mouthing an invocation, he caused four spiraled circles to form in the air in front of the ward. More words were spoken, and sparks of teal overlaid them until one circle disappeared. Cory's lips kinked into something between a smile and a smirk as the teal spread over the second gold circle, flashed, and disappeared. The gold circle remained intact. Leaning forward, he studied the circle.

"What's your plan again?" he asked absently, his fingers striking the air again. Teal and deep rose danced through the air, merged, and covered the gold circles. Moments after it twined around the gold circle, the circle disappeared.

"It's not going to change on the fifth iteration, Cory." I sighed. The conversation was getting tedious. I had gone over the plan at his house before the whiskey slipped us into a midday nap, and again after lunch, reminded him before I went home, and again this morning when I picked him up. My exasperation or frustration with him never affected him. He was working on the third circle when he stopped mid-spell to look at me.

"'I'm going to charm them,' you said, so I was expecting more. Unless you plan on doing a spell that will compel them, I'm not exactly sure how that's going to work."

I lightheartedly smacked him on the arm. "Are you saying I can't be charming?"

"That's exactly what I'm saying. I thought I was being quite clear about that." He flashed me a smile.

"First of all, I'm charming as fuck—"

"Yep, you sound charming as fuck."

"I don't need to be charming, just persuasive, and I can do that. It's an offer they won't be able to refuse."

His brows inched together and I heard it the moment the words left my lips. Definitely more aggressive than intended. As if I was going to make them an offer they couldn't refuse or one they better not refuse—mafia style.

"Just like *The Godfather*." He beamed at the reference to his favorite classic movie. Then the smile faded and replaced by a look of dismay at me not showing the same fondness for the movie. He gave me the same look every time I dared voice my lack of understanding as to why it was considered a classic. Apparently, my lack of cinematic appreciation for it was an unforgivable sin, sacrilegious.

He finished the third spell, leaving one gold spiraling circle. Sipping air through his teeth, he sounded like a malfunctioning kettle.

"This is the easier option of the two," I said. "I don't have to travel or steal. This could turn out to be a very good situation."

"Easy? They aren't going to welcome you with open arms."

"I didn't say it would be easy, just easier. That's where me being charming comes in." I flashed him a smile, showing all my teeth.

With a playfully derisive sneer and flick of his hand, he batted away my assertion. "I'm not on board with a plan that hinges on you being charming. What else you got?"

"A pretty good persuasive argument as to why they will want to give it to me and possibly work with me in the future. Just open the ward and go back to the car. I have this."

If only I actually felt the amount of confidence I had put into my words. Charm—I wasn't first in line to get my share. But I could be persuasive and I was good at reading people. I thought that would work. I hoped it would.

Before he brought down the final circle, he asked, "Are you sure you don't want me to go with you?"

I shook my head. "If I bring you, they'll sense your magic and it could be a sign of aggression. Just wait in the car."

"And get you down once I see you dangling from a dragon's leg?"

I nodded and flashed a grin. His disapproving scowl deepened at the seemingly flippant way I was handling the potentially dangerous situation. He was wrong, I had a plan, but a large component depended on improvising, and he'd worry even more if he knew that.

The last ward dropped, the gate opened, and Cory reluctantly walked backward a few feet. I could feel his worried gaze on me as I entered.

Halfway to the house, the occupants met me on the unpaved driveway. The witch's shock of red hair was now a bob of wavy, ear-length hair. It looked good, but based on the arctic glare she pinned me with, she preferred her original style. The waves softened her features to the point that she seemed innocent and demure. Vibrant, expressive round eyes were framed by light-auburn lashes. Her pert nose had a point that, if her slight height of five feet would have allowed, she would have gathered a great deal of pleasure looking down at me from. Dressed in shorts, flip-flops, and oversized t-shirt, the threat of her magic seemed diminished. But I knew better. She was strong.

The younger of the two men fixed the light glow of his eyes on me as he slipped from formation. No matter how many times I saw it, a shifter's glow was menacing. He looked to be in his mid-twenties. The cleft chin that both men had led me to believe they were related. Even if I ignored the cleft, the thick waves of chestnut hair, the broad mouths that both formed perilous snarls, something about their in-tune mannerisms signaled a familial connection. The other brother, the man from the robbery, looked older but not by much. Maybe four or five years. The younger dragon shifter was the taller of the two men, standing a little over six feet. Behind the glow of their eyes were hints of amber. Once they turned off the danger lights, I probably could get a better look.

"Hi," I said brightly, flashing a smile that no one returned. "I'm Erin."

"What do you want?"

I'd been anticipating a lighter, more melodic sound, so the witch's harsh voice was grating. I stood taller, pulled out the envelope, and extended it to her.

"This is for you, if you can do me a favor," I said, getting straight to the point. Nicety and affability weren't going to happen, not on this visit. Her jaw clenched. When I stepped forward to hand it to her, her fingers spread and filled with a bright blue pulsing sphere. I didn't miss the young shifter using that opportunity to move a little closer. I tossed the envelope at the feet of the older shifter. His scowl had relaxed enough to give him a pleasant look, and the shifter glow was gone, revealing gentle hazel eyes.

He picked up the envelope, opened it, and turned it to show the money to the others.

"Is that for the things you stole?" the witch huffed out, giving the money a dismissive look.

"You stole them first," I snapped. The gall of her made my temper rise, and that was the last thing I needed. I took in a slow breath and released it through pursed lips. "Do you have any idea who you stole from? Landon, who is the official liaison for the Master of the city. Landon, who has been acting in an official capacity as the Master due to the Master's absence."

Her eyes widened and her mouth parted slightly.

"When you did your second little crime spree," I went on, "you stole from the Alpha of the Northwest Pack and some other people who you really don't want to anger."

The young shifter eased a few more inches in my direction. The electric pellet in my hand slipped, splattering a bright explosive charge that served as nothing more than a distraction. The witch instinctively released her sphere in its direction and I used the precious moments to spin out of sight, yank the Glanin claw from my belt, grab the young shifter's arm, and snap the cuff around it. The teeth of the cuff scraped against his skin. Safely positioned behind him, I used his body as a shield.

"This doesn't have to end badly," I said, panting lightly and trying to calm the startled shifter, who hadn't seen it coming. And I was lucky he hadn't. Whether he was part of a pack or not, shifters were fast. His instincts weren't as honed as other shifters I had dealt with. A history of broken bones, bruises, and scratches were a testament to how difficult it was to get a Glanin claw on a shifter. My arm started to tremble from the strain of holding him steady. It was the unknown object around his arm that kept him from fighting harder.

"If you don't stop moving, I'll have no choice but to engage it," I growled. "You don't want me to do that."

The older shifter's scowl returned and sparks of magic flickered along the witch's fingers. Knowing she was preparing something nasty for me, I made sure the young dragon was firmly blocking me. I could see they couldn't identify what the claw was, so I used that lack of knowledge to my advantage.

"This is a Glanin claw on him. All I have to do is press the button and he won't be able to shift."

I left off the part about it being for just a few hours, at worst a couple of days.

My panting had subsided. My mouth was a Sahara. I was in desperate need of water. Even improvising, this hadn't gone nearly how I anticipated. The envelope of money was supposed to open a dialogue.

"I get it. Vamps have to vamp, which involves drinking blood and being the mysterious type. Shifters have to be shifters, exhibiting pack loyalty and being predators by nature. Dragons have to dragon. But here's the thing: You're not just dragoning and hoarding treasures for your trove because you're compelled to by your nature. I understand the valuable objects. But the expensive liquor, high-end electronics, and jewelry are just theft. That's not a dragon being a dragon, so who's the thief?"

Calling them out on their avaricious behavior might not have been the best move, but I wanted all the cards on the table. To know where we all stood.

The witch's eyes lifted to meet mine. Her lips puckered as she glowered at me. My demeanor calmer than I felt, I spoke in an even voice.

"I don't really care what you do, but you have something I need. In fact, you have several things I might need. Keep your little treasures, and if by chance you have anything I need in the future, I promise I'll pay you for it. I'm looking for a—" Partner wasn't the word. I didn't trust them enough to partner with them, and there was something truly off-putting about the witch and the troublemaking baby dragon. I suspected the only thing he had in common with other shifters was that he might be an ass. "Mutually beneficial relationship."

The older shifter moved to the witch and whispered something to her. From his intimate angle and gentle touches, it was obvious they were in a relationship. It only took one glimpse of his profile and the sound of his relaxed and gentle cadence to get the impression that of the two, he was the pragmatic and equitable one. He was the one at the game. He was also the more level-headed of the two shifters, that much was evident from the tense, corded muscles of the one I was holding on to. The older one was the one I'd prefer to deal with in the future.

"What do you want?" the witch asked through clenched teeth, tetchy and refusing to be mollified. She might not be able to be assuaged, but she might listen to reason and cash.

"I need the D'Siren. The cash is yours if you give it to me. I'm pretty sure we can do business again, and it will be worth your while." *And mine.* "Stop it," I hissed at the younger dragon, who was clawing at the arm I had around his neck. "I'm not even applying any pressure. But you're going to make me lose my balance and my fingers might just slip. Is that what you want? I'm pretty sure that's not what you want."

The calmer dragon shifter seemed willing to work out a deal, but not Ms. Witchy. Sneering, she asked, "If we don't?"

I really thought I wasn't going to have to do a scene from *The Godfather*. Why can't people just play nice?

"I'm going to steal it, and while I failed to give your location to the Master of the Vampires and Alpha, I'm not going feel as obligated to continue extending such courtesies."

The shifter kept moving because he was bent in an awkward position to accommodate the height difference between us. I wasn't sure how long they had lived in this place, but they looked settled enough that it was doubtful they wanted to move. The decision was playing out on the witch's face, her pixie-like features hardening into severity.

"You didn't tell them?" Her eyes narrowed on my face, assessing me.

"Nope. I saw what you have up there and figured we might work together. We wouldn't have that opportunity if I had told. The mage and shifter who were with me were spelled. They don't remember this place."

She didn't believe me because there wasn't any magic on me. I explained.

"I work with a witch, a powerful witch. As you can see, I got through your ward, which, by the way, he did with minimal effort. He was playing on his phone the whole time."

That last part was unnecessarily bitchy and partially untrue. He looked at his phone, twice. What was with all the questions? Take the pile of money and give me your stolen goods. How hard was that?

Her extended consideration of my offer pricked at my growing annoyance. Slowly she started to back away, and when she turned her back to me to go to the house, I knew we had a deal. I moved from the shifter, keeping my finger on the activator until I could see his face and get an idea of where we stood. His attention was on his brother, and after a silent exchange of looks and slight head tilts, he calmed.

When I moved toward the claw, he flinched.

"I'm taking it off," I told him. He seemed fascinated by it and was paying close attention to the removal. Curiosity became surprise when I handed it to him. Ingratiating myself to him might not have the benefits I hoped, but I figured it couldn't hurt.

He bent down to study it, examining the teeth and the release. "Don't touch that," I warned him. "It's a single use. Once activated, it's useless."

A slow smile emerged on his face that looked much better on him than the sneer.

"I'm Maddox and he's—" His eyes moved to his brother and he stopped abruptly, giving him the courtesy to offer his name if he wanted.

"Zack."

The stiff silence remained. Even Maddox could feel it. "Thank you," he said, lifting the claw, "I'm sure it will come in handy."

"Not as handy as you think," I admitted, my smile wry from experience. "It's a great defense against a shifter." It was odd speaking to him like he wasn't one. But he wasn't part of the Northwest Pack and that's a different story. "But you only win *that* fight. Then you have an enemy for life. It's the whole battle/war scenario. Shifters, like magic wielders, don't like being neutered. Take away a shifter's ability to shift . . ." I let his imagination fill in the rest. He wasn't part of the pack but exhibited some of their surly countenance. He only had to imagine how he'd respond.

Look at that, he's just giving out smiles like candy on Halloween.

Running his fingers through his hair, Maddox kept looking at me and only stopped when the witch returned, her face folded into a painful-looking frown that would wipe the smile off anyone's face. Her dagger gaze bored into me as she approached. We definitely weren't going to have an amiable relationship. The D'Siren, along with a piece of paper, was shoved into my chest.

"If you want to do business in the future, don't break my wards and just show up. It's rude. Learn some manners and call first," she said.

These weren't dragons being dragons—they were thieves, plain and simple. I'm sure some of the items were tied to their dragon need to hoard treasures, but there was more to them.

Backing away, the D'Siren secured close to me in case they changed their minds, I gave them a half wave. "Thanks, Maddox, Zack, and . . ."

"Lexi. You can call me Lexi."

Maddox and Zack might be their real names, but Lexi sure wasn't hers.

"Are you playing a game on your phone!"

Pulling his eyes from the screen, Cory gave me a once-over. "What else am I supposed to do while I wait for you to be ejected from a lair by means of dragon flight? Although, as I didn't have to work any magic to keep you from plummeting to your death, dare I say you actually charmed them into compliance?"

I showed him the D'Siren. "No. The witch hates my guts. One of the dragons doesn't hate me, but I'm sure he's okay with never seeing me again, and the other might have a crush."

Cory grinned. "Did you have to kick someone's ass? Let me guess, the one whose ass you had to kick is the shifter with the crush."

"He liked my offerings."

With a naughty grin, he said, "Yeah, he did."

Playfully, I hammered into the curve of his bicep. "I had to put the claw on him but didn't have to engage it. I ended up giving it to him. That won him over. If anyone had wanted to drop me from several hundred feet, it was him."

"And all it took was a threat and a gift and he's crushing on you." He shook his head and made a derisive snort. "Shifters are going to be shifters."

CHAPTER 21

J tried to keep the irritation out of my voice when Benton's voice came over the speaker asking if I was expected. No, I wasn't. It was an impulse visit. Victoria wasn't available, or so I assumed since she hadn't answered my call or returned the message I left. Visiting Mephisto was just the next thing to do.

"Ms. Jensen," purred Mephisto from the speaker. "I wasn't expecting you."

"I know. I should have called. Do you have a moment to talk?"

"For you, of course. What would you like to talk about?"

"Not like this. I need to see you."

His deep laugh resounded with a level of amusement I didn't understand. "If you *need* me, then who am I to deny you of that?" The gate opened and my eyes fluttered from the effort of keeping them from rolling.

Instead of Benton meeting me at the door, Mephisto stood there, dressed in his signature black, the surrounding trees casting a shadow over his striking features. He watched me intently as I got out of the car. In silence, I followed as he ushered me to his office past Benton, who was seated in his leather chair, sipping on coffee, a paperback in his hand. He raised his cup in greeting as I passed.

Mephisto closed the door behind me once we were in his office and moved to his desk, where he rested against it with his arms crossed over his chest. His expression was blank as his gaze immediately went to the palladium cuff around my wrist.

"Is that the reason you needed to see me?" he asked.

"Yes. What are you? I've borrowed magic from many sources and you're the only person who reacted that way."

"Which way is that?"

Was he messing with me?

"Nothing happened to you," I spat out. "Remember, you were there."

"You didn't see anything happen, but I assure you something did. I just don't respond to your magic as others do."

"What happens to you?"

"I won't be nearly as strong. Your magic requires a sacrifice. You're just used to it being a life. If you are able to help me, then the payment I make will be far greater than any monetary compensation."

He slowly moved toward me, his magic stronger than it had ever been, an alluring embrace that I felt over every part of me.

"Stop doing that," I demanded.

"Doing what?"

"Whatever you're doing with your magic. Making it more intense."

His dark chuckle filled the room and lingered. "Erin, you really need to make up your mind. Do you want to see if the cuff works or not?" He slipped it off my wrist and put it on his, tightening it enough that it was secure. He was definitely familiar with them. Braces needed full contact; I learned that the hard way in the field. Without full contact, it's just an ineffective piece of jewelry.

The intensity of his magic remained. Closing my eyes briefly, I let it wash over me. A carnal promise that I wanted to explore. I snapped my eyes open. Taking several steps back, I removed myself from the temptation. Or rather I attempted to. The magic-drenched room was impossible to ignore, and so was Mephisto. My thoughts were a wave of thoughts and plans to divest him of his magic. Take it and make it mine. Inhaling and exhaling a ragged breath, I blurted, "I need water." It was rude, but it would have been ruder to make a play for his magic, again.

Rushing out of the room, I sped through the hall and to his kitchen. Before I could get to the fridge, the cook turned from whatever he was preparing for dinner, at the sound of my arrival. Wide-eyed concern slipped from his face after a few moments, and he forced what I assumed was an attempt at a warm smile.

"May I get you something?"

"Water. Please."

He nodded and retrieved a bottle of water. "Would you like anything in it? Mint, cucumber, berries, lemon?"

"No, just plain water. In the bottle is fine."

At least his look was subtle. *How dare I want something as prosaic as plain water out of a bottle. How uncouth.*

Leaving the water on the island, my gaze went to the window that drew Mephisto's attention during breakfast. I pressed against the island, closed my eyes, and tried a quick meditation. Slow breaths, clear my head, imagine myself on the beach. The comforting feeling of the warm sand nestled between my toes, sun bathing my skin in warmth, lulling sounds of ocean waves and a gentle breeze. It usually worked. Within minutes, I should've found myself in a better space, but instead, my calm was overtaken by the stifling feeling of coveted magic. Then cool plastic pressed against my arm. I opened my eyes to find Mephisto inches from me, offering me the bottle of water.

"You needed water," he reminded me. I nodded and took it. Increasing the distance between us, I went to the bay window and looked at the breathtaking view. I pressed my forehead against the window. The cool glass was better than a compress. I sighed into it, feeling the strum of magic washing over me.

Mephisto's cautious, curious eyes watched me. Without taking his eyes off me, he said, "Jasper, I'll be on my own for dinner. I'll see you tomorrow."

"I can finish it," Jasper replied.

"No, I can take care of it."

I could hear Jasper moving quickly, clearing things away, then he left without a word, leaving me and Mephisto alone.

I gulped another mouthful of water, working hard to tamp down my desire to take his magic, to feel it once again. His eyes darkened, a reminder of what happened when I attempted to take his magic before.

"Do your parents find it as difficult?"

Did I want to have this conversation with him? Give him insight into my life? Would it give him an advantage?

I shook my head. "My mother's half death mage and she doesn't seem to have a problem. My dad is human."

"Raven Cursed," he corrected, with the same type of haughty offense a person might correct someone using the wrong fork during a formal dinner. "It's tragic that they consider what you are a curse. The ability to make magic your own and manipulate it to perform to your desires seems far from a curse."

"Raven Cursed," I amended. "My mother doesn't use magic. She said it's better if she never does. The urges don't get exacerbated. My dad is human, so he doesn't have any problems."

I made a face, recalling my childhood and seeing how easy it was for my mother. It was as if she couldn't care less about the magic. The pity in her eyes as I struggled with taming my desires and ignoring the urges that flared in me when I was around Madison, her mother, and her father. The look on her face during the *incident*, when Madison called in every favor, pulled rank where she could, and accumulated debts and favors she'd never be able to repay. It wasn't as if she hadn't had a strong case for me to be put in the Stygian.

"Your mother's half?" Mephisto asked, his brow furrowing. He looked past me. "And your father is human," he added as an afterthought. The frown deepened, and when he noticed I was looking at him, he relaxed it. "Oh," he said in a tight voice.

Focused on the magic that thrummed off him, his questioning seemed mundane, irrelevant. Narrowing the distance between us, I closed my eyes, leaned in. Was it because I knew what it felt like? Was it the strength of it and the things I could do with it that made being around him impossible? Was I drawn to slipping effortlessly into the Veil, seeing fascinating new worlds previously unavailable to me?

He lowered his head so that our eyes met. His long, strong fingers lazily traced the angle of my jaw, traveling until they came to my lips. Tracing my bottom lip with his thumb, he inched closer and waited for me to respond. I closed my eyes, relaxing, and leaned into his kiss. The attraction to him apparent, the need undeniable, the lust unable to be contained. I kissed him hard, my fingers laced at the nape of his neck. My kiss was so hungry and uncontrolled, he panted at the voraciousness of it.

He cupped my butt and lifted me, my legs entwined around his waist, only releasing me when he'd set me on the island. Urgent fingers worked the buttons of his shirt until they were almost undone. When the last ones seemed to take too long, I forcibly jerked at his shirt, pulling the buttons from it. Cufflinks hit the floor, followed by his shirt. Reluctantly, I pulled away to let him slip off my shirt. Being so far away from him seemed wrong, unnatural. Roughly I tugged him back to me, my legs wrapped around him, to keep him close. He shivered when my fingernails grazed the muscles of his back and traveled along the indentations of his abs. My hands moved over him in long sweeps, exploring the defined sinew of his body often hidden by his suits.

He kissed me again, hard and fervent, before pulling back to allow his gaze to rove slowly over me: my lips, my shoulders, the swell of my breasts. He dragged his eyes over the exposed skin and to his position between my legs. His lips covered mine again, raw and hungry, before easing away to look at me again. Desire and curiosity competed in his eyes. I knew the question he wanted to know; it had vaguely crossed my mind. Was this real? Or was the desire, the want, and the need born from my yearning to have his magic?

I knew it and he saw it. When I relaxed my legs from around him, he stepped back, and in a graceful sweeping move, he grabbed his shirt, cufflinks, and buttons from the floor. In stilted silence we both dressed. He was the most disheveled I'd ever seen him: hair mussed, shirt wrinkled with gaps where the buttons had been torn off. His eyes never left mine as I put on my shirt.

Dressed, he moved his finger slowly and thoughtfully over his lips. I scooted off the island and grabbed the forgotten water and took a drink, pushing away the urge to douse myself with it to cool off.

Mephisto's eyes moved from me to the island. The very spot where we were moments from having sex. "I'm confident that won't be the last time. Perhaps you'll finally give in to it and not mistake what you feel as magical desire with what it really is—simply desire."

Moving away from the island to the center of the large kitchen, I shook my head slightly.

"Nothing's wrong with a little confidence, no matter how misdirected."

His light taunting chuckle filled the room. With a great

amount of effort, I pulled my attention away from his tongue, which was moistening his bottom lip, and busied myself with looking out of the window, getting drawn in by what fascinated him about his backyard. Aside from the beautiful arboreta and vegetation, he had a menagerie of animals. Deer, and rabbits that kept darting between the trees, making their presence known and jetting back into the thicket. The same with two plump squirrels that moved slower than any I'd ever seen. And then there was an animal I wasn't familiar with. White stripes marking its legs merged into dark-brown fur.

"Okapi," Mephisto offered from behind me. "A gift from a friend."

"My friends give me gift cards and laptop bags, not exotic animals," I joked, trying to ease the tension. His gaze resting on me was a reminder of what had just happened, and the closeness of him was a reminder of the fragility of my willpower. And a glaring indictment that I wanted my willpower to snap.

"We should see if you can remove things from the Veil," he suggested in a low, rough voice, running his fingers through his hair and mussing it more than I had. "That's the next step."

"Tomorrow." I backed away. "I have something to deliver to Victoria today."

Before he could answer, I was heading for the door. I was curious about whether I could retrieve things from the Veil as well; after all, it was the pathway to me completing my job for him. But satisfying our curiosity had to be delayed. I needed it to be the final step. There wasn't any way I could borrow his magic and walk away. I just couldn't. The tendril between my willpower and causing chaos had been pulled so taut, it was moments from breaking. I needed a day or two to replenish my weakening resolve.

. . .

The air conditioner's cold air blasted me in the face, shocking sense into me. It felt wonderful. For five minutes, I remained in my car in Mephisto's driveway, scrolling through my missed calls and messages. I had five missed calls, all from Victoria, along with a text message and voice-mail. Apparently she was excited to get her item. I had a couple of hours before I had to be at her home at the requested time of nine, so I drove around, music blasting and air conditioner blowing, ignoring the goose bumps on my arms and Cory's "I told you so face" that was sure to be there if I even hinted at what happened between Mephisto and me. The hours before meeting Victoria were going to be spent listing all the reasons I needed to keep a professional relationship with Mephisto. Number one on that list: I had no idea what he was.

CHAPTER 22

I had just jerked the car into park in Victoria's driveway when the front window of her house exploded, sending shards of glass flying. The front door was dangling from one hinge. From my vantage point, I saw a hole in the wall opposite it. Grabbing my karambit, I shoved my Ruger LCP into the holster on my right leg and checked the knives in my ankle sheath with the same efficiency and practiced manner I'd done many times. This was an "I told you so" moment that Cory would hear about. It might finally stop him mocking me for carrying a cache of weaponry to simple visits. At a disadvantage when up against the magically inclined, I found my toys necessary. It was easy to think they were excessive when you could conjure up a spell, smack someone around with defensive magic, or thrash them with the elements. I didn't have those options.

Dense magic that blanketed the air met me at the front door. Victoria shot a bolt of magic that I suspected was intended for the man standing a few inches to the right of the door. It smashed hard into my chest, jolting me back several feet and right back out the door. Losing the grip on my karambit, I got a glimpse of it being lifted away but was unable to get a visual of where it landed. I rolled to my feet as soon as I crashed to the ground, pulled out my gun, and raced into the house. The missed target had Victoria affixed to the wall, her arms magically bound to the side. Her teeth were clenched in anger. Untethered rage sharpened the glare she was giving him.

Magic pulsed and the scent of rosemary with hints of tannin inundated the air. I couldn't quite put my finger on the other smell that lingered behind it. As if it had been aged. Arcane, weathered, and powerful. Reminiscent of an old book. The distinctive smell nearly masked Victoria's magic, which seemed to have been subdued.

While the missed mark held her against the wall, another man, taller and broader, twisted and contorted his fingers in strange angles, hooks, and shapes. Fluid rhythms caused symbols to weave up Victoria's arm, where the ripped sleeves of her shirt left skin exposed. Panic overtook her face as she looked at the marks scrawling up her arm.

The missed mark's attention went to my hand.

"Go away," he growled.

Not likely.

As the markings continued to cover Victoria's arms and hands, I ran toward the man performing the spell. The force of my gun's handle slamming into his hand broke his chain of movement along with a bone—or more. I heard the crack. He stumbled to the side.

A flick of his finger and orange and blue sparks turned the gun into a metal inferno. I dropped it, fast. His uninjured hand lifted, shooting out a wave of magic. It was crude and uncontrolled but no less powerful. Dropping to the ground, I felt the breeze of its wild energy move overhead. Plaster from the demolished wall rained down on my back and head. *Damn. I wouldn't have survived that blast*, I thought, surveying the wall's damage. Another wave of his hand, and my gun moved out of reach.

Readying to grab my knives, I spotted my karambit a few feet away. I dodged the shots of magic pelted in my direction as I went for the karambit. Snatching it up, I charged the man but stopped midway when his eyes slipped past me.

I whipped around to find a third man quickly approaching, his glacial stare fixed on me, his hands moving in the same graceful, rote, sharp movements of the other man. I moved at him fast, directing a front kick at his hands. My foot grazed them but didn't stop the hand movements. The roundhouse kick got him squarely in the jaw. Shocked, he stumbled but caught his fall. Shifting my weight to the other leg, I got enough momentum for the spin kick. He jumped back, exhibiting the lithe movement of a trained martial artist.

I risked a look at Victoria, who was still being spelled by the man whose hand I broke. The hand moved as if there wasn't an injury. *What the fuck?*

Karambit swirling in a figure eight, I charged the powerful wielder, the slash into his hand ending his magical assault. The karambit slashing in hard and fast figure eights and strikes in varied patterns gave me a tactical advantage of surprise. Before I could corner him, he dropped to the ground to swipe at my leg, grazing it enough to unbalance me. I hit the ground and twisted enough to jab the point of my karambit in his leg. He crashed to the ground. I hovered over him, preparing to spew the words of power to disable him and grab his magic to use against the other two.

His eyes were chasms of darkness. I'd never hesitated about taking magic, but this gave me a moment of pause before I leaned into him.

The power words spilled from my lips. His face relaxed and his mouth slackened and his eyes glassed over, but he didn't drift into the in-between. He looked dazed. Magic coursed through me, but without the usual intoxicating flow. This magic was toxic—wrong. Its heaviness consumed me, and heat flamed in my chest and made breathing difficult. I choked on it, feeling the need to expel it. I realized this wasn't magic I could use before I even tried to form a defensive ball to use against the other two. Nothing.

Mouth still slack, the man whispered something. I gasped at the shock of his magic being ripped from me. His eyes widened.

"The Raven," he whispered.

Then he was gone. Wynded away.

Cursing, I pulled myself to stand and rushed toward Victoria, only to find her gone. They were all gone. Tangs of magic lingered in the air along with the dankness of my failure. A burst of the ominous magic and the clammy feel that accompanied it ripped through the air. I whipped around to the body that Wynded in on my right. Before I could strike, before I could process what had just happened, the bloody karambit was snatched from my grip.

At that moment, I felt the unthinkable: unrelenting hate for magic.

Light footsteps moved behind me. I snatched my knife from its sheath and whirled around. Mephisto, and I was pointing a knife at his chest. Seemingly unbothered by it, he placed his hand on the blade and lowered it to my side.

"Victoria's gone," I said, giving the area the same once-over that Mephisto was giving it. The room was in shambles, strong magic soiled the air, broken glass and shattered ceramics and soil from upturned plants littered the floor. There weren't any signs of blood. "From the looks of it, Victoria put up a fight before I got here." I looked at him. "Why are you here?" My voice was rougher than intended.

"I had several missed calls from her, and she didn't answer when I returned them," he offered, then fell silent.

Why would she call him? As he took inventory of the room, I paid more attention to him.

He had ditched the impeccably tailored suit for jeans,

leather boots, and a black t-shirt that stretched over lean muscles. The way he was dressed wasn't just a response to a call. It was a response to a call for action. When he knelt down to where the bloodstain should have been from where I cut the attacker, I eyed the rune-marked handle of the sword affixed to his back. He leaned over to inhale, and my mind flashed back to when he found the dragon's blood on the shingle. Unfortunately, there wasn't any blood here.

The man that had come in with Mephisto was dressed similarly, and his sword had similar strange markings on it. I took a few steps back as he moved farther into the room, in order to reconcile the subtle differences and similarities of his magic to Mephisto's and how powerful it felt. How did they walk around without people clearing the area to get away from such raw, undiluted energy? The intensity of it was simultaneously captivating and repelling.

Cedar and smoke marked the magic of the other man. His lean frame showed a svelte, toned body. Small veins rose from the powerful swell of muscles on his arms. His sharp, terracotta eyes were veiled by thick lashes several shades darker than his champagne-colored hair. There was a dewy glow over his warm ivory-colored skin. His hair was a direct contrast to Mephisto's midnight mane. Full, wide lips bowed into a frown. His magic possessed the same intensity as his person. I'd never considered that someone could possess too much magic, but it seemed as if eight feet of magic was packed into his six-five frame. It reminded me of a blizzard. He moved as if he was very well versed in the use of the impressive sword he carried, but I suspected magic was his weapon of choice.

The newcomer tensed at the sight of Pearl wandering in slowly, her gait sluggish and eyes glassy. She looked drugged, but based on the assailants, she'd probably been bespelled. The man's eyes narrowed as he watched her carefully. She stopped and looked at us all before meandering to the man with an odd familiarity. She curled at his feet.

Mephisto's magic was a peculiar mélange of the newcomer's magic. Briefly, my mind drifted to that, wondering if he too could have his magic borrowed without the usual consequences. *Erin,* I chastised myself, but I couldn't drown out the thoughts. Potentials.

"Tell me what happened," Mephisto said.

It was hard to focus on answering because the taller man with the cedar and smoke magic was kneeling next to Pearl and asking her the same question as if he were addressing a human, his voice a comforting tenor. My eyes widened.

"Erin." Mephisto's voice was sharp and commanding. But my focus remained on the man whose eyes deepened to darker shades and emanated a shimmer of glow. The snow leopard's head lifted to look into the man's eyes and then she made several chuffing and mewing sounds. The animal whisperer nodded, giving the massive predator who'd adopted domestic cat mannerisms a sympathetic stroke. His large size and commanding appearance were belied by the gentleness of his interaction with the animal as he languidly ran his hand over the cat's fur. I tried to pull my attention from him, but there was a magnetic lure, and I couldn't decipher if it was his magic, him, or his mystical affinity with animals.

Speaking to animals. There had been rumors of a spell weaver having the ability to control them, although the endless hours I spent with my classmates testing them proved otherwise. Unless they wanted the cat to scratch them, the dog to snap at them for bothering them, or the bird to poop on them, I was inclined to think it was more wishful thinking.

"Erin, I need you to save your fascination with Simeon for later. You are not alone. Most mammals are drawn to him."

But it was more than his magic. How could I focus when

someone was having a conversation with an animal? With great effort, I dragged my gaze from Simeon and relayed everything that happened to Mephisto. He didn't seem shocked by the level of magic Victoria possessed or that the abductors were immune to it.

"Continue," he urged.

"I tried to disable him by taking his magic, but nothing happened."

Simeon's gaze shifted from the animal briefly to meet Mephisto's eyes and then he raked his eyes over me, his brows inching together in inquiry, but he didn't ask whatever questions he had.

"What do you mean, you attempted to take his magic?" Mephisto asked in a husky voice. He was putting notable effort into keeping his face devoid of emotion.

After telling him everything that happened, he seemed to be having even more difficulty maintaining his impassive demeanor.

"Then he called you 'The Raven'?"

I wondered if part of the story should have been edited, especially that part. Mephisto was thinking about things too much and not sharing.

"What did he mean by that? 'The Raven'?"

"I have no idea," he admitted, and I doubted that even Mephisto could pretend to be that baffled. He struck me as a man who was rarely without the answers and found it challenging to be in this position.

"Did you see any markings on them?"

I did my best to describe the markings I saw on the inside of their arms. The design was difficult to describe, and the best I could do was to compare it to a sphere within a sphere.

"Is Victoria a Caste?" Simeon asked when I had finished.

"I long suspected it, but she denied it." Mephisto looked around the destroyed space. "I guess I have my confirmation." His voice sounded strained. "The Immortalis took her."

Answering my confused look, Mephisto gave me a weak smile.

"Caste. I guess you would consider them witches. Their spell-weaving, disarming magic, and protection spells have their limits. In fact, their magic is weak in comparison to fae, mages, and witches. They excel at curses, which is what makes them different from mere witches, who can't hex."

"They cursed the Immortalis?"

"Over fifty years ago. Expelled them from the Veil and weakened their magic, preventing them from ever going into the Veil again."

Panic and frustration mounting with each new piece of information, I split my attention between listening to them and surveying the room for anything that would help find Victoria.

"Why would Victoria deny being a Caste?"

"The Immortalis responded to the curse with anger. Their goal was to destroy the Caste, but it didn't take them long to realize that the Caste were the only ones able to remove the curse. However, their thirst for revenge meant it was too late. They nearly decimated the race, and the remaining Caste, if they could pass for human, did. The ones I've encountered don't even practice magic, hoping to never be discovered by an Immortalis. In the past, that would have meant immediate death. Of course they fear Immortalis. Caste defensive magic wasn't very strong to begin with, and years of having half-human children has significantly decreased what magic they had. And killing an Immortalis is nearly impossible."

"If they are immortal, how do we kill them? I mean, I know no one is ever truly immortal. Vampires are hard to kill, but it is possible. Beheading works." Vampire speed, strength, and preternatural reflexes made it nearly impossible to kill them. Could be done with a Dracon dagger, though.

"Amber Crocus can kill vampires. It's hard to find, but if

you stake them with anything laced with that, they will die. I haven't seen it in years. I suspect they've had their hand in finding and destroying the plant."

I made a mental note to investigate, search for, and possibly find some of my own. Nothing is ever completely destroyed, and if by some chance they had succeeded in eradicating the world of it, perhaps a manufactured version could be made.

"The Immortalis are nearly immortal, but they can be killed with an Obitus blade."

My eyes shot to the blades they both carried.

"The Immortalis can only be killed with an Obitus blade," I confirmed.

Mephisto's head shifted ever so lightly into a nod. "Obitus blades. They don't heal from any wounds inflicted by one. Behead them with it and they can't return." Beheading them with something else and them not dying was unsettling. Headless Horseman images came to mind.

Simeon's brow furrowed. "Victoria couldn't possibly remove a curse made by a coven."

Mephisto looked grim as he considered. "I suspect they found a workaround, a magical object of some sort. Fifty years of looking, they were bound to find something. Let's go. We need to find out what they have."

"I need to search the house," I said. "Maybe there's something here that can help me find Victoria."

The first place I searched was her bedroom, for anything with hair fibers on the off chance there was a blood sample. A search of her room, bathroom, and what I suspected was Pearl's room came up empty. The kitchen yielded no results. Stopping in front of Pearl when the search ended, I looked at Simeon. "I need to check her paws." It was a long shot, but there was a chance she might have a sample.

There wasn't any peculiar vocalization as before. "Will you please get on your side?" he asked her. Pearl plopped down and rolled onto her side, allowing me access to her paws. Crouched down, I examined them.

"There's nothing there," Mephisto informed me without giving the limbs a look. Although I knew he had detected the dragon's blood, it made me feel better to check. Magic didn't work like a CSI team; there actually had to be visuals, not trace amounts that could only be examined in a lab.

After I finished, Mephisto started for the door. I wanted to continue my search. I needed to do something. The feeling of not having any form of a lead nagged at me.

"If we can find the object they're using, it won't be hard to find her. They won't have her far from it. Hopefully, Elizabeth knows something."

Simeon rose to follow after making a sound that mimicked the chuffing noise Pearl made. She stood and followed him. Mephisto stopped mid-step once he realized that Simeon had invited the cat along. He raised an inquiring brow.

"We can't leave the animal here defenseless," Simeon said firmly, apparently offended at the mere idea that Mephisto had considered leaving her.

It's a hundred-pound cat with claws and fangs, it's hardly defenseless.

There were a few seconds of sharp looks passed between the two before Mephisto reluctantly conceded and continued toward the car.

"Who's Elizabeth?" I asked Mephisto before they could get into the SUV.

After several moments of appraisal and contemplation, he said, "I think you all refer to her as the Woman in Black or the Woman of the Forest." His abhorrence of the moniker was evident. Was he offended no one called him the Man in Black?

My mouth dropped open and I snapped it shut. Was it that easy for him? Did he just call up *Liz* for help? I needed to get to this meeting—not just to find Victoria but to ask her about Mystic Souls.

"You continue to do what you can to find Victoria," he said, "and I'll call Elizabeth." He was in his car with Simeon and Pearl before I could dispute his suggestion.

The thought that he was going significantly over the speed limit to either shake me off his tail or to see if I'd get pulled over crossed my mind as we sped through the city to his house. I rode his bumper as he drove to the gate and parked his car. Then he got out and sauntered over to mine.

"May I help you, Ms. Erin Katherine Jensen?" he asked in an airy tone, bending down enough that we were eye to eye.

"Yes, you can, Mephisto Lucifer Beelzebub."

His lips twitched.

"Why are you at home and not going to see Elizabeth?"

"Because I need to check my collection to make sure nothing is missing." Mephisto in possession of magical objects that could remove a curse was no surprise to me.

"I'll help."

"No need, I will keep you informed."

"Or I can keep myself informed," I said, getting out of the car. "I need to find Victoria. If you have a lead, I'm going with you."

He closed the garage door and after several moments, the front door opened. Leaning against the doorframe, he crossed his arms across his chest, looking exasperated. I wasn't sure why.

"Give me a minute," he said, but he didn't move immediately, instead focusing on me. "The Raven," he whispered. Something passed over his face that I couldn't quite place. His brows knitted together. He repeated the words. Snapping his attention from me, he moved quickly down the hall, past his office, and disappeared. The urge to follow was quickly squashed when Simeon said, "I wouldn't."

Waiting for Mephisto to return, I rested against the wall and watched Simeon. The more I observed him, the more curious I became about him and his magic. It was so similar to Mephisto's, yet as different as their personalities. The similarities were what interested me.

"The Immortalis are power-hungry, vile beings who will do anything to be returned to their former selves. It can't be allowed," Simeon said softly from his position on the rug in the middle of the room. He had moved the furniture off it to make more room for him and Pearl. Either he and Mephisto were extremely close or he had very little respect for personal boundaries. His eyes never moved from Pearl, who had his undivided attention as he absently stroked her. "Great magic far too often leads to great thirst for power to destroy others, or at the very least assert power over them. No one could expect any less from them—similar to their creator, Malific. A cadre that thirsted for death, power, and destruction as much as she does."

"Creator? Malific is a god?"

He nodded. "She's among the many that exist. Brilliant, talented, and ruthless. Possessing powerful magic and no restraint, she wanted to control all that fell under the Veil. Much like someone wanting to overthrow a country. The Immortalis ensured she had the force to do it. To stop her, they had to stop them." Frowning, his eyes were fiery with anger. "Shifters in the Veil are immune to magic. It makes them an asset to have and great allies. There was a small community where the shifters and a coven of witches lived as allies and friends. A rare camaraderie since the prevailing belief is that it was a spell that turned men into shifters. Malific wanted to use the shifters as her battle animals to terrorize others into submission and the witches as an addition to her army.

217

When they declined her offer, the Immortalis slaughtered shifters during the full moon and killed the witches, binding them with iridium braces and torturing them. There are more stories like that, but people lived in fear and hope that she wouldn't take an interest in their community."

I assumed the rules of engagement were similar to what they were on this side of the Veil. Most shifters changed fast, but no one attacked them during their full moon transition when they possessed very little control.

It wasn't until I relaxed the scowl on my face that he continued.

"It was after years of Malific terrorizing so many in the Veil, conquering for no other reason than to assert her power, that eventually, with persuasion from others, the Caste intervened. They pride themselves on being neutral…" He considered his words for a second. "Not neutral as much as too self-absorbed to care about more than themselves. Self-absorption, which is often seen as a flaw, serves as an asset for Caste. They tend to overindulge and prefer extravagant lifestyles. Their exceptional ability to curse has never made them power hungry. Attaining and maintaining power is difficult and of no interest to them." Briefly he looked up from Pearl, his eyes meeting mine. "The Blood Moon is in two days."

Uh, okay. I had no idea what he was talking about.

"Excuse me?" Obviously, I had missed an important part of the conversation.

Giving me a small smile, he said, "It's not a coincidence that they abducted her two days before the Blood Moon. It's the most optimal time to do a spell, particularly if they have something that can remove the curse. They've secured a Caste, because only Caste blood can be used to remove the curse. As long as a Caste exists in the world, the curse will remain. Unless it's lifted."

"How can you two be so confident that a magical object is involved and that they don't have several Caste?"

"Because it took the magic coven to weave the curse. It is doubtful that one person could lift it, no matter how strong they are, which is why there has to be a magical object involved. Even if they have more than one Caste, it's doubtful there are enough of them to remove the curse. A magical object has to be involved. Hopefully Elizabeth will be able to offer us more help, perhaps find the object and nullify it."

Maybe we did have time. But not a lot. *Where are you, Mephisto?*

Pearl was devouring the attention Simeon bestowed on her but still decided that it wasn't enough. She bumped her head against my leg in a request to pet her.

You're not a house cat no matter how many houses you end up in! The look I gave her relayed that thought. Pearl simply bumped me again. Eagerness to know more about Simeon kept me seated next to him, halfheartedly stroking Pearl. She made some chuffing noises and Simeon laughed and covered my hand with his, guiding it over her fur, showing me how she preferred to be stroked. Content, she snuggled her head closer to me. Despite her belief, she wasn't a house cat and was at risk of unbalancing me. I switched position and sat on my butt, unsuccessfully trying to ignore Simeon's magic. Weary from drowning in magic, I was relieved that Simeon's was decidedly the less tempting of the two. I chalked it up to the fact that I knew Mephisto's and its facets and ignoring it was more difficult. *And* Simeon hadn't ever had me on the kitchen island shirtless, panting, clawing at him.

I was confident that wasn't likely to happen. He was infinitely a better choice than Mephisto to share magic with, if it were possible. And if he were as open about Mephisto as he was about the Caste and Immortalis, then I might be able to find out more about him and Mephisto. It was a situation where I just couldn't lose.

"She likes you," he soothed, removing his hand from over mine.

Or she wants me to be an appetizer. The fact that on her hind legs, she stretched to a length that would put her just a few inches shorter than me made it difficult not to see her as anything less than a predator. No matter how friendly Pearl was, one overly playful or aggressive lunge could floor me, and her claws and fangs were designed to damage. She tolerated my unguided stroking of her velvet fur for a few minutes before shrugging me off and returning to Simeon, who apparently had superior stroking skills.

That gave me an opportunity to move away from Simeon, whose magic was inducing urges that were getting harder to ignore. Leaning against the wall, I watched him.

"You can communicate with all animals?" I asked.

He nodded. I gathered he preferred the company of four-legged animals. Studying him with greater scrutiny, I could see flecks of green in his terracotta eyes. The intensity of them swung from the animal to me in anticipation of more questions.

"Can you only speak to animals or can you read their minds as well?"

His lips slowly formed a smile. "That's not the question you want to ask. I prefer directness. What you want to know is whether I can read your mind, because humans are animals, too."

I barely moved my head into my nod. The *kitten* had fallen asleep, and he moved from under her to standing with imperceptible grace, then quickly closed the distance between us. I was mistaken; his magic wasn't less tempting than Mephisto's. The similarities and the stark contrasts were apparent but no less enticing.

"Mephisto enjoys his games," he said, "and his indulgences. I don't share those qualities. Be direct with me and I'll be direct with you."

I liked him. I liked him a lot.

"You know who I am, right?" I asked.

"Yes. Erin Jensen."

He might be direct, but questioning him was going to be difficult. It was like asking a robot: I wasn't going to get any more than what I asked.

"Do you know what I am?" I modified.

"I know what Mephisto thinks you are and the capabilities he is hopeful you possess." A shrewd smile appeared and disappeared. "I know what people think you are. Raven Cursed." He frowned. "Crudely referred to as 'death mage' in a demonstration of the slow extirpation of history and respect for words. Mage magic is diametric to what you are."

"Diametric?"

"Your magic comes from loss—most of the time, life. Theirs, like witches', is created, it's vitality and conception. Witch and mage are new magic, yours isn't. It is a curse, but it can't be traced to the Caste—so I suspect it predates them. An arche."

Although his words were cold and somewhat cruel, his tone held a gentle timbre. Paying more attention to our conversation, it wasn't until I felt the pulsating energy of his magic near me, waking my senses, that I realized how close we were to each other. Fully aware how easily he moved undetected, I watched him more carefully.

"Are you and Mephisto the same? I mean magic wise."

"No. He can't communicate with animals, his defensive magic is stronger than mine, and he can Wynd. I can't." He tilted his head at me. "You're not asking the questions you want to ask."

"If I were to borrow magic from you, what would happen?"

"What do you think would happen?"

"I thought you valued directness. You don't seem to have the same feelings about vagueness."

His smile radiated mischief and reticence. A duality I wasn't fond of.

"Because that's not what you really want to know. Ask your question, Erin," he urged. His patience appeared to be thinning.

"Mephisto didn't die when I borrowed magic from him, and something about your magic feels the same. I'm wondering if you'd respond in the same way."

There was so little space between us that if I wanted, I could just say the words of power and find out for myself. Remembering the massive headache I suffered when I tried to do it to Mephisto without his permission was the only thing stopping me. I wish it was because it was wrong, but it wasn't.

There was a slight spark of irritation when Simeon's gaze drifted to the entrance, where Mephisto was now standing, and then back to me.

"Perhaps," he said, "but I don't have a desire to find out."

He glided away from me with the same ease he had moved toward me and went back to take a position next to the napping cat.

"I assume you've filled her in on the Caste and Immortalis?" Mephisto asked.

Simeon nodded, ignoring the sharp look Mephisto was giving him as he addressed me.

"My knowledge is your knowledge," he offered. I had no idea what that meant.

"You're offering her use of your library?" Mephisto asked.

"If she'd like. Your interest in her makes it necessary that she doesn't remain as ignorant as she is now."

Becoming less fond of his directness since it seemed to come with a side of insults, I glowered. But he was offering me his library, his knowledge was mine. And I had a lot more to learn.

"That's quite an offer," Mephisto said, his tone smooth

and professional despite his speculative gaze. "Simeon's library is impressive. Many originals, before they were modified to present what they want the general public to know. Books that are no longer in circulation, and handwritten accounts of many events. It will be an experience you should enjoy."

Mephisto's gaze narrowed on Simeon and they stared at each other. Finally breaking the eye contact, Simeon looked down at the napping snow leopard.

"Should I leave her here?" he asked.

Irritation moved over Mephisto's face.

"No, put her in the basement."

"Who will watch her?"

She's an apex predator, she doesn't need to be "watched."

"Benton will be here soon, he can do something with her," Mephisto groused, heading for the door. Guardian of the door to leopard babysitter cannot be considered a professional lateral move.

He turned and gave Simeon a wicked smile. "Maybe if she's hungry later, he can take her into the backyard. She might find the okapi interesting."

Simeon scowled and shot a laser-sharp glare at Mephisto. I looked from one to the other, puzzled, and then it dawned on me that Simeon must be the friend who'd given Mephisto the okapi.

Mephisto laughed and Simeon nudged Pearl awake. "I don't find your humor funny," Simeon asserted.

"Of course not, you never do." Mephisto looked quite pleased with himself.

CHAPTER 23

*W*e drove down the empty street of Mephisto's subdivision, flanked by trees that obscured the few neighbors from each other, interspersed with small ponds and fountains. As we approached the gate, it opened and two motorcycles sped in, the drivers slowing their machines to look in our window. Giving Mephisto a small nod, they turned and raced away.

"That's Kai and Clayton," he informed me. By the time we were through the gate, they were so far ahead, I couldn't see anything more than the ruffle of their shirts from the wind as they tore through the streets.

In the gravel parking area were the two motorcycles, parked. The taller of the two men rested against his bike. Deep, dusk-brown skin melted along the angles of his face and high cheekbones. His lips twitched as he watched the slight man bound back and forth. They couldn't have been waiting long, but from watching the tawny-skinned man pace, you would have thought they'd been waiting hours.

I got out of the car and was immediately hit with the wave of magic flowing from them. It was more than magic coming off the pacing man. Bounding energy like that couldn't be functional. I wouldn't be likely to forget experiencing his magic. It was an effort to drag my gaze from his finely carved features, but I managed because staring is rude. I did keep taking peeks at him, though. His ethereal beauty made it difficult not to watch him to determine what was the most alluring thing about him. Could it be his sharp nose, his expressive eyes, or his enviable flawless skin? When he caught me looking, he stopped pacing.

"I'm Kai," he said softly, his cognac-colored eyes meeting mine briefly before he returned to walking, slower now, but he obviously needed to move.

The taller man, who I assumed was Clayton, was as fluid and effortless in his movements as if he were gliding in water, which, based on his broad build that narrowed at the hips, was something he did often. A swimmer's build. Full lips remained in a relaxed line, resisting a smile of greeting. His curious eyes looked me over. His nostrils widened a little to inhale and he leaned slightly into the air. Did he sense magic the way I did? Did I smell like Riesling and strawberries the way Grayson said I smelled?

"We didn't think you would take so long, Mephisto," Clayton teased, but his voice tightened on the name. Simeon's gaze wrenched in my direction, hyperaware of my presence. I knew he was used to calling Mephisto something else.

"Erin was in the car."

"Ah, protect the breakable Erin. That's your excuse." His head went back in laughter that Mephisto didn't share.

So, they weren't as breakable. Today was full of new information, including the fact there were more people like Mephisto. Even in the open space, their unique thrum of magic couldn't be ignored.

Although Clayton continued to address Mephisto, his eyes stayed as glued to me as mine were to his. After several moments of us gazing at each other, his lips settled into a welcoming smile.

"Clayton," he said, extending his hand. My gaze held his before dropping to his long dreadlocks of intricate twists, coils, and waves that he had secured back with a loose-fitting band.

"Hi," I breathed out, hating the sound of my voice. It wasn't him. I felt like I was drowning in magic that I couldn't have, and I hated the feeling.

One brow hitched up and he smiled, exposing brilliant white teeth. I had zoned out. Trying to force myself to think of anything other than magic, I blurted, "I like your dreadlocks."

"I'm confused. Do you like them, or do you find my locs dreadful?"

"No, not dreadful at all." Confused, I looked at Mephisto, whose pursed lips indicated he'd heard this line before.

"You can just call them locs." Clayton grinned in Mephisto's direction. "I'll save her the history lesson." He winked at me.

"Well that hardly seems fair since I've had to hear it . . . what is it, twenty times?"

"There's nothing wrong with a refresher on history. Isn't that what you always say? But of course, if it were up to you, my locs would be gone, right, M? Sharing the attention has always been difficult for you."

Mephisto chuckled. The sound held an ebullience very different to the darkness he leaned into. This man brought it out of him. I looked at him with renewed interest.

"M, you're bringing a Raven Cursed to see Elizabeth. I don't see how anything could go wrong with that." Clayton cast a sympathetic look at Kai, whose pace had quickened.

"It'll be fine," Mephisto said in a neutral voice that lacked the confidence needed to sound believable.

Mephisto navigated the area with the awareness of someone who had been there before. I fell back and allowed the Others to pass so they would encounter the imp first. Worst-case scenario, while they were dealing with the imperious duplicitous red devil, I could sneak by.

But there wasn't an imp or sharp-toothed fishes. Instead, at my approach, the bridge collapsed and a small blaze ignited that quickly spread to surround us. I bolted toward the untouched area, hoping to cross before it was engulfed in flames, but it was too late. Encircled in the flames, heat licked the air and brushed at my skin. I looked around anxiously. It was only a matter of time before the forest would be engulfed in wildfire. That didn't happen. The orange-and-blue flames danced around in a controlled circle with a life of its own, restricted to the small area.

"Step back," Simeon instructed.

I did. Backed away until I was in the middle of the forest. The fire faded, leaving the ground unmarred. The bridge reassembled and yellow flowers twined around the handrails.

"It's you," said Kai, in a whisper, when the flames ignited again at my next approach.

Really? I never would have come to that conclusion.

Mephisto sighed and a frown tugged down his lips. Exasperation whetted his words. "Elizabeth." He said her name with a combination of reverence and annoyance. An appreciation of her display of power and irritation that it was being used against him.

Mephisto whispered a few words, and the flames disappeared then reignited. A spark of fire lashed out and nearly burned Mephisto, who jumped out of reach just in time. It was a reprimand for his behavior.

"It will be worse if we attempt to disable it," Mephisto said. He studied the fire. "I don't believe Elizabeth is happy with us."

"*Us?*" Clay looked at me cautiously.

"You all should go. Obviously you are welcome and I'm not," I said. I'd have to find an alternative way of getting to her. Worse, all information from her would come second-hand and possibly edited.

Mephisto placed his hands close to the flames. "It's an illusion."

Illusion my ass. I'd seen illusions and very convincing replications, and this was neither. Illusions didn't give off heat.

"It's a Mirra," he offered in explanation.

A spell, I presumed, one I wasn't familiar with. I reveled in new information, as a rule, so I should have been pleased to learn about Mirras. I wasn't. I was being reminded that I knew little about this world and I desperately wanted to learn more. Like this magic. Elizabeth's magic. It had to be powerful beyond imagination to create such a realistic illusion.

"We need to walk through it," Kai said, his voice just above a whisper.

Like hell I'm walking through fire.

Without preamble or further consideration, he walked through it. His strained groan that changed to a shrill sound of pain wasn't encouraging, nor was the silence that followed.

"Kai?"

No response.

Clay followed. You don't follow after hearing that. You stop, assess, and move away from the danger. But they didn't. And seconds after Clay went through it, Simeon did as well, because apparently that was their logical response to someone groaning in pain and then falling silent. It's like hearing a crash and a bloodcurdling scream. I see it as a sign of danger, whereas obviously they looked at it as an invitation.

"It's going to feel like you're going through a fire, but you won't have any injuries," Mephisto informed me.

"That's reassuring." Fear softened my sarcasm.

Mephisto moved closer to me. His fingers splayed over my back, giving me a reassuring touch that didn't help. Three people went through, followed by silence. There wasn't anything he could do to embolden me.

I can't believe I'm doing this.

Vaulting through it, I hoped my speed would make it easier. It didn't. The small line of fire became a tunnel of flames. My skin burned, the blaze engulfed me, labored breathing from the pain choked me. I wailed. The sound was captured in a void, leaving me bent over, panting, waiting for the pain to subside.

Lifting my head, I saw the Others looking at me. By their flushed faces, I knew they'd felt the same.

"Erin." Mephisto's voice was soft as he pressed his hand to my back.

My jaw ached from clenching it so hard. I folded over again. My skin wasn't burning, but the pain of going through the fire was etched in my mind, and for a few moments, I relived it over and over. Once calm, I stood and looked at the Others, who weren't showing any signs of distress. In fact, they were far too relaxed for people who had gone through a fire. It was as if we hadn't had the same experience. My gut was telling me it was because they'd probably experienced worse. Standing taller, I no longer ignored Mephisto's look or his gentle touch on my back. Balmy coolness spread over me like a blanket, easing the warmth to something tolerable. Then it faded to nothing. I blinked back the tears that formed in my eyes and cursed Elizabeth in every language I knew, adding some special names that made me feel better just saying them.

Mephisto straightened his shirt and brushed off his pants

because heaven forbid he walk through a fire and be in shambles.

"Dealing with Elizabeth, you learn to appreciate her eccentric welcomes and her unique ways of showing displeasure," Mephisto said dryly.

"Yeah, making us walk through fire is a totally normal way to show your displeasure. It's not possibly the behavior of a sadist," I said, eliciting a rumble of laughter from Clayton.

Within feet of the cottage, I definitely felt pulled into a fairytale. Not the updated version that wasn't intended to scare the hell out of children. The atmosphere was dark and ominous, heightening my feeling of foreboding, and the magic that swirled around me wasn't as captivating as the Others' magic. I was biased against the woman, it was true. How could I not be after the fire and the blatant cheating? I had a moment of pause for the first time. It was warranted. So many things could go wrong when dealing with a person who peddled in dark magic and irrevocable consequences.

I drew in a breath and blew it out gently as I followed them into the home, entering the opened door to a spacious entryway. A comfortable-looking sitting room on the right and library on the left. The leather-bound books visible from my position at the entryway were in Latin, Greek, and two other languages I didn't recognize. There wasn't a desk, just an oversized chair in the far corner and a table with an electric teapot. Pale hues of yellow and eggshell white should have felt soothing, but my guard was up and I suspected it was a strategic effort to relax the suspicions and apprehensions of guests who came requesting help.

"Are you all going to just stand there at the door, or do you plan on entering?" asked a dulcet voice from another room. Now, I could see how people fell for this. It wasn't the house of horrors but a genteel woman with a library. And tea. If you wanted to just visit for a few minutes, there was a cozy sitting area. The closer we'd got, the more I'd been expecting a baby-eating trollish person with discolored fangs and bottomless black eyes. Hunched posture and long knobby fingers that pointed menacingly at us. Okay, I'll admit it. I was thinking of every evil witch in the old Disney cartoons.

Turning to face us was a slender woman in her early thirties. Rosy cheeks stood out on her smooth, alabaster skin and gave her deep-ginger eyes a brighter look. Her nut-brown hair was pulled back into a sleek ponytail. It was hard to imagine such power and knowledge was hidden behind a woman more than five inches shorter than me. The black leggings and oversized chambray shirt, rolled to the forearms, made me feel foolish about how I'd imagined her. But yet, despite her nonthreatening appearance, something more lurked behind the illusion she presented to us.

A hint of her magic brushed over me. The fae didn't want to claim her as one of theirs, but she definitely was. Florid undertone, hints of dark chocolate, mixed with traces of much more. A mélange of tone and textures. She was a fae, a powerful and unique one.

"Fire. The answer was fire," she simpered. She seemed quite pleased with herself. Maybe it was symbolic or ironic. Or just the actions of a madwoman. Silence swelled as I studied her, trying to figure out if I was dealing with a quirky magical virtuoso or the mercurial tirades of a powerful magical being.

"I'm not what you expected?" she asked, keeping a significant distance between the two of us. Her eyes were alight with amusement. I felt like I'd been dropped into this bizarre world and presented with the most innocuous-looking person with the worst reputation, and I wasn't sure how to deal with it. I liked my danger to look dangerous.

I shook my head, and she chuckled, a melodic sound. Maintaining the strategic distance, she moved her gaze from me and swept it over the cadre behind me. Dense magic swirled in a warm mist over us. An iridescent glow covered our arms, and when it vanished, it left behind marks. On my forearm, a raven perched on a gilded branch, several archaic-looking symbols around it. On the Others, a shield with two crossing swords encircled by markings similar to those on the swords Simeon and Mephisto carried. She smiled, then her brows furrowed as she studied them. Silent for several moments, she finally said, "Mephisto," and nodded in his direction. Then she recalled the names of the others—or rather the names they were now using—and I was willing to bet there had been changes in their appearance since she'd last encountered them. It wasn't beyond speculation that they could modify their appearance, similar to what fae could do. It wasn't unreasonable that, unlike the fae, they could do it at will and for extended periods. I studied them as thoroughly as she did.

"Kai." Her gaze went to the tawny man with the chaotic energy. She moistened her lips as her gaze bounced back and forth. Why didn't she just ask who was who? The brightness of her smile, the glow of her cheeks, and the liveliness of her eyes showed she was having fun. A puzzle she was determined to solve.

"Go over there," she directed me without taking her eyes off the two men she had yet to identify.

When I didn't move, she looked at the fading raven on my arm, jabbed her finger in my direction, and pointed to an area near the corner. Slowly, I walked to the small corner and stepped in the sigil circle. Once in place, she whispered an incantation and the enclosure blazed with magic, netting around me, forming a circle of frenetic energy that caused my skin to tingle. The potent magic was intoxicating. The reputation and misdeeds of the person behind this magic was no longer a deterrent to coveting her magic.

Once I was no longer near them, she moved to Simeon. The craggy man with the kind smile allowed it to widen at her approach. Her hand pressed his cheek and he moved into her gentle touch. Her lips brushed his lightly and the tender kiss quickly devolved into rapacious interlocking, Simeon's fingers digging into her back, pulling her closer to him.

"Simeon," she breathed out when they released each other.

She moved to Clayton and I wondered if he was going to get the same identification process. Her finger wisped playfully over the bridge of his nose. "Clay."

He nodded. Simeon had his thumb pressed against his lips, his disappointment at the ending of the kiss clear.

I scrutinized the men, trying to see the break in the façade in their appearance. Four pairs of eyes were looking at me, and there wasn't any way they couldn't see my curiosity.

What are you?

"Whose idea was it to bring a Raven into my house?"

The casual, kind tone was gone. Now it was cold, harsh, and promising a violent response if the answer wasn't acceptable. It wasn't my imagination; she was keeping her distance from me. I was in the corner for misbehaving supernaturals and I hadn't even done anything. But if thoughts were intentions, I was guilty. For a brief moment, I considered what it would be like to possess such strong, arcane magic. It was like inhaling the aromatic smell of freesia, a light breeze at midnight, the serenity of a beach. And it was aged to perfection. I coveted it more than Mephisto's or anyone's that I had ever encountered, and she had to have noticed, which was why she'd put a safeguard in place. Why she maintained a distance that wouldn't allow me the opportunity.

"I don't want your magic," I snapped, defiant and definitely more indignant than I had the right to be. I'd only thought about it . . . once. Twice. Maybe three times. But I hadn't considered acting on it. I had to get credit for that. Half a gold star, maybe?

Ignoring me, her gaze breezed over Simeon to Mephisto. "It's been so long," she said.

"It has been. We need your help," he answered.

"Of course you do or you wouldn't be here. No one ever visits me just to say hello."

Her lips puckered into a pout that was in no way cute. It was hard not to gawk as I tried to figure out where the term Woman in Black came from. A slow dramatic turn had her facing me with a guarded smile as she took in my face, which had to express exactly what I was feeling: blatant curiosity and bewilderment. This wasn't the Woman in Black. She was the Woman in Yoga Pants.

With a small twirl of her finger, her makeup darkened. Lips colored to a deep wine that looked black. It was the only makeup she had on, but it transformed her to something that matched the stories and her reputation. A black high-collared bodice complemented her new gothic look; a black satin skirt billowed out from the corset. A black serpent bracelet twined around her arm until it reached the bend of her wrist, where it lifted ever so slightly to reveal the snake's open mouth. The details were so stunningly intricate that I wondered if it was in fact an actual snake. This was what I'd expected to see. Was this what she presented to people once she'd agreed to help them?

"Elizabeth," Mephisto said softly, getting her attention. The distraction was good. Her intensity and the amount of magic stifling the air was overwhelming. I didn't want her to see the effect it was having on me. "The Immortalis have returned."

"Returned? They never left, just living a mortal existence.

I never understood it. They still possess so much power and yet they chose to live a life of banality."

I guess she wanted company, living in the forest, being sought out for help and making most people regret it.

"Not banality but biding their time. Concealment has been their strength. Anonymity is power. The knowledge of one's existence allows people to discover your strengths and learn your weaknesses. Weakness that gives them power over you." Mephisto shifted his eyes to me as if offering me the same explanation for his concealment and anonymity.

"Aw, do you two miss each other?" she teased, examining the distance between me and Mephisto. Trying to be as stolid as Mephisto was difficult, since what she implied was so far from the reality of what existed between us.

"Do I have your word you won't take what isn't yours?" Elizabeth asked me.

It dawned on me that perhaps my reputation was just as sordid as hers. Depending on the storyteller, what I was, my lack of control, the risks I took, my addiction to adrenaline and magic, didn't make a pretty picture.

"I don't want your magic." It was the truth, as long as she didn't have the ability to determine a lie.

"Arius," she called. Within moments, the imp manifested.

Was his nose just permanently upturned? He had traded his suit for a vest and slacks in a hunter green that looked better against his red skin. Cool, castigating eyes roved over me as if he was warning me not to break my agreement. He took a seat in a chair just a few feet from me.

I simply rolled my eyes and moved from the sigil circle once Elizabeth waved me forward. The weight of the magic that I had been encircled in fell from me like a shawl. When I moved back to my position in front of Mephisto, she smiled. The beauty of the circle was that the magic I felt there was all the magic I felt. It was like being in a magical deprivation tank. Now I was standing in a room full of the entrancing, intoxicating, powerful stuff.

Mephisto pressed his hand against my back. It was a gentle, reassuring touch and it did absolutely nothing to stifle the urge. He was just another hit of the cigarette for a smoker, another sip for the alcoholic, another tumble in bed for the sex addict, one more indulgence of your drug of choice. He was the addiction, not the cure.

My discomfort signaled everyone to look down at the raven on my arm that, unlike the others' marks, still hadn't disappeared.

"What do you want from me?" Elizabeth asked.

"They have a Caste," Mephisto said. "I need to know what objects can be used to break a Caste's curse."

Elizabeth scoffed. "After all this time, I thought they would have given up. Moved on. Accepted this as their new existence."

"They never would have done that. Especially with Malific being imprisoned. I suspect their sole purpose of wanting their magic restored is to return to the Veil and free her."

Elizabeth shuddered. "If she's bound by an Omni ward, are they strong enough to remove the binding and free her?"

"Her knowledge is extensive. She'll use them to find a way to be freed. To ensure that never happens, we need to make sure they never return to the Veil," Clayton said.

"Do they have one Caste or a coven?" she asked.

"We don't know," I offered.

Elizabeth's gaze slipped in my direction.

"Caste no longer have covens. I doubt they'd be able to undo that curse, even if there was one. I'm confident the Immortalis have discovered a magical object, or a spell to undo. But the Immortalis will still need to boost their magic enough for it to be effective at removing the curse," Mephisto offered.

Keeping a substantial distance from me, Elizabeth flounced about. It would seem more theatrical if her face hadn't become so severe. Her look of worry heightened the same feeling in me.

"Perhaps you should be concerned with finding the Caste that was taken and not the object. A person is easier to find. Without the Caste, no removal of the curse," she argued.

Finding people was substantially easier if you had a sample of their blood, or even a hair with the root. Finding a magical object was nearly impossible unless you had a piece from it, or blood from the person who created it. Blood was limiting, though, because you'd find anything linked to that blood. If you were fortunate enough to have magical objects, life got a lot easier. You could find the object by doing a spell to find the object's match.

"We don't have anything to locate her. Neither she nor any other Caste will ever be safe as long as the Immortalis have whatever object they plan to use. Finding the object needs to be the priority." Mephisto said.

I didn't have any experience with removal of curses and wondered if they just needed Victoria's blood to do it, or her life. My mind quickly ran through all the scenarios. What if they only needed her blood and released her after the curse was done? If the Immortalis went back to the Veil, it wasn't definite that they could unbind Malific, and if they couldn't, she'd still be confined to the Veil.

"If I knew the object, then I could possibly nullify it," Elizabeth offered. "The list of magical objects that could be used to weaken the curse or enhance Victoria's magic enough to remove the curse has to be limited—an ipsimus." Layman terms: class five objects; the most powerful and potentially dangerous of the magical objects. After several moments of contemplation, she said, "The Myrx can mimic any magic, therefore allowing them to each mimic hers."

Mephisto shook his head. "There are only two in the world and I have them both."

And they're on the top of the STF list of illegal objects. Mephisto eyes narrowed; a subtle challenge. The unrepentant look he gave me said: "Yes, Ms. Jensen, I have those and so much more…your move." I didn't have a move, because I was sure we'd find that we held similar views regarding the STF list.

Elizabeth rattled off several more objects, all of which seemed to be in one of the four's possession. She closed her eyes and audibly inhaled. When she opened her eyes, they were ringed in black.

"I can try to locate all the ipsimus in this area."

Relief flooded me. That would narrow down the search significantly. Most of them would show in a concentrated area: the STF, probably at Asher's, and, based on recent admissions, the homes of Mephisto, Simeon, Clayton, and Kai.

Kneeling at the table, she whispered an incantation and a map appeared. Opening the table drawer, she pulled out a knife. Most people look a little reluctant to cut themselves, but not the goddess of magic, who seemed to gather pleasure from swiping the knife over her hand and watching the blood well. At the invocation, the map flashed and quickly went black. Brow furrowed, Elizabeth repeated her actions, but this time the map didn't even light up. The flat, dulled map was nothing more than dark lines and shapes. The black rings reclaimed her eyes, which were wide with incredulity. Her mouth twisted into a snarl. Magic pooled around her and clouded the air. She spat out her incantation and when nothing happened, she shrieked and slammed her hand on the map. A dark cloud blanketed the air. Anger, fervid and toxic, overwhelmed the space. Magic pushed away from her like a tornado, sweeping up anything in its path, and we had to move to not fall victim to a magical goddess's big-girl tantrum.

"No!" she wailed in a bloodcurdling scream. Even Simeon, who had received such a special greeting, looked shaken. Magically neutered Elizabeth wasn't dealing with it. The house shook, art fell from the walls, raining glass everywhere. Doors slammed. Cracks spiraled up the walls and the floor shook.

"Elizabeth," Arius said, hesitating before coming to her side. More incantations fell from her lips without success. It was obvious that her magic had never failed. When her hand healed from the cut, she violently slashed it again and blared out more spells, to no avail. The floor rumbled underneath us. Mephisto's arms encircled my waist, his breath warm against my ear as we crouched a little to keep balanced.

"Elizabeth," Mephisto snapped uselessly, Elizabeth's focus staying on the unlit map.

"Mistress," Arius soothed.

Mephisto shot Simeon a look. Whatever their past was, Simeon lacked confidence that it mattered and it showed in the tentative way he approached her. "Elizabeth," he soothed. "Liz." He knelt next to her. Glassy-eyed, she rested against him. He was as gentle with her as he was with Pearl, stroking her skin softly, whispering words of affirmation.

"They are stronger than I am," she admitted.

Watching her succumb to the frailty of her magic, to grudgingly accept defeat, was disheartening. It was an awakening for me. I fully accepted the situation. The curse couldn't be removed from the Immortalis. They were strong, cunning, and flexing their power.

The power that emanated from Elizabeth wasn't luring or inviting. It was a blast of a water hose into my face. I shuffled away from her.

"I can nullify all the ipsimus." She lifted her eyes to meet

Mephisto's, then she met everyone's eyes for mere seconds, and I knew why we had come to her. She had power like no other. I doubted my magic senses now. Maybe she wasn't just a simple wielder of magic. What she was and possessed transcended fae, witch, mage, and whatever the hell the Others were.

"It will not be without consequences. *All* ipsimus will no longer work."

"Can it be reversed, once you do it?" I asked.

"No."

Class five objects didn't necessarily mean that they would be used for evil. The Enclave, the supernatural prison, used them for security. Some had been used for healing both in the human and supernatural world, and they could be used for protection spells, to undo chaos spells, and to counter dark magic. I'd criticized the STF for vilifying all objects that could cause harm when compiling their list of illegal objects, so I couldn't turn around and do the same.

"Give us a day," I blurted. I turned to Simeon. "How sure are you that they'll try to remove the curse during the Blood Moon?"

"Nothing is ever a hundred percent, but if I were them, knowing this could be their one shot, I'd want it to be under perfect conditions."

There had to be another way. We needed to exhaust all options. Elizabeth nodded in agreement. She knew the consequences.

Desperation had us back at Victoria's, scouring the home, being less discriminating about the items we chose to attempt to track her: clean hairbrush, clothing, tweezers, and pretty much anything that she came in contact with.

In her kitchen, I took inventory of the items Clayton and Kai had stacked on the island.

Kai moved with quiet self-assurance in the space. A magical signature placed subtle differences in their magic. Traces of aged cognac. Intense, powerful, and different enough from the others to pique my interest. Clayton's had a spicy signature, but his magic wasn't as tightly wound as Kai's.

It wasn't until their attention turned to me that I realized I wasn't just watching—but staring. It was an effort to look away. I couldn't seem to stop eyeing Kai, whose magic pulsed like a malfunctioning electrical outlet. I desperately wanted to know what the hell they were.

There were too many similarities in their magic for them not to be the same. Their familiarity with each other suggested they'd known each other for a long time, maybe even a familial bond. Their appearances didn't lead to them being related, but there was a sameness to their movements, their magic, the intensity of their gazes, as if the world looked different to them.

Clayton appeared darkly amused by my attention, but Kai was disconcerted. I could see why; it was probably creepy as hell.

"You're staring," pointed out Kai, Captain of the Obvious.

"Your magic reminds me of the elves."

Kai stopped moving, his skin flushing ever so lightly. There was a notable shift in his demeanor, which became guarded. He looked at me with reservation.

"How so?" Clay's sepia eyes lit with a dark curiosity and narrowed on me.

"Their magic is just as strong as yours and not like anyone else's."

"When was the last time you were around an elf?" Kai asked.

Most people didn't like to lie, but it was an occupational necessity sometimes, and I counted this as one of those times. Before I could tell him that it had been a couple years,

Mephisto entered and handed me his haul. It seemed like everyone was grateful for the interruption. I didn't have to come up with a plausible lie, and they didn't have to deflect or avoid giving me any information.

The search yielded three bags of items that I promptly took to Cory's.

CHAPTER 24

*M*y body melted into the sofa, one arm over my eyes to block the sunlight that streamed in through a small opening in the drapes. Apparently, Dr. Sumner decided that the curtains still needed to be drawn when I came because I was too distractible. But in his haste to close them, he left an opening. Not enough to see anything, but the light that peeked through was a distraction.

I'd called him to make the appointment, so obviously I wanted to talk to him. Seeing him would fulfill the obligatory session, serve as a distraction from thinking about Cory attempting a location spell on the bags, and allow me to unburden myself. But instead of venting, I found myself wondering what type of quack could get me in within half an hour of me calling. Didn't he have other patients? If not, why not?

He wasn't a quack. I was a case study, a person he'd reform and once again he'd be hailed for his therapy brilliance. I was a priority. That was why he made space for me.

"Erin," he said, his voice low and soothing. I guessed I should say something since it had been ten minutes since I last spoke. I'm not sure why I didn't speak, or why I had the overwhelming need to be in his office, around him, soaking up his non-magic-ness. It was a wonder why he was the safe space, a placid place that made me feel like I was floating on a lazy river. Victoria, Veil, Immortalis, class five objects, and gods, for an hour, were pushed from the forefront of my mind.

I closed my eyes and let the nothingness of his office wash over me. There had to be a happy medium for my life. Right now, I was living in a sea of magic and potentially life-changing problems and it was too much.

"What did you speak to Dr. Wilmer about?" I asked. Apparently they were meeting quite often.

"Why did you want to see me today, when you've done nothing but lie on the sofa?" He allowed a small smile to feather over his lips in an effort to compensate for his tone.

"It's been a rough couple of days," I admitted.

He probably saw this as a breakthrough, and maybe it was. I just wanted to say it out loud. Take the power out of it and make the situation seem less dire. The other day, the world appeared to be opening up to me. I had two possibilities: Mephisto and the Mystic Souls. Those options seemed less certain now—at least Mephisto. Learning what I had of the Veil, who was in it and how the Immortalis would use it, going into the Veil seemed too dangerous. The Mystic Souls had been iffy from the start. The damn raven was still on my arm. Born of fire, I had immersed it in cold water, hoping it would disappear. It hadn't. Just got fainter.

The Raven—how was that different from Raven Cursed? What was the look the Others gave each other when their marks faded and mine remained?

"Let's discuss the *incident* that brought you here." Sumner's tone had softened, and removing his glasses did exactly what he wanted it to do. It endeared me. Softened the walls I'd erected between us and made him and this situation seem less formal.

"I don't remember what happened," I whispered, sitting up to face him.

Under the scrutiny of his gaze, I stilled. Moments ticked by, the serene silence becoming airless and uncomfortable.

"What do you mean, you don't remember?"

"There are pieces of that night I don't remember."

"Do you remember taking the magic?" His voice lowered to match my quiet confession.

I nodded. "I remember almost everything about that, it's just fragments of that day are missing. I took the magic, left the room, and I remember sitting down to practice some spells. Then there's a gap. Like minutes were taken from me…" I trailed off, seeing the doubt in his face that he quickly mastered. He slipped his glasses back on.

"Maybe it was the spell you were working on. Is it possible it did something to you?"

I regretted telling him, but the past couple of days had opened my mind to possibilities. I wasn't without fault—I wanted to take magic and wasn't particularly concerned about the trail of bodies I'd leave behind if there wouldn't have been consequences. But I would get caught. With so few death mages in the world, it would simply be a process of elimination.

I hated missing that piece of time. Not being aware of the nudge my body gave me to return the magic.

Dr. Sumner relaxed back. He was scribbling, and the placid silence was welcome until I felt the shift. The toxins in the air, the pressure in the room changing. *Fuck.*

"Get in there!" I commanded, pointing at the closet. "Now!" I barked when he didn't move.

It wasn't until I retrieved the knife sheathed at my leg that he moved to the closet. I took inventory of the room: Visible to my right was the extinguisher. Good. I might need it. I dumped out my bag, looking for anything that could be used as a weapon. I was relieved when the flask tumbled out, but I

245

didn't have a lighter. What little vodka was in it, I drank earlier. It had been a rough day. I snatched up the Taser that fell out with it. Fire extinguisher, Taser, and knife were all I had when the Immortalis Wynded in next to the couch.

It was the one who'd bested me before. His overly confident smile fell quick when pressurized CO_2 hit his face. I targeted his eyes and he blindly expelled magic. Immortal didn't mean exempt from the fragility of a human—or human-like—body. With his compromised vision, I easily ducked and weaved around the indiscriminate magic he hurled. When he brought his hand to his face to work his magic on it, I smashed the extinguisher into him. The second thrash of the metal made him lose his footing. I dropped the extinguisher and went for my knife. I slashed his wrist, blood pooled, then I jammed the knife into his arm, coating it with his blood. Blood that could be tracked.

Shuddering, he made an attempt to Wynd. His body flickered and became partially translucent before returning to corporeal. A growl of determination followed his next attempt. Shudder and a flash, nothing. Another quick shake. Partial disappearance and then nothing.

Good. My gaze swept the room. Nothing I could use to bind him. I guess it would be weird if Dr. Sumner had anything like that. It didn't stop me from looking. When I spotted the extension cord in the corner, the Immortalis propelled a silver ball of magic at me that I barely dodged. It punched into the wall but didn't cause any damage. It wasn't an attempt to kill me, but retaliation.

His face was now clear of the CO_2. He shuddered hard. One of the wounds I'd inflicted meshed, leaving a light line, but other than that, there were no signs that he'd been cut. This time his Wynd was successful.

"Sumner," I yelled. He peeked from the closet and I glanced at the metal in his hand. A gun that he had trained on where the Immortalis had been standing.

"We should go," I said, using my shirt to dab up some of the Immortalis's blood and ignoring Dr. Sumner's grimace of disgust. Despite the claims he made of his knowledge of the supernatural world, he was still ignorant about a lot. Or, me dabbing up blood added credence to my score on the personality test. From his perspective, it couldn't be a good look.

"I need it to track him," I explained.

He nodded, but there was a true lack of comprehension in his eyes.

He followed me, his back to me and his gun trained, while I kept an eye on anything they could Wynd in front of, and stayed alert to any change in the air that would indicate more coming.

Outside the building, I thought Sumner would interrogate me, but he didn't. He stared at me, his face blank, eyes dulled. In a flat voice, he said, "We'll need to reschedule this appointment." As I moved closer, he tensed.

"Are you okay?" I asked. I started to touch his arm but stopped after seeing his apprehensive look. Face stolid, he blinked once, turned on his heels, and headed for the parking lot.

The car was the safest place because it couldn't be Wynded into. The last thing a person needed was to be driving and have someone just pop into the car. I tried not to think about the Immortalis coming after me. I wasn't convinced he'd wanted to hurt me, but to take me. And I had no idea why. Did my magic make me an added bonus to their objective? Dammit, I hated not having answers.

CHAPTER 25

*E*xcitement, shock, astonishment were emotions I was prepared for, but when I walked into his home, Mephisto spent the first few minutes scanning me for injuries. It made me wish Cory was my first call. In hindsight, Cory should have been my first visit, but Mephisto persuaded me to go to him. Cory was relieved when I let him know about the blood. It had to be demoralizing spending the day doing location spells that were likely to fail. Now that I had a blood sample, the next one he did wouldn't.

"He attacked you?"

"No, well…I don't know. I didn't give him a chance to attack me. I went on the offensive when he popped in."

"Only one?" he asked for the third time. Rolling my eyes, I blew out a breath and recounted the entire situation play by play while he listened carefully.

"The Raven," he whispered. His thumb trailed over his lips as he continued his annoying pacing. "The Immortalis are Malific's creations, her soldiers. A magical army, powerful, immortal beings. If they wanted you dead, you would be. So, what do they want with you?"

"M," I said, trying to get his attention.

"Don't call me that."

You're okay with me calling you Satan and Lucifer, but M is where you draw the line? Strange.

"We can track them. We need to go get Victoria," I redirected him. My curiosity about me being The Raven and my link to the Veil was still there, but I needed to get Victoria and prevent the Immortalis from releasing Malific.

He stared at the bloodstained knife and shirt in the sealed bag for a minute before he pulled his attention from it to me. Dark, unwavering eyes stayed on me for such a long time that it made me uncomfortable. Not the intensity of the look, but the bewilderment and hints of aversion that were now present.

"What's the matter?"

"I don't know what they think you are," he admitted with the troubled look of someone who typically had the answers.

"Victoria first, and worry about that later," I urged. "Cory can do the locating spell, unless you can do it?"

"I'd rather have Cory do it. Locating spells leave a footprint."

That answered that question. Never leave a footprint or enough information that could identify his magic.

"Can you do wards?" I asked, taking out my phone to text Cory. He placed his hand over mine to prevent me texting. His head barely moved into a nod. I made a mental note.

"We have to wait," he said.

"Wait? We can't wait."

"What if they can detect that a locating spell is being done? You have the blood of one of them. We'll locate where he is but not all of them. They'll all be present when they attempt to remove the curse. There's no guarantee Victoria will be with them right now, but tomorrow during the moonrise, she will be. And we will, too. The only way to truly protect her and prevent this happening again is to wait. One day."

I nodded. "Get her and destroy the object so it can't be used again."

His lips pursed and he offered a reluctant nod. Hmm, clearly I'd have to get to the object first to destroy it, because it appeared Mephisto wanted to add it to his collection.

Tactically, his plan was the best course of action, but it didn't sit well with me. I needed to be proactive. Do something, but there wasn't much I could do.

Mephisto glanced at his watch. "It's getting late and I just received some Léoville Las Cases and red Bordeaux." All I heard was *blah, blah, blah, Bordeaux*, but he sounded happy. "Would you care to have dinner with me and try it?"

I could try it, but I doubted I'd appreciate it any more than a ten-dollar bottle of wine from the grocery store. The appreciation of the legs, the aromas primary or tertiary, the exquisite taste would be lost on me. He waited as I contemplated the motives of his dinner and expensive wine invitation. I didn't mean to be so cynical, but it was hard not to be. Mephisto didn't do anything without an ulterior motive.

Eyes narrowed on him, I took in his appearance again. His appeal was hard to deny and as far as bad decisions went, this was the worst.

"Are you trying to seduce me?" I asked.

His riotous laugh filled the room, and when he finished, his full lips twisted into a bemused smirk. "You would know if I were seducing you, Erin Katherine Jensen." My name spilling from his lips in a velvety lilt made me think I was right.

"And how would I know that?"

"Because if I were, you'd be waking up with me," he said confidently. "And I'd never try to seduce you over dinner and wine, it's so cliché. And if I ever decide to seduce you, I don't want alcohol or anything else to detract from your full enjoyment of the experience."

"I like your confidence. You'll go far with it. Not with me, but a lot of women find that type of arrogant confidence sexy," I said brightly.

His rich laughter boasted a confidence that nothing I said could diminish it.

"Will you join me?" he asked.

I nodded and followed him to the empty kitchen.

"Who's cooking?" No longer running on adrenaline, I realized I hadn't had anything substantial to eat all day.

"Me."

Oh. I was hungry and didn't feel like eating someone's cooking experiment. He looked at me, clearly amused at my dejected expression.

"Just because I don't do something doesn't mean I can't. Do you think I'm incapable of finding missing objects, negotiating with others, and guarding myself?"

Worst-case scenario, I would have a nice glass of wine and pizza.

Taking a seat at the table in front of the window that so captivated Mephisto, I watched the wildlife absently as the sun faded, creating a dusk haze over everything. Mephisto filled my glass with wine, going into great detail about it as if he were an enologist. The five ounces in my glass was a reminder that his pour was the correct serving size, and me filling my glass up to the top and sipping it down enough to walk to the living room to watch TV without spilling it wasn't the proper way to drink wine. Seeing my disappointment, he filled it a little more.

I could tell the difference between it and the ten-dollar wine. After a quick search on my phone, I savored it a little longer, appreciating the feel of it against my tongue, the aroma, and the full taste because it was highly unlikely I'd ever taste it again.

My interest soon moved from the wildlife outside to the man indoors. He moved around the kitchen with an expertise and proficiency I hadn't expected.

. . .

When he sat the plate in front of me, I wondered why he even bothered with a chef. Braised lamb, sautéed vegetables, and white beans. I felt guilty when he filled my glass again, but he didn't seem to have a problem and gave me a faint smile when he filled his glass to match what he'd given me.

"I'm like the type O blood of magic," I offered between bites. I know I should have stopped eating while talking, but it wasn't going to happen. I was starving and the food was delicious and worth the two-hour preparation time. Wildlife gazing while he cooked gave me time to consider possible reasons the Immortalis wanted me.

Putting down his fork, he gave me his undivided attention. It would have been polite to extend the same courtesy to him. I didn't, but I did take smaller bites and longer breaks between bites.

"They don't want me dead. Well, I don't think they do. You said that yourself—if they wanted me dead, I would be. If they are trying to remove the curse, maybe I'm just a source to stack the deck. Ensure success."

Mephisto had abandoned his meal, slipping it away from him and taking an appreciative sip from his glass. "What can you do with magic?"

"Everything. It's not lack of ability that stops me, it's lack of sources." I gave him a pointed look. "I've shifted to an animal before, too, but I've never borrowed magic from a shifter." Now I was more curious than ever. The Raven, could that be more than just Raven Cursed, more than just a death mage?

"If that is true, then it is advisable that you stay here —with me."

My laugh came out as an odd snort. "Stay with you? I thought you weren't going to try to seduce me."

"I have no intention of trying to seduce you . . . tonight.

They tried to abduct you the day before they plan to remove their spell. Do you think they won't try again? Stay with Madison, Cory, or whomever you wish, but I own an Obitus blade, the only thing that can kill them, so they're less likely to come here."

"Cory's wards are resilient enough to stop most."

"Good for him. But the operative word is 'most.' I've gotten past my share of them—"

"Because you're a…"

"Very clever man," he offered, his eyes lit with amusement. He shrugged. "Choose where you'd like to go, but I think you'll be safer here."

Ignoring his food, he continued to sip on the wine, leisurely, as he waited for more questions. It was the first time I'd seen Mephisto exhibit any hints of worry. It creased his brow. He finished his wine, emptied the bottle into his glass, and drank more. "We need more wine," he announced.

Refilling both our glasses with more than the initial serving size, he then lifted his glass to me and took a sip.

"You make the Veil seem like a terrible place, but what I saw seemed so peaceful and beautiful." It was hard to believe that part of it harbored vicious, power hungry, destructive gods.

"Parts of it are beautiful, filled with those who choose to live there rather than among the…" It took him a moment to find the right word, his voice devoid of any emotion. "Unremarkable."

It appeared we were having haughty judgment as a side with our wine. The look that passed over his face showed that he didn't count himself among the "unremarkable."

"Then there are other parts that aren't as beautiful, and some are downright dangerous, where people are bound by magic."

"Imprisoned." *Don't make it sound lovelier than it is.*

"I prefer 'bound.' They roam nearly as freely as we do, just restricted to a larger area."

"Is that where your box is, in one of the bound places?"

"I don't know. All I know is that it's in the Veil."

"And the contents of the box are...?" I pressed, hoping the four glasses of wine had made him more open to sharing information.

"Erin Katherine Jensen, our agreement hasn't been suspended because of this situation. If I've given you the impression that it has, please accept my apology and know that whatever happens between us, that still stands." His tone had suddenly become impassively professional, reducing the cozy moment of dinner and wine to something that would take place in his office, with his lawyer present.

His dinner remained untouched. After emptying our plates and placing them in the dishwasher, he came back to finish the rest of his wine. I didn't want the conversation to end. I needed to find out more about the Immortalis, the very thing that their anonymity gave them—ignorance of their weaknesses. I needed to know their weaknesses.

"An Obitus blade, where can I get one?"

"Rumor has it that Simeon, Clay, Kai, and I have the only ones in existence, but I don't place great confidence in that claim. If I acquire another, it is yours."

My gaze scanned all the places visible from the kitchen, but it was highly unlikely he had it lying haphazardly in his home. It was probably locked somewhere—maybe in his bedroom.

Mephisto's gaze followed mine, then he finished the remainder of the wine in his glass. "Let me show you where you will be staying."

CHAPTER 26

J wondered when a house was no longer considered a home but rather an estate as Mephisto escorted me to the guest room, which reminded me of an upscale hotel suite. The clothes I retrieved from my overnight bag made me feel like I'd be underdressed. Before I had a chance to step into the room, Mephisto spoke.

"Is this where you want to sleep?"

"What other option do I have?" I asked, assuming he meant there were several rooms to choose from.

A sly smile crept over his lips. "My room is that way," he said, lifting his chin in the opposite direction.

Looking down the hall toward it, I said, "And?"

He shrugged, a mischievous spark in his eyes. "Just information I thought you should have."

Stepping into the room, I watched him as he backed away.

"There's more than just the magic between us, Erin. We both know it."

He turned and headed down the hallway, giving me a view of the muscled body I'd seen in a threadbare t-shirt and fitted jeans and could recall with ease. Even as he disappeared around the corner, I could imagine his body under the tailored midnight-blue shirt and slacks. The adrenaline hangover and kindled curiosity had me wondering what it would be like to spend a night with the Dark Prince. *Satan, Lucifer, the man with no name,* I coolly reminded myself. Calling him the Dark Prince made him sexier, more alluring and mysterious. It stripped away the wariness with which I needed to deal with Mephisto. And I needed that wariness to use as a shield. The voice that I couldn't stifle considered a tour of his room, if only to look for the Obitus blade. *Yeah, right.*

My bag dropped to the floor as I looked around at the room. Large windows took up one wall. The curtains were drawn back, and I was sure there'd be a stunning view if it wasn't blanketed by the night. My feet sank into plush carpet. An expensive-looking rug was placed in front of the king-size bed. There wasn't any art on the soft-gray walls, making the expansive space seem comfortable. Next to the table in the sitting area were built-in bookshelves filled with classics and genre fiction.

In the bathroom, I was forced to make the decision between a waterfall shower or a Jacuzzi bath. I wanted a shower, and what typically took ten minutes became an hour of letting water cascade over me as my mind sifted through what I'd learned over the past few days, especially about Mephisto. I wanted to know why he no longer lived in the Veil. Was he cast out as a preemptive measure to save others from him, or did he choose to leave? If so, why?

Curled up in the bed, smelling of lilac and honey from the shower, my senses were inundated by the intermittent scent of lavender that filled the room from a diffuser I couldn't see. It seemed to be intermingled with Mephisto's magic, but surely I was mistaken. I couldn't feel his magic from this distance. Or was it the lingering redolence, residual memories of the energy he emanated that I was forced to ignore during dinner? It was very distracting. I needed something to take my mind off it. Looking at the five texts Cory had sent me asking where I was, I responded.

A minute hadn't passed before my phone lit up and his face appeared on video chat.

"What?" I asked.

"You're texting me while with Hot and Broody. You tell me what."

"Why does your mind always go to that? What if I were injured and couldn't make it home, or he was holding me hostage?"

"And you texted me that you're at his house and not 'help me, this crazy MF abducted me' or 'bring help, I broke my pinky finger'?"

His lips rested into an expectant smirk. "Tell me, how did you end up in Satan's lair in what looks like one luxurious dungeon?"

Slowly moving the phone, I gave him a panoramic view of the bedroom and then the bathroom.

"Where's the man of mystery?"

"I'm assuming in his room."

"You're not going to check on him? Make sure he's okay?"

"He's fine."

"Hmmm. So," he nearly sang, "you're at tall, sexy, and mysterious's home. If the walls could talk." He was finding way too much enjoyment in my frustration.

"The walls wouldn't have a thing to say because It's. Work. Related."

Cory sighed. "Mephisto's not wrong about anonymity being a good strategic maneuver. It brings comfort to the humans, even those who still have a problem with us being around and living among them. We all have weaknesses that can be used to rein in our magic. No one is exempt. Immortalis, and whatever the hell Mephisto is. Damn, Erin, this is…" Graduating from magic school still hadn't prepared him for everything out there. "A lot," he finally admitted.

There was dead air for several moments.

"I wonder if I can see the Veil?" he said.

"Doubtful. You've done a lot of extraordinary things with your magic, so if you were able to see the Veil, I think it would have happened by now."

"Maybe there's a spell that can help," he mused. Looking for one was going to dominate his night. "Okay, goodnight and have fun with your work-related sleepover." His voice was jocular and teasing. This was something I was definitely going to hear about over and over.

"Night, and be here an hour before the Blood Moon."

CHAPTER 27

*C*hampagne-colored light spilled into Mephisto's library when I opened the curtains. The small storage room in my apartment afforded me space to keep most of my books—and I had acquired a lot. Mephisto's collection was extensive. The first hour, I perused the titles under his heavy gaze. My eyes flicked away from one wall, which contained nothing but books on war strategies and great battles, to return the same look of interest he'd been giving me for the past hour.

"Stop that," I demanded. Giving him the benefit of the doubt, I figured what I was feeling was just his unrestrained magic that he normally had to subdue when around others. During breakfast, it hadn't seemed so potent, although I was ever aware of it. Now I was drowning in it and resisting was getting harder.

There was a reprieve when he left, and I spent the two hours in the library. Surprisingly, there weren't many spell books. Nothing in there gave away what he and the others were, although he had extensive information on magical objects and one old weathered book that touched on the Veil, confirming everything Mephisto had told me about it. Each division was like a city in a state, with delimitations more restrictive than anything seen in cities.

My visit had been like walking through neighboring subdivisions, easy transitions. Stronger magic was required to move through the other barriers. Entrance to a Veil city didn't necessarily guarantee an exit from it, a fact that Mephisto had failed to mention. It made me question what I was willing to do to have magic. It was life changing—but nothing was guaranteed.

In the past, others had risked their lives for me to have magic. Was I willing to do the same?

A familiar ring tone interrupted me. I hadn't returned Madison's three calls, reluctant to tell her what was going on. Madison was a bureaucrat and sworn to uphold the law, and what I was doing was definitely in a gray area. Telling her about the Caste, Immortalis, and the Veil would require her to make that information available to others, and there didn't seem to be any benefit to doing that other than to stoke fear.

"Hey," I said, voice neutral.

"Victoria Kelsey is missing. River said you had a meeting with her the day before her disappearance. He thinks you're involved." No greeting, just straight to the point. Along with the inquiry, there was concern. She probably thought me ignoring her calls was an indicator I was in a situation. "It's his goal to see you off the streets. He's been vocal that any cases involving you should be handled by the police department because you have too many connections in the STF and your victims will never get justice if we're involved."

Victims? He'd adopted a distorted picture of me of being an unconscionable magic-stealing psycho who left trails of bodies in my wake. What the hell?

"I was the last person to see her and I was there when she was abducted," I admitted.

It didn't sound good, and the uneasiness about the past

260

few days lay heavy over my words. This wasn't going to be a situation that Madison had to fix—I wouldn't let it.

"I'm taking off my badge."

It was a symbolic gesture letting me know she was being Madison, my sister, and not a divisional head of STF division.

It spilled like water from a broken dam. I told her everything, from the moment Victoria was abducted, meeting the Others, the rune-covered weapons, my response to taking their magic, visiting Elizabeth, the Immortalis's appearance at my therapy session, our plans for getting Victoria back during the Blood Moon, and the Veil. The only part I edited was me entering the Veil and possibly going back to it, and since I hadn't told her about my travel into the Veil, I didn't need to tell her about the deal I struck with Mephisto. Omitting the information was better than ignoring her disapproval and the impending suggestion to reject his offer. She didn't understand my situation and I couldn't make her.

She let out a wispy sounding "oh" before falling into silence. Then there were strings of curses in French, English, and combinations of the two. A few words I think she just made up.

"Why wouldn't you tell me this? I need to be involved."

"I don't know if you should be," I countered. "If it can be stopped quietly, wouldn't that be better than you all storming in, fighting people you might not be able to defeat?"

"I'll assemble a team—"

"A team who will be on the news the next day. People will panic. If Victoria, a person who doesn't obviously possess magic, can be abducted by the Immortalis, then anyone can. Not only will there be mass panic, but we'll also put Victoria in danger, and what if they get a whiff of a large team coming for them and abandon their plan?"

"I'll assemble a team," she repeated, ignoring my objection. "People I know I can trust and who can keep a secret. If you believe the Veil exists—then it exists. That's all I need to know. Do you know what they plan to use? Wait…" I could hear her on her computer. "There's nothing on the outstanding objects list that can be used."

"We didn't know about the Veil. It's probably an object we had no idea existed."

She whooshed out a frustrated groan. I could imagine the rigid furrow of her brow, nose scrunched in frustration, and lips stretched into a painful straight line. I'd seen the expression too often.

"I need to be in on this," she said. "Not accepting help is arrogant. Even if we don't have weapons that can permanently stop them, we can help."

"I agree." I wasn't sure how the others would feel, but the priority was to stop the Immortalis.

Madison stopped me before I ended the call. "Promise me that the object will be destroyed. I don't want to be responsible for keeping it from falling into the wrong hands. I want it destroyed." There was a long silence, then, "Don't let him persuade you otherwise."

"Of course."

———

"I agree with her on both counts," I told Mephisto, trying to figure out what held his attention the most about his backyard. Was it the blue sky, the lush abundance of trees, the exotic flowers, the animals, the peach-and-gold glow the sun placed over it all? Was it a reminder of places in the Veil?

He glanced at me. "They can't kill them. Only we can, with the blades."

"She knows that, but even with Cory, there'll only be five of us and an army of them. I'd prefer some backup."

"And the object?"

"STF doesn't want it. Madison wants it destroyed and it

should be. If Malific is as dangerous as you say, I want her in the Veil and bound."

An internal debate played out on his face. It wasn't Madison's assistance that was the issue, it was the object. I didn't think he wanted it destroyed.

Eventually he said, "I'll let them know."

His face was unreadable, but his intentions were loud and clear. My objective was to save Victoria and get to the object before Mephisto could. And destroy it.

CHAPTER 28

I *would risk my life for this magic.*

It sounded so melodramatic, Oscar winning, the queen of theatrics, and all things over the top, but that's how I felt with Clay, Simeon, and Mephisto in the SUV. Cory's magic became a trace, barely detectable among their overpowering magic. Kai refusing to ride with us was fortunate. It would have been too much.

Midway to our destination, I fought the urge to make them stop so I could get in one of the two cars following us. It wouldn't have been a reprieve from magic, just a change of magic—adrenaline-heavy magic. There wasn't a good situation. Remembering my agreement with Mephisto eased some of my discomfort. In a short time, this wouldn't be an issue. The thought consumed me as we drove into the night.

Getting out of the car, Cory sidled up next to me. I wished he'd taken my advice to stay behind, but I couldn't come up with an acceptable reason to keep him away. He wasn't at any more risk than Madison and the STF because their magic and weapons weren't effective against the Immortalis.

We all looked at the barren land. Stretches and stretches

264

of fallow land, lightly lit by the emerging moon. Madison moved next to me, a reassuring hand pressing against my back. It was a little unnerving how well she knew me. Unobtrusively, she slid between me and Mephisto. Claire slipped between me and Clay, but not before she gave him an over-enthusiastic smile, showing all her teeth. A flash of brightness in the dim night. Based on the arch of his brow and the discomforted look he cast in her direction, if it wouldn't have been rude to move away from her, I was pretty sure he would have.

"This is the right place," Mephisto confirmed, raising his hand to lightly touch the air. "A Mirra."

Mirras were at the top of my least favorite things list. They were different than wards, where hints of magic drifting off them gave away their existence, and if you were especially skilled, the diaphanous patches of discoloration that never quite blended could be detected. Mirras were indistinguishable from what they mimicked. The scent of dry destitute earth soaked the air and wisps of oak breezed in from the trees that I could see in the distance. I would have driven past the place completely unaware that something more existed behind the illusion.

Everyone did another quick weapons check, even me: backup double-edged karambit, cuffs clipped at my back, Asher's knife at my waist, another knife sheathed at my ankle, and the holstered Glock. I was fully aware that none of them could kill the Immortalis—just injure them momentarily. It was disheartening. I wanted to be more than a distraction; I wanted to permanently stop them.

As we did with the fire at Elizabeth's, we walked through the deceptive cloaking screen and into a crowd of dense trees, magic-laden air and vibrant lush grass. The lively beauty didn't belie the dark and ominous energy that coursed through forest. If we had doubted the location, this confirmed it.

"This is it," said one of Madison's team. "I hear invocations."

He changed into his animal form, nudging the other shifters to follow. The first to move in the direction of the invocations, the three shifters made use of their long, powerful legs and cleared the area fast enough that I had to run to keep up.

Mephisto pulled in behind the others, his movements mirroring mine with just a second's delay. It only took several zags of movement in an attempt to get around him to make me realize that he was purposely keeping me back, slowing my advance.

"What are you doing?" I snapped.

He stopped abruptly, blocking my way. Two large trees flanked me and a massive oak a few inches beyond narrowed the path enough that I'd have to turn sideways to get past him.

"I'm trying to decide if it's a good idea for you to go," he admitted.

"It is. Move." I gave him a little shove.

"You took magic from one, without the penalty of death. They came after you and we don't know why. I'm not sure you'll be safe," he offered.

The others were getting too far ahead, dispersing to cover all areas.

"We're having this discussion *now*? They don't want me dead. If they did, as you so eloquently said, I would be."

"They wanted you."

My bravado made me appear far more confident than I felt, and I recalled the putrid feeling of death that overtook me the moment I took the Immortalis's magic. I could happily go a lifetime without feeling that again, but if that's all I had to stop them, it was still an option.

"I stopped him before, I'll do it again."

He frowned. "Just don't die," he said, drawing his sword.

"Great advice," I mumbled. "Before you said that, my go-to plan was just to die." The cynic in me wondered if they wanted me to stay behind to ensure that I didn't destroy the object.

He scowled at me before moving aside and letting me pass. After several more feet, the narrow pathway opened up. The light rhythmic sway of the branches moved faster the farther in we went, the leaves whipping erratically and violently.

A mere touch of a dehydrated and brittle tree trunk caused bark to crumble from it. The verdant grass turned brown and crunched underfoot. The wilted trees and dead grass led us to Victoria better than any of our senses. Madison was already taking magic from the earth.

There were about twenty Immortalis working quickly around an incensed-looking Victoria, who was secured to a tree. The fiery rage on her face promised violent retaliation the moment she was capable of it. The intricate tannin markings on her face and arms guaranteed she wouldn't be given the opportunity to seek revenge. Her furious eyes moved over her clothing and then the markings, and I wasn't sure which disgusted her more, the poly-blend fabric of the formless tank dress they had her in, the bindings on her limbs, or the markings stained on her body to restrict her magic. A glance at Mephisto, who looked equally disgusted, made me guess the poly-blend fashion.

The Immortalis were using intricate hand movements, their lips moving just as fervently as their hands. A blade lay next to Victoria, and a black icosahedron-shaped object lay on a white cloth. The ground shook, a small tremble that startled the Immortalis, drawing their attention from Victoria. Madison's hand pressed to the earth, her eyes intense as she caused the ground to quake. The Immortalis turned to us, using various methodical movements to cast spells and violent waves of magic in our direction. Dodging a bolt, I saw a shifter blasted hard into a tree.

A mage waved his hand and patches of dirt and grass ripped from the ground in front of one of the Immortalis, the dirt flying up into his face and reddening his eyes. The Immortalis's hand movements changed and the mage dropped to his knees. He howled in pain before collapsing on his back, convulsing. The Immortalis switched his attention from the jerking mage to Mephisto, sword in hand, charging him. The rote movements of the Immortalis stopped abruptly as he seemed to focus on the markings on the blade. Mephisto shoved the blade into him. The Immortalis dropped to his knees. Mephisto yanked the sword out and shifted his weight. I couldn't turn my head away fast enough to miss the swift arc of movement that beheaded the Immortalis. Blood dampened the ground.

Bolting toward Victoria, Simeon kept pace with me before diverging to the right. The gust of wind from an Immortalis hit me hard, knocking me off my feet. The hammering blast continued battering into my side before abruptly stopping when the Immortalis suffered the same fate from Simeon's sword that the other had.

A wave from Claire and fire roared around them. Moments later, the blaze was briefly frozen in thick ice until it exploded into shards of ice that sprayed the area. A magical guard was erected, but I couldn't see who had done it. Probably Cory, but it fell just as quickly as it was created.

A large wolf soared past me and hit the ground with a thud. It howled in pain but managed to come to its feet, only to have a spiraling bolt of magic thrash into its side, knocking it down again. It was breathing, but it was labored and inconsistent.

Sharp cries of pain pulled my attention to the leopard tearing into the arm of the Immortalis who injured the wolf.

The fighting paused when another Immortalis fell victim

to Mephisto's blade. The commotion stopped entirely when his lifeless, headless body dropped to the ground. No movement. The Immortalis eyed the blade and quickly retreated from the only weapon that could kill them.

I placed my focus on the magical object, which was being guarded by the Immortalis I'd tangled with in Sumner's office. His fingers curling into claws, his hands circled one another, growing in speed with each revolution until he'd conjured a lilac ball that he hurled at me. They might have wanted me alive, but they didn't care in what condition. I dropped to the ground and it smashed into the tree behind me. Bark pelted me. Drawing my gun, I came to my feet and shot, hitting him in the chest. Crimson colored his shirt, and he staggered back but did not fall.

"Your left," Victoria yelled, but I couldn't move fast enough. The arrow-shaped magic didn't penetrate like an arrow, but it delivered concentrated pain. Hunched over, I searched for the assailant. I watched him drop to his knees, face folding into a painful grimace before he fell face forward to the ground. Kai pulled the dagger from the Immortalis's back and gave me a quick nod.

Shooting him a sign of appreciation, I ignored the chaos around me, the tree bark splattering, shaking ground, magic-drenched air, leaves fluttering, howls and cries of pain. Focused on Victoria and the magical object, I moved toward them. From my peripheral vision, I saw a wave of magic coming at me. I lunged for the white cloth, my hands shielding my head as the magic scraped over my skin. It was like sandpaper. Pain seared through me. I grabbed the object. It was far lighter than I expected. And stronger. Smashing it against a tree didn't even crack it.

Five Immortalis stalked toward me, their hands moving rapidly, lips working, magic thrashing off them. They ignored the object in my hand and focused solely on me. One of them held a blade. A vibrant wave of color rippled next to me. Their approach came faster and so did their words. I let the object slip from my hand and dropped to a crouch. Karambit in hand, I planted my feet and crouched lower to get better balance. It wasn't enough to resist the swell of magic. Dropping the karambit, I grabbed Asher's blade and stabbed it into the ground, tethering me. My arms strained from gripping it. I took a chance and removed one of my hands to grab the karambit and hurl it at them. It was enough of a distraction for them to lose the rhythm of the spell. The magic's intensity decreased.

A blade punctured one of them and brought him to his knees. Life left him as fast as the blade had pierced him. Kai moved with a swift grace as the other Immortalis veered away, afraid to fall victim to his weapon. They didn't use magic against him. When Simeon charged with his sword in hand, they retreated, again without using magic in defense. Two Immortalis fell to Simeon's blade. Another Immortalis Wynded away. That left one, whose determination to reach me didn't waver. What the hell did he want from me?

The karambit blade blocked the knife he thrust at me. I ripped Asher's blade from the ground and plunged it into his thigh. He stumbled back and I yanked it out, watching blood spread over his pants and then the wound mesh and heal as if it had never been. I cursed under my breath and attacked. Slashes with the karambit, figure eights, moving smooth and fast, jabs of the blade, the sole purpose to keep him on the defensive and unable to use his magic.

He Wynded from me and I heard the distinctive whoosh behind me. I whirled to find him trying to grab the magical object. Distracted by the wave of magic Madison thrust at him that left him untouched, I snatched up the magical object and secured it close to me. Madison's hand went to the tree next to her, which dried and shriveled, dead leaves falling from it as she pulled its energy to make more magic. Magic that didn't have any effect on him. But Mephisto advancing, wielding his sword, had him retreating. The Immortalis used the trees to do his fighting, adopting the same tactic we used on them, using magic against objects as a defense. It confirmed what I suspected: Their magic didn't work on Mephisto and the Others. Branches tore from the tree and speared in Mephisto's direction. Then he Wynded out, the branches falling uselessly to the ground.

Mephisto turned to me. "Do you have it?"

I held the object out.

"A Roboro gem," he whispered, inching closer and extending his hand for it.

Shaking my head, I secured it to me.

"Erin, give it to me," he demanded.

"I can't. It needs to be destroyed." There were rules I'd violate on a whim, laws that I bucked at, but a promise to Madison was something I couldn't break.

"Erin." His voice was sharp and commanding. Mephisto was a collector of powerful objects. Arrogant and overly confident enough to think he could keep it from falling into the wrong hands. I didn't share that confidence. Even if I did, I never wanted to be in this situation again.

"I don't care what you think you need it for, I can't risk the Immortalis getting their hands on it again. We can't risk it. I won't risk it."

Mephisto surveyed the area in silence. "Erin," he entreated. "Please."

"I promised Madison I would destroy it," I explained. A dense cloud of Mephisto's magic smoothed the air as he coveted the object in my hand. I watched him carefully, fully expecting him to use magic to take it from me.

"I promised Madison," I repeated, the words weighted with the importance of my commitment. The awareness was expressed in his. I kept my promises. If I made a promise to him, I would keep it and I'm sure he would hold me to it.

His magic feathered along my skin. And then there was

the Immortalis magic that lingered as a heavy musk in the air. Hints of it that floated in the air seemed forbidden.

Placing the Roboro gem against the tree closest to me, I smashed the mother of pearl handle of Asher's gifted blade into it. Chips fell, and more crumbled with repeated assaults.

Holding Mephisto's gaze, I spread the chipped pieces about, surreptitiously keeping several chips for myself so that it could never be made whole.

It was done. And couldn't be undone.

CHAPTER 29

*T*he balance in my account made me grin. Victoria had paid me with a bonus to ensure discretion and send another subtle "snitches get stitches" warning. I would keep her secret as long as I could, but the Immortalis were out there, and although the Roboro gem had been destroyed, they would be looking for other objects that could restore their magic. Victoria wasn't safe. The extra money was a payment for silence but also for bodyguard work. It seemed easy enough, to make sure she wasn't snatched again.

My phone rang with a notification showing a text from Asher.

I came by your home with your requested item. You weren't there. I waited with your Ms. Harp. She's delightful. Call me.

I wasn't sure who this joker had waited with, but it definitely wasn't Ms. Harp. I was just about to call and tell him he had been with an imposter when I was interrupted by a knock at the door. Ms. Harp's silver-gray hair was all I could see from the peephole. I swung open the door.

"Is everything okay? Are you okay?" The rush of panic elevated my voice, and she frowned.

"Honey, are you always like this? Calm down, no one should be this anxious."

I was astonished to see her at my door. Her cane was hooked around her arm and occasionally she scanned the hallways, presumably on the lookout for Chatty Cathys she'd have to avoid to get back to her apartment and Judge Judy.

"I'm fine…. You never come to visit. I just wanted to make sure you were okay."

It was an effort not to point out that we had exchanged more words in the past few minutes than we had in the last three months.

"I won't take up much of your time, just wanted to make sure you called your friend. He was waiting for you. Seems like a nice man." Her words sounded casual, but the smile that flourished on her face told a different story. Even cranky Ms. Harp had been swayed by Asher's charm.

"Thank you. Next time you don't have to host him. He can just text me and wait for me to return."

"It was my pleasure. He's a very nice man and he enjoys Judy as much as I do."

Really?

Before I could get "too chatty" with her, she waved me a goodbye and started for her apartment, her cane still hooked on her arm.

"You enjoy Judge Judy?" I asked as soon as Asher answered the phone.

"I enjoyed it with Ms. Harp," he corrected. My cynicism never rested. I wondered why he was ingratiating himself to her? "She's someone I've wanted to meet for a long time. There have been many rumors and I wanted to see if there was any truth to them."

"Ms. Harp?"

"Shifter."

"No."

People with weak magical signatures often slipped by me,

but shifter magic was hard to miss, even if you could ignore the torrid bursts of primal energy that pulsed from them. One look at their eyes would clue you in that they weren't just human. The intensity of their otherness was too strong to ignore. And their eyes. They glowed at night.

"She's actually a witch/shifter hybrid," Asher clarified.

"What?" I prided myself on my extensive knowledge of this world, but now I felt like a fledgling. I didn't like the feeling.

Asher went on. "A rarity, as you know. I think it's important to be aware of those who manage to evade shifter magic. Her mother was a shifter and her dad a witch."

"Maybe she knew a spell," I suggested.

It didn't make sense. Shifter magic dominated to a fault. No one could mate with a shifter and not bear shifter children. Ms. Harp, my neighbor—distant, evasive, and peculiar. It put a different perspective on her mannerisms. Did she not shift but still possess all the preternatural senses? Could she perform magic, or had the shifter genes canceled out the ability? Or could she turn? Ms. Harp was an anomaly, a significant one.

"My understanding is that a spell wasn't done, and spells have been done in the past without success." Asher's voice dropped. "You are aware that this isn't common knowledge and what it would mean if it were to get out."

You're supposed to say that before. Something like "Hey, triple pinky swear not to reveal what I'm about to share with you."

I sucked in a long, frustrated breath. Retroactive confidentiality agreements annoyed me. If it was an afterthought, how important was it?

"Shouldn't you have requested the oath of secrecy before revealing it?"

"Perhaps, but I have the Mystic Souls, and unless I have your vow that Ms. Harp will remain a secret between the two of us, then with me is where it stays."

Asher, always playing his little wolf games.

Ms. Harp's situation wasn't something most shifters would care about. They seemed proud to be shifters and had no qualms about voicing it. A level of arrogance accompanied their ability to glide effortlessly between man and animal, keeping all the benefits of their predatory nature when in human form. It undeniably had advantages, and their extensive wealth and place in the hierarchy of supernaturals was a testament of that. Human reaction to Ms. Harp is what would concern them. She went against the prevailing knowledge we had about shifters. Humans reacted unkindly to anything that contradicted it. When we came out, classes were taken, books written, interviews constantly requested, so humans could know everything they could about supernaturals.

Residing down the hall was a woman who didn't align with human knowledge. I would never tell her secret—or whatever it was. But I was intrigued. How did an anomaly like her happen?

"Are there more like her?" I asked.

"No, she's the only one I'm aware of."

"You have my word," I said. After several seconds of silence, I added, "Finally, I know a pack secret."

"She's not part of my pack." Asher would never reveal one and he wanted to make sure I knew that. "But she's now what I consider a friend of the pack."

Meaning I wouldn't be disclosing pack secrets, but I would be betraying a friend of the pack, and that had severe consequences as well.

"Yeah, yeah. Snitches get stitches. I hear you," I huffed.

"Hear what?"

"You heard me. You didn't miss anything. You just want me to believe you're too sophisticated to say it."

"You'll have your book tomorrow."

. . .

Finding out about Ms. Harp and gaining access to a Mystic Souls made me hopeful. Magic was obtuse, with inconsistencies and anomalies. I could be one: an inconsistency and an anomaly. Not just a Raven Cursed. And I wouldn't be beholden to Mephisto. He had my attention, and I wanted to know what was in that box of his, but now I had the option to walk away. I liked having options.

The firm rap on the door had hints of demand befitting Mephisto. He was back in his uniform of charcoal jacket with tie-less black shirt and slacks, but I'd seen him. I knew there was a warrior under the exquisite suits, and powerful magic behind his enigmatic restraint.

His dark eyes narrowed on the spot where Elizabeth had revealed my mark. To my relief, I had awoken to find it gone. He stared as if he could still see it. I invited him in, and he entered and stood some distance from me. Behind his dark eyes, something lingered that I couldn't quite place—was it fear, aversion, apprehension, or leeriness . . . That was it. He was leery. Of me.

Breaking the silence, I said, "Are we going to see if I can remove things from the Veil?"

"No," he whispered. "I don't think that's necessary anymore."

"Why not?"

"You have another job you should focus on."

"That is?"

"Finding out who your real parents are, because they're not who you think they are."

"What are you talking about? My parents are Vera and Gene."

It didn't sound very convincing, even to me.

"By your own accounts, your mother is half Raven Cursed, your father human. But you've never seen your mother use magic. She doesn't have the difficulty you have—the difficulty that others have had. You borrowed magic from the Immortalis, something that brought death to those who tried it. By your own admission, you can do extraordinary things with your magic."

He spoke in a measured tone as if listing my various crimes. The distance between us bothered me. The relationship, camaraderie, whatever it was we had, was gone.

Pensive dark eyes stayed fixed on mine.

"I know who The Raven is," he said.

I tensed.

"The Raven is Malific's daughter."

Well damn.

MESSAGE TO THE READER

———

Thank you for choosing *Fireborne* from the many titles available to you. My goal is to create an engaging world, compelling characters, and an interesting experience for you. I hope I've accomplished that. Reviews are very important to authors and help other readers discover our books. Please take a moment to leave a review. I'd love to know your thoughts about the book.

For notifications about new releases, *exclusive* contests and giveaways, and cover reveals, please sign up for my mailing list at McKenzieHunter.com.

Printed in Great Britain
by Amazon

71508322R00170